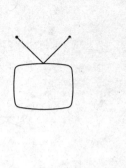

NOT SUITABLE
FOR
FAMILY VIEWING

VICKI GRANT

HarperTrophyCanada™
An imprint of HarperCollinsPublishersLtd

Published by Harper*Trophy*Canada, an imprint of HarperCollins
Publishers Ltd.

First published by Harper*Trophy*Canada in an
original trade paperback edition: 2009
This digest paperback edition: 2011

Harper*Trophy*Canada™ is a trademark of HarperCollins Publishers.

HarperCollins books may be purchased for educational, business, or
sales promotional use through our Special Markets Department.

HarperCollins Publishers Ltd
2 Bloor Street East, 20th Floor
Toronto, Ontario, Canada
M4W 1A8

www.harpercollins.ca

Library and Archives Canada Cataloguing in Publication
Grant, Vicki
Not suitable for family viewing / Vicki Grant.

ISBN 978-1-55468-181-5

I. Title.
PS8613.R367N68 2011   jC813'.6   C2011-903884-6

Printed and bound in Canada

Text design by Sharon Kish
9 8 7 6 5 4 3 2 1

This book is dedicated to all the "celebrities"
who allowed me to sully their good names
in support of John Martin Junior High.

1

The man is a movie star. When my mother sees him, she slaps her hand over her mouth and gasps. He smiles and walks toward her. She jumps up and throws her arms open. They hug. She says something to him that I can't hear. He tosses back his head and laughs. (I bet she says the same thing to all of them.)

She takes his hand and they sit down on her big leather couch. It's kind of a gold colour and, today at least, it matches her hair almost exactly. (Who knows what colour her hair will be next week?) Their knees touch. She tells him he looks fabulous. He tells her the same thing. She sticks her lips out like she's some cheesy swimsuit model and says it pays to have a good plastic surgeon. She winks. They laugh. She takes a sip of water, then asks him about work, the ranch, his sister's illness. They talk and talk. She doesn't take her eyes off him the whole time. It's classic Mimi. The guy totally falls for it.

She softens him up a while, then she comes right out and asks. When is he going to stop fooling around? When is he going to settle down, get married? He sighs, shakes his head, looks down. He opens his mouth to say something—but my mother stops him. She puts her hand on his arm and says, "I love you. You know that. I really do. And there's so much else I want to talk to you about. . . ." She turns away but doesn't let go of his arm. "First, though, this word from our sponsors!" She looks right into the camera. "Stay where you are," she says. "When we come back, George Tasiopoulos is going to tell us all about his remarkable love life!"

The camera zooms in on George's face. He acts horrified, as if that's not what he came here to talk about at all. The *You, You and Mimi* theme music kicks in. My mother leans against him and whispers in his ear. It's so embarrassing. He wags his finger at her. The studio audience eats it up. They're on their feet, clapping, laughing, checking the monitors to see if they got on TV.

I pick up the remote. This is sick. I'm a seventeen-year-old girl sitting in a dark room on a beautiful summer day watching my mother on TV.

Again.

Or should I say "still"?

What's the matter with me? Why am I doing this?

I'm going to turn off the television. Get up. Walk out. Do something with my life—or at least my hair.

I am.

Right after this next segment.

2

Friday, 3 p.m.
Mimi Marathon

The 72-hour *You, You and Mimi* marathon
continues. If for no other reason, watch it to see
how Mimi's nose morphs over the years. Five big
sparkling stars if you love lifestyle TV. A no-go
zone if you don't.

Anita doesn't even knock. She just barges in like she owns
the place and yanks open the drapes. The sun practically
blinds me but she doesn't care. I cover my eyes with my
arm. I don't groan. I won't give her the satisfaction.

"Up. Get going," she says. "I've had enough of this non-
sense." She flicks off the TV, stuffs the empty chip bags into
her uniform pocket and kicks the stool out from under my

feet. My legs thump onto the floor as if they belong to a corpse.

Which, come to think of it, I guess they do.

"C'mon. I told you. Up!" She pulls the cushion out from under my head, pushes up my chin.

What does she think this is? A police interrogation?

I can feel her staring at me. I can picture her lips all puckered up, her eyes squinting, her whole head just ready to blow. You'd think she'd learn. You'd think after all this time she'd know that's only going to make things worse. No way am I moving now.

She clears her throat. She starts tapping her foot. What? Is that supposed to scare me or something?

She can tap a hole in the floor for all the good it's going to do her. She can fry my brain with those X-ray eyes of hers. She can spray me all over with her beloved Lemon Pledge and buff me to a high shine. It's not going to make any difference. It's my life. It's none of her business what I do with it. I can spend it watching reruns if I want.

The tapping stops. I brace myself. I figure she's going to freak out any second.

But she doesn't. She freaks *me* out instead. She flops down on the couch—and starts hugging me.

Hugging me! Like what's with that?

This is not what I need right now. Seriously. I clench my face. I try not to move. I hold my breath. She is not going to do this to me. I won't let her.

Crying is so lame. Why do I feel like crying?

She's got so much product in her hair it makes a crunching sound in my ear. She tickles my arm with her fingernails. She pushes my lips up into a smile. She rubs her cheek against my face and starts making these big, wet kissing sounds. She thinks she's going to make me laugh and then—just like that—everything will be all better.

Doesn't she get it?

Why doesn't *anyone* around here get it?

"Tickle her."

"Give her a candy."

"Buy her a new car . . .

"a new computer . . .

"a new friend . . ."

Whatever. It's always the same thing. "Throw her a bone. She'll be okay."

My face hurts. I don't know how much more of this I can take. I've got to blank her out. I try to concentrate on the orange and grey pattern flickering on the inside of my eyelids. I do the yoga breathing thing that Mimi forces on her audience just before the credits roll.

It doesn't take long before I feel like I'm floating in jelly. I love that feeling. I'm barely here. *Anita*'s barely here. She's just this sort of distant wobbly voice—the cartoon teacher yammering away at the daydreaming kid.

It makes me think: why does everyone always feel sorry for people in comas? The comatose guys should be feeling sorry for *us*. They've got it so easy. No worries. No expectations. No wondering how you're going to fill your day. (Next time the guidance counsellor asks me what I want to be, that's what I'm going to say: comatose. If nothing else, it'll make picking my courses easier.)

I start to relax. Anita has to have noticed that her little kissy-kissy ploy isn't working. So now what? She's too scrawny to drag me out of the room. There's no way she'd ever consider calling up my mother and "bothering" her about me. She can't stand my father. (She's never said so, but please. I'm not blind.)

Her only other option? That little temper tantrum she's been holding out on.

I'm almost looking forward to it. At least it's real. At

least she's not being "nice" to me just because I'm Mimi's kid. I've always been able to count on her for that.

I know exactly what will happen. (Despite what Mimi's Thanksgiving Special might lead one to believe, this is as close as we get to a family tradition around here.) Anita will go ballistic. She'll do/say something she regrets. She'll slam out of the room and go clean the fridge. She'll put a note on my pillow saying she's sorry. She'll leave me alone for a day or two. By then, I should be gone to Dad's for a few weeks. (Or at least I think I should. When am I supposed to go to Dad's? How long have I been at Mom's? How would I even know?) Anita'll be happy to see me when I get back. For a while she'll even cut me some slack.

Problem more or less solved.

But I'm wrong again. Anita doesn't go berserk. She doesn't stomp out of the room. She starts rubbing the tip of my nose with her feather duster and singing that stupid song she made up when I was little. "*Birdie, Birdie, fly away . . .*"

I want to rise above all this—make *her* look like the childish one—but I can't. There's something about that song that just gets me.

I do exactly what I promised myself I wouldn't do. I jump up. I go, "Why. Are. You. Bugging me?"

Anita's got this huge smile on her face. "Because you *always* bug the ones you love," she says. She swishes her duster at me again and winks.

"Very funny," I say. My bottom teeth are jutting out and my nostrils are huge. I know exactly how ugly I look. Who's her little Birdie now? "Why don't you just do your job and leave me alone?"

"Then I wouldn't be doing my job, would I?" She plumps up the cushions. "I'm paid to do everything your mother would do if she weren't out working like a dog to give you this fabulous life. That means cleaning the house, buying the groceries, making the meals—and getting you up off your sorry behind."

Oh, yes. My *fabulous* life! It always comes down to that. The nerve of me! I don't have a thing to complain about! I have everything a girl could ever want!

Or at least buy.

I'm all ready to say something—something mean—but I don't have to. The doorbell rings. It's my turn to smile. Ha! Anita's got to go answer it now. And when she does, I'll lock myself in. (Why didn't I think of that

before? I'm usually pretty good at finding ways to keep
people out.)

She doesn't move. She just raises her eyebrows. "Robin,
be a good girl. Go get that, would you?"

I can't believe her.

"*Me* go get it? You're the hired help. You go get it!"

She puts her hands on her hips and looks me up and
down like she's some tough chick from the 'hood.

The doorbell rings again. She flicks her head toward it.
"Off you go now! And be polite. Nobody likes a rude girl."

I'm so mad all I can do is hiss at her. She waves her
hand in front of her nose.

"You should brush your teeth too, honey. Fresh breath
is important if you ever want to be an active member of
society again."

I storm out of the room. "I'm only answering the door
so I can get away from *you*!"

I hate myself for saying it. I hate her for making me say
it.

Something sad and cold pours over me. This is how I
treat the one person who loves me? Like really loves me, I
mean. No wonder those girls at school dumped me. Why
would anyone like me?

I do what I'm supposed to do. I stand up straight. I put an almost-pleasant look on my face. So long, Robin.

I open the door and say, "Hello."

For one horrible second, I could swear it's another Anita staring back at me.

3

Friday, 3:30 p.m.
Radio Mimi

In "Cleaning the House, Cleansing the Soul,"
psychologist Adele Currie tells us what we can
discover about ourselves through our housekeeping
styles. Clean freak Mimi Schwartz reveals a
surprising secret.

I haven't seen Selena in ages. Must be since I started going
to boarding school. (When was that? Four years ago? Five
years ago? A lifetime?)

Selena didn't wear makeup back then—or a push-up
bra for that matter—but it doesn't take me long to recognize her. She looks exactly like her mother now. The
skinny hips, the skinny nose, the massive hair, the perfect

nails. She's wearing one of those ugly orange and purple Chili Willie's uniforms, complete with matching hat and burrito stain. You'd think it would bother her but it doesn't. The way she's standing, you'd swear she was wearing the latest Dolce & Gabbana. It makes me feel sort of embarrassed that she caught me in my sweats. I can't believe we used to be best friends.

From the look on her face, neither can she.

"What's your problem? Ma on your case?" she says.

What is this, voodoo or something? How come she and Anita can always see right through me?

I shake my head as if it's nothing and let her in. I'm suddenly nervous, suspicious. I feel like I'm surrounded. Is this one of Anita's little schemes? Find me a friend? Get me out of the house?

I don't think so. Anita gives Selena a big kiss but sounds as surprised to see her as I was. "What are *you* doing here?"

Selena tries to look offended. "What? It's a crime for a girl to want to see her mother occasionally?"

Anita just lowers her chin at that.

I get the feeling Selena didn't really expect to get away with it. "Okay. Fine. I need a ride home. I missed my bus. I'm babysitting the Lombardo kids at six."

Anita explodes. "Six! It's almost four!"

She's forgotten all about me. She's glaring at Selena now. (I never thought of that before. That's how to get Anita off my back! Feed her fresh meat. Let her "love" somebody else for a while.) She looks at her watch. She does this full-body exasperation thing—shrug, sigh, eye-roll, slump. "Well, you're going to have to help me then! I've still got Mimi's *entire* room to do!" She's so mad her lips keep moving even after she's stopped talking.

Selena follows Anita down the hall. I head the other way. I've got a TV in my room. It's calling me home.

Anita doesn't even turn around. "You too, Robin," she says.

She knows I wouldn't scream at her with Selena there. I'm trapped. I follow her too.

Anita is making a big deal about nothing. Mom's room is spotless as usual. Doesn't matter what time she has to be at the studio or how late she was out the night before, Mom always hangs up her clothes. She always lines up her shoes by colour and heel height. Her bedroom always looks exactly the way it did the day the interior designer placed the last expensive knick-knack on the mantelpiece. It's like a fancy hotel room. The only thing that looks out of place is that old picture of me on the bedside table.

Anita hands us each a cloth. She points at two high-back antique chairs that no one's ever sat in and says, "Dust." She heads off to the other side of the room and powers up the vacuum.

I take the left chair, Selena takes the right. She immediately starts rushing around as if this is some type of *Survivor* challenge. I turn my back to her and kind of swish away at the chair. What a waste of time. I feel like I'm on *CSI* or something. The chair's already clean. What am I trying to pick up here anyway? Traces of DNA?

I swish some more. I back up to see how I'm doing. I guess Selena does the same thing. Whatever. We smash butt-first into each other. That little ass of hers is surprisingly powerful. I go hurtling forward like I just got rear-ended by a Greyhound bus. I grab an arm of the chair to keep my face from smashing into the wall.

Brilliant.

As if a spindly thing like that could hold a tank like me.

The chair flips over and I end up doing this flying-hippo belly flop right on top of it. I try to get up but the floor is slippery and I can't manoeuvre with the seat of the chair wedged into my gut. It's so embarrassing. I must look like a dead moose tied to the roof of a Smart Car.

Luckily, Anita's still vacuuming the walk-in closet. She doesn't hear anything.

Selena, though, sees me splopped over this upside-down chair and goes nuts enough for the two of them. She slaps her hands on either side of her head and starts mouthing swear words at me. She clearly thinks this is my fault. (Can someone please explain why my ass is more to blame than hers?) She digs her little feet into the carpet and starts yanking me by the arm.

That's a big help.

Every time she pulls, my face slams into the leg of the chair. It doesn't stop her. She just yanks harder.

I don't know why but I suddenly find this all hilarious. Me totally klutzed out on the back of some priceless antique. Selena bashing my brains in. Even the thought of what Anita's going to do when she catches us. It totally cracks me up.

Selena's still swearing and sweating and yanking but pretty soon she's laughing too. She's pulled me halfway across the room and I'm still no closer to getting upright. We nearly pee ourselves when we realize that my lip's bleeding all over everything.

The sound of the vacuum suddenly gets louder. I turn and see Anita backing out of the closet.

We are so getting killed.

Selena cranks up the lip-swearing. She yanks harder. The chair tips over on its side. Something shiny hits the floor. We both see it. I mouth a swear word too, then freeze. Now we've gone and broken something.

Selena is better in a crisis than I am. She immediately goes into her Flashgirl superhero mode. I half expect her eyes to start glowing and little fluorescent whirlwinds to blow up around her. In a nanosecond, she plucks the thing off the floor, stuffs it in her pocket, grabs a fistful of my pants and pulls. That's all it takes—a Class A wedgie—and I'm on my feet an instant before Anita turns around.

Unfortunately, Anita's no fool. She immediately notices that I have the leg of a chair caught in my hair.

The way she screeches you'd swear she'd just stumbled on the decapitated remains of her entire family. She drops the vacuum, races over and rips the chair out of my hair. (And my hair out of my head, but, like, whatever.) She falls to her knees as if she's going to start giving the chair CPR or something.

She flails an arm at us. "Get out! *Get out!*"

We know better than to say anything. We get out.

Somehow we manage not to laugh until we're safely in my room.

4

Mimi: The Magazine

Friends, enemies or frenemies? Find out where you stand. Also, don't be chicken: ten bold new ways to serve your favourite fowl. Available on newsstands now.

Selena's rolling on the floor, killing herself laughing, when all of a sudden she winces. "Yowch! What the . . . ?"

She gets up, rubbing her hip. She's annoyed for a second, then her face just, like, blooms. She reaches into her pocket and goes, "The thing! . . . I forgot about the thing!"

She jumps onto the bed beside me, all excited. I get this little memory of being about nine and the two of us finding something—I can't remember what, an old key maybe—and thinking it was magic. We were too old to actually believe that kind of stuff but it didn't matter. It was our own little world. We could believe whatever we wanted to back then.

I'm looking at Selena still sort of bouncing on the bed and I suddenly remember the whole concept of "fun." It's like I stumbled on a picture of someplace I forgot I ever even visited and, just like that, all the fabulous things I did on the trip start coming back to me. I get this happy feeling in my stomach. I almost laugh. Life's so weird. Half an hour ago, I didn't even want to answer the door. Now, I don't know, I feel part of something again.

Selena slumps against the wall and goes, "Damn." She tosses the thing at me. "I thought it was some big honking sapphire," she says, "but it's just some ugly football ring."

I smile and shake my head. Who cares what it is? I slip the ring over my thumb and try to read what's written on it. It's kind of grubby, as if it's been through a lot. "'Port Mutton, N.S. . . .'"

"That's Minton, you moron." Selena makes this little one-ha laugh. "Port Mutton. Are you nuts? Who'd name a place Port Mutton?" She gives me this squiggly eyebrow look.

I squiggle my eyebrows right back at her. Old buddies. I say, "Yeah, well, someone named a place Boca Raton. You know, like, Mouth of Zee Rat? Doesn't stop rich people from going there."

"And I guess you'd know about that, wouldn't you," she says.

My face goes hot. Is she pissed off? Does she think I'm bragging? Why would I brag about being rich? Like I need to be anyone else's target.

Selena clicks her tongue. "Still doesn't make it Port Mutton."

Relax. She's okay. She's just joking.

I say, "Fine. So it's Port *Minton* High School Panthers. Whatever. What's my mother doing with a high school football ring in her bedroom?"

She winks. "Do you really want to know?"

Anita would kill her if she heard her say something like that. I just gag.

Selena says, "Sorry," and gags too. We both laugh.

I stare at the ring. It's huge, even for me. Mimi could no doubt wear it as a bracelet.

If I'd found it anywhere else, it would have been *yeah, so what? A football ring. Big deal.* But finding it in Mom's room is just plain bizarre. Mimi has nothing in her room. Nothing, I mean, that a decorator or a stylist or an assistant of some type didn't pick out, buy and unpack for her. Even that picture of me came from Anita one Christmas. Where would Mimi get something like this?

And where did it come from exactly? It couldn't have been on the chair. I would have noticed. Was it *inside* the chair? That's even weirder.

I say, "Seriously though. Don't you think someone like Mimi would be more likely to have a big honking sapphire than a football ring? I mean, really. A *high school* football ring? Not her style at all."

Selena doesn't disagree. She just doesn't seem to find it all that interesting.

"Who's to say it's even Mimi's?"

Good point.

"Maybe it's your Dad's."

I go, "*My Dad's?*"

Selena bugs out her eyes and says, "Joke."

We crack up. Dad's the lead singer in this lame rock band. He's the only person I know with a smaller ass than Selena's. He's hardly the type to play football—unless, of course, they needed someone to play goal post. Besides,

Mom hasn't talked to Dad in at least five years. (I can't imagine how long it's been since he was in her bedroom. Ick. Don't even want to think about that.)

"Okay, then whose is it?" I say.

Selena's looking for split ends. "How am I supposed to know? Could be anyone's. Maybe the guy who upholstered the chair hid it there. Maybe the moving man dropped it. Maybe"—she goes totally cross-eyed trying to inspect this big hunk of hair—"you should just ask your mother. Seems easy enough to me."

"Yeah," I say—but what I think is *As if . . .* No way would I mention this to Mimi. Selena has completely misread our relationship. (She shouldn't believe everything she hears on TV.)

I let it drop. The silence starts getting awkward. I wish we were both laughing again but too much time has already passed for me to go, *Wasn't that hilarious when the chair . . . ,* or, *Did you see the look on Anita's face when . . .* That kind of stuff has got to be natural to work.

I rack my brain for something to say but all I can think is, *Danger. Danger.* I'm so weird around people now.

Why wouldn't I be?

You think someone's your friend and you're all happy

and relaxed until you find out they just want tickets to the show or a chance to meet Robert Pattinson or even—and this is my favourite—a good shot of the dimples in your thighs so they can plaster it all over the Internet. How many times do you have to let yourself get burned before you say, "I'm not playing any more"? How many times do you have to get sucker-punched before you realize you can't trust anyone?

Selena's still picking through her hair. It's like she couldn't care less about me. That's somehow reassuring.

I should just chill out. We've known each other since we were babies. Selena could get tickets to *You, You and Mimi* whenever she wants. She was here when Beyoncé and Pink and all those girls came for Mimi's Celebrity Sleepover. She must have lots of incriminating pictures of me. She's never done anything with them. She wouldn't. Anita would kill her.

What am I afraid of? We're having fun. It's okay.

I wet my lips. I say, "So, like, what are you up to these days?"

She's going at her cuticles now. She's clearly not trying to impress me. That's good.

"The usual," she says. She doesn't even look up. "Working

full-time at Willie's for the summer. Babysitting most nights. When I find the time, hanging with my friends. What about you?"

"Uh . . . Nothing," I say.

Now she looks up. "Nothing? No job?"

She doesn't wait for an answer "No. I guess you don't need a job, do you. So whaddya do, then?"

"Don't know," I say. I try to smile. "Not much."

"You still draw?"

"No."

"Read?"

"Not unless I have to."

"Go shopping?"

I shake my head. What have I started?

"You must do *something*. C'mon. Go to movies? Get your nails done? Commit acts of vandalism? . . . Stop me if I'm getting warm."

I'm not sure if that's contempt or sarcasm I'm hearing but it doesn't matter. I recognize the signs. She's seen who I really am and she doesn't like it. Oh well. So much for my little trip to Funsville.

I wipe my tongue over my teeth and look away.

"Seriously. What do you do all day? Stare at the walls?"

I go, "Whatever." I'm so pathetic. Getting all excited! Did I really think we were going to be friends again, just like that?

I start looking at my hands as if it's *my* turn to fix my cuticles. My skin is dry and scaly. My thumbnails are all weird and ridged and stubby. I bunch my hands up into fists so she can't see them.

She gets up off the bed. "People like you make me so mad."

I can't believe it. "Why am I making *you* mad?"

She pauses, I presume, for effect. "I'll tell you why. Because I work two jobs all summer long. I pay my mother a hundred and fifty bucks a month room-and-board. I work for every T-shirt I own, every lip gloss, every minute of my cellphone plan. I'd love to learn to dance or take guitar lessons or do Pilates, but I can't because I have to clean the apartment and do the laundry and buy the groceries. Meanwhile, you! . . . You! You've got all the time in the world. You live in a penthouse overlooking Central Park. You've got your own Visa and a bank account that somebody else fills up for you. You've got the life I dream of. And what do you do? You waste it! You apparently don't even wash your hair. I can't stand it."

She thinks she's so smart but she doesn't get it at all.

"Like, seriously. Why don't you quit schlepping around and just *do* something?"

I make it as simple for her as I can. "Like what? There's nothing to do here."

She holds her mouth open as if she's too shocked to speak. (I should be so lucky.)

"Right. Nothing to do here!" She makes a big point of looking at my computer, my sound system, my drum kit, my clothes. "Okay. Then go somewhere else!"

Sure. Where's this miracle place that would make everything better? My eyes can look as scary as hers. I say, "Oh yeah? Like where?"

She pretends to strangle me. "What difference does it make? Paris . . . Rome . . . Hong Kong!"

I smile. "Been there. Done that."

She picks the ring off the bed and biffs it at me. "Go to frigging Port Minton, then! Find the guy who gave this to your mother. Join the cheerleading squad. Sell peanuts at halftime. I don't care. Quit being such a spoiled brat. Get up off your ass and do something!"

She wipes the corner of her mouth and smooths out her polyester tunic. She looks me up and down. "I don't get it.

How come you got to be so lucky? You got money. You got brains. You even got boobs! You won the jackpot—and you're too stupid to enjoy it."

She sashays over to the door.

"See you later," she says. "Unlike some people, *I've* got things to do."

Oh, she loved that snappy little rejoinder! I try my best to laugh.

5

Friday, 5 p.m.
***You, You and Mimi* (rerun)**

"Streamlined Living." Five leading organizational
experts show you how to declutter your home,
your life and your personal relationships.

Selena's standing by the elevator. She looks like she's
watching for cops while her buddies rob the joint. Anita's
dragged me to the door so she can keep giving orders
all the way out. I don't fight it. The longer I can keep my
mouth shut, the faster they'll both get out of here.

"There's a nice low-fat meal for you in the oven. I got the
recipe from Tuesday's show. Eat the vegetables. I'll know
if you throw them out. Don't forget—tomorrow's Saturday.
You're going to your dad's. Tony will pick you up for the

airpoit at twelve forty-five. That leaves you plenty of time to see your grandfather in the morning. Visiting hours are ten to twelve. Don't look at me that way. Just because he doesn't recognize you, doesn't mean he doesn't care about you. What else? . . . Oh yes. I packed some gym gear in your bag. You need to get some exercise. It'll help you get out of this slump. Remember to bring your retainer. I don't want to have to FedEx it all the way to San Francisco again. That's expensive. Don't wear those sweats on the plane. They're disgusting. It's not fair to the other passengers—and besides, you're a beautiful girl. You should flaunt it. Quit sneering at me. It's true. You have lots of lovely clothes to wear. That nice blue-green shirt your mother brought back from Barcelona matches your eyes perfectly. I laid it out in your room with a new pair of jeans. They have angled back pockets that are very flattering for your figure type. It's time you washed your hair. People would kill to have that gorgeous auburn hair—so look after it. Believe me, that new girlfriend of your father's is not the kind to understand dirty hair. And why don't you start wearing your contacts again? It doesn't make sense, you going around in those ugly old glasses when you're so pretty in your contacts. Tony will make sure you've got your purse. Your passport is in the zippered pocket on the right. I also put in a couple hundred bucks just in case you don't have time to get to the ATM or your dad forgets to pick you up at the airport again. In the meantime, turn off the TV, for heaven's sake! Why do you need to watch that endless "Mimi Marathon"? You can see your mother when she comes home. Which reminds me. She called. She's very upset. She hates to miss your last evening home but this new syndication deal is more complicated than she thought. She'll try to get back before you go to bed—which, by the way, should be no later than eleven. You look exhausted. Use some of that Visine I left in your bathroom."

Selena sighs. "Ma, c'mon! The elevator."

Anita waves her off like a cat batting away a mouse. "I'll meet you downstairs."

She turns back and looks me right in the eye. "What am I forgetting? Money, ID, retainer, clothes, grandfather, father, mother . . ." She bites her lip. "I guess that's everything. No. There's one more thing. . . ."

I know what's coming. It's going to hurt.

She reaches up and puts her arms around me. I pull back but she just hangs on tighter.

"I forgot to tell you how much I love you. I'm going to miss you. I don't know what's bothering you but I know things have been rough for you lately. I know we've been at each other's throats. You need a break. Maybe when you get back, you, me and Selena can all go out somewhere. Just like old times . . ." She kisses my cheek and, even though she's way smaller than me, rocks me back and forth like I'm a baby or something. She mumbles, "My little Birdie . . ."

I can feel her face is wet. I'm going away for three weeks and she's crying.

I should ignore her but I can't. For a second, I feel myself kind of melt. I lean on her. I want to just let go, give in. I take a breath and stop myself.

"Fine, okay," I say. "See ya." I should say I love her too, but I don't. I turn away.

Anita rubs my hand against her face before I can pry it loose.

"Text me as soon as you get there. . . . And lock the door behind you," she says. "I'm staying here until I hear the dead bolt click."

6

Friday, 8 p.m.

You, You and Mimi (rerun)

"Sweet Treats." Remember when Mimi was a
redhead? This early episode is an interesting trip
down fashion's memory lane. It also features a
particularly cute cooking segment.

This is an old episode. I know that because there are pictures of me in the opening montage. Mom and me riding
a tandem bike. Me getting my hair cut for the first time.
That cranky English lady teaching us which fork to use. I
forgot I used to be in the opening. When did they change
it?

Why?

What did I do?

This must be a Wednesday show. "Eating Like a Birdie" is on. I remember it perfectly. This girl named Mattea Cacchione was a production assistant back then. She was so nice. Anita would bring me to the studio about an hour before start time. Mattea would meet us in the lobby and take me upstairs. They'd put me in my little white chef's uniform. Annalise would do my makeup and fix my hair. It was bright red and really curly back then. If I was lucky, Mom would get her makeup done at the same time. Sometimes she was too busy and I wouldn't see her until my segment came on. I'd be really excited by then. The audience would all go *oooh* when I ran out and hugged her.

Here I am now. I don't look nervous at all. Funny. I'd be freaked if I had to do it today. Back then it was just natural. My life.

I walk out on set. I have to keep pushing my chef's hat up out of my eyes. It's kind of cute. The wardrobe person probably made it too big on purpose. (What was his name? Darryl? Darrin? He acted nice but he wasn't really. He kept on mentioning my "nice round tummy." I wonder how he'd feel if I kept talking about his "nice bulbous nose.")

Mom's waiting for me on the kitchen set in her *I'm just following orders!* apron. I scramble up onto the stool so I

can see above the counter. She says "Hello, Little Birdie!"—
something she picked up from Anita—and I say, "Hello,
Big Mama!" She pretends she doesn't like to be called
"Big." How dumb is that? I'm probably the only person
in the whole studio who'd think she's big. I'm about five.
Everyone's big to me.

She asks me what I'm going to cook today. I say, "Peanut
butter truffles!" just like Anita and I practised. It comes out
"twuffles." The audience loves it.

The truffles aren't much more than sugar, peanut butter
and chocolate chips. Mom and I each have a bowl and a
big wooden spoon. I tell her what to do. She always says,
"Yes, ma'am!" or "Right away!" I mix everything together,
then take a fistful of dough and roll it into a ball. I'm con-
centrating. I don't want to make a mistake. Anita's told me
to make just three truffles, not the whole batch. I'm old
enough now to know that you can't take too long doing
stuff on TV. You have to leave time for the commercials.

I push my hat up again. Everybody laughs really hard. (I
remember this so well!) I didn't know why. I look around
to see what's so funny. The camera zooms in on this big
smear of peanut butter across my forehead. A chocolate
chip is stuck right in the middle. Close-up on Mimi. She's

screwing her face up in this really exaggerated way, like, *Should I tell her—or shouldn't I?*

I'm worried we're taking too long. Why isn't she doing anything? She hasn't even started to roll out her truffles. I say, "Hurry, Mommy, or there won't be time for our sponsors!" Huge laugh at that.

Mimi jumps into action. She's being very messy. I don't understand. She's never messy at home. She'd be mad if I ever did that. This can't be good. I'm not sure what to do. The show had just started to get big. Lots of people are watching. People in twenty-three countries worldwide! I know that because Anita lets me watch the show every day while she's making supper. Mom shouldn't be making a mess in front of everybody.

I say, "You better stop, Mommy. You're not doing a very good job."

I'm surprised the audience laughs at that. Mimi pretends to be hurt.

Even then, I sort of know she's joking, but I hug her anyway. I love her so much. I don't want to make her unhappy. I pat her with my sticky hands and say, "That's okay. Don't be sad. You can have one of my twuffles!"

The audience does that *awww* thing. I know that's good.

I say, "Which one do you want?"

Mom says, "Can I really have *any* one I want?"

I give this big, slow nod.

Mom thinks about it for a second, then she suddenly leans over and licks the dough off my forehead. I'm so surprised my eyes fly wide open like I'm a character in an anime cartoon or something.

Mom goes, "Mmm-mmm good!" and hugs me.

We cut to a commercial. No one can hear her telling me what a great job I did, but I remember.

I have to admit—that was a really good segment. I was so cute! The hair, the hat, the funny voice. It makes me laugh seeing it again.

Then it makes me cry.

7

Friday, 10 p.m.

You, You and Mimi

Mimi and world-renowned nutritional psychologist
Dr. Zita Fenwick-Wilson explore the roots and
causes of emotional eating in "Food Is Love."

I can't stop bawling. I keep changing the channel but it
doesn't help. Mimi's on three other stations. What kind
of pathetic person is watching this stuff at ten o'clock on
a Friday night? I chuck the remote at the TV and get out.

I go to the kitchen. I'm going to stuff my face with something. Nutella. Bagel chips. A row or two of Fudgee-Os. I
don't care. Just something to fill the hole. I pull open a
cupboard door. I see the food and I think of "Eating Like
a Birdie." I start crying all over again. I slam the door so
hard it bounces back open.

I've got to get out of the kitchen before I break something. I make it to the door but can't go any farther. I don't know what to do. I look up and down the hall as if I've never seen this place before. As if I have no idea where to go.

And I don't. I'm too scared to move. I'm too scared to even think about moving because I know there will be something somewhere that will get me crying again. For a second, I consider racing down the hall and locking myself in my room, but even thinking that makes my eyes sting again. I know I'm not safe there either.

I get this picture in my head of the tall blond designer Mom had on that segment "Decorating for Your Teen" and something about that one word—Your—just practically kills me. I slide down onto the floor and bang and bang and bang my head against the wall until I stop thinking about that stuff. . . .

I'm not sure how much time has passed, but I'm calmer now. I have to do something. Mom can't find me like this. I get up. I go into the kitchen and make sure the cupboard door is closed. I leave one light on, over the stove. Mimi will turn it off when she gets home. (She can't stand wasting electricity. Viewers would be surprised to see how cheap she can be.)

I go to the TV room. I find the remote I threw and put it on the coffee table. I turn off the television. I line the magazines up neatly. I fold the blanket over the back of the couch.

I wasn't anywhere else. I didn't leave a mess anywhere else. I checked. I'm sure. I can go to bed now.

Except that I don't.

I go to Mom's room.

8

Friday, 11 p.m.

Late Night with Campbell Irving

Guest star Mimi Schwartz discloses the almost comical lengths she's gone to for a little privacy in her floodlit life.

At first, all I do is stand in the doorway and stare. I don't know why. I just feel like I want to look at it.

Next thing I know though, I'm going through her bedside table, rifling through her closet, checking her medicine cabinet, her desk. I have no idea what I expect to find. I don't know what I'm looking for. Some clue, I guess.

There's a folder in her desk with my grandmother's obituary and my parents' marriage certificate and my report cards and other documents like that. I don't bother reading any of them. They won't have the type of clue I'm look-ing for. I don't want facts. I want something real.

Nothing in this room is real. It's all designer clothing, European face creams, the latest magazines. There's no Mimi here.

I see that picture of me on her bedside table and pick it up. When they took it, I hadn't even got braces or glasses or fat yet. I was just chubby. It hits me that this is like some upside-down version of a "Before and After" segment. This time it's the "Before" that's cute and happy and almost pulled-together. It's the "After" that's big and lumpy and mad and totally, totally hopeless.

I ram my palm into my forehead and scrunch my eyes closed. I don't want to remember the last time I was on Mimi's show but it's in my head now and it won't go away.

I was about eleven, I guess. It had been a while since I'd been on-air even then, but Mother's Day was coming up. I had to make an appearance. The wardrobe people wanted to put Mom and me in matching outfits but it didn't take them long to change their minds. It was pretty clear that everything that looked good on her was going to look ter-rible on me.

I had a belly and frizzy hair and bad posture and I couldn't stop rubbing my nose with the back of my wrist. They made me keep my hands in my pockets and they straightened my hair and put me in black pants and a jacket that accentuated my so-called waist—but none of it helped. Nobody went *awww* when I came on this time. The hour-long special they'd planned of our mother-and-daughter excursion got edited down to a five-minute segment. The producers tried to fluff it up with fuzzy lenses and long shots of us holding hands and Mimi's sappy voice-over about our special time together—but even then the problem was obvious.

Me.

Big, ugly, awkward me.

Where did I come from? How could perfect little Mimi Schwartz produce someone like me? No wonder she took me off the air. No wonder she sent me to boarding school.

I start making these little shivery sobs, but I bite my lip until they stop. I hold my breath.

Mimi could be home any second. I've got to get out of her room—but I can't. Not yet. Because suddenly I know why I'm here.

I pull the chair out. I check the curtains behind it and

the table beside it. I look for a box, a safe, a hole in the floor. I need to find out where that ring came from. I rub my hands over the upholstery and down the legs. I flip the chair over. The cloth on the bottom is beige and rough. It's attached to the frame with little round-topped tacks. One of them is missing.

It's as if an alarm goes off in my head. I stick my finger in the gap where the tack should be. I can't feel anything. I shake the chair. I hear something sliding over the fabric.

I get the letter opener from Mimi's desk and pry out a few more tacks. I tip the chair again. The corner of an old photo pokes out of the hole. I can't get at it. I take out a few more tacks. The picture drops onto the floor.

I don't have time to look at it. I've got to fix the chair before Mom comes home. I have to do it right. Otherwise, she'll notice.

I run for the little hammer Anita keeps in the broom closet. I sort of laugh. There was a segment on the other day about how to reupholster a chair. I remember the guy telling Mimi that you have to pull the fabric tight and tack the centre of each side first. It's sort of funny—Mom has actually managed to teach me quite a bit over the years. Me and millions of others of course.

I bang in the tacks. I turn the chair over and check to make sure it's lined up the way Anita likes. I back out of the room, wiping my footprints off the carpet as I go. That's overkill, I know. Mimi would never notice a little thing like that.

Or would she?

I'm safely back in my room, looking at the photo, when I hear her come in. I've seen this picture before, or at least one like it. There aren't many shots of Mom as a kid. Their house burned down when she was a teenager. They lost almost everything.

This one looks like it was taken on a class trip. There are a bunch of kids leaning against this lady. There's a boulder in the background and maybe a beach. Most people are laughing, as if the guy taking the picture just mooned them or something. Mom's off to one side. She's not laughing, just sort of smiling. She's either nervous (hard to believe) or the photographer caught her off guard. There are some names on the back of the photo. They don't mean anything to me. I don't remember Mom ever mentioning a Tracy-Lynn or a Lenore.

I hear Mom walk down the hall. She stops outside my room. I want to ask her when the photo was taken and why she hid it—but I don't.

I slip it under my pillow and turn off the light. She knows I'm awake but she doesn't open the door. She doesn't knock. After a couple of seconds, she just turns and walks back to her room.

That's when I decide to go.

9

Saturday, 10 a.m.
Radio Mimi

In "True or False," Mimi welcomes family counsellor
Deni Ogunrinde, author of *Teen-y, Weeny Lies:
Coping with Adolescent Dishonesty*.

Hi Mom,

Sorry I didn't get up in time to say goodbye in
person. Gone to Dad's. You can reach me on my
cell. I know you're busy though, so don't worry if
you don't have time.

I'm wearing that new shirt you got me in
Barcelona. Thanks. I really like it.

See you on the 21st,

Robin

"Hello."

"Ah . . . hi. Kelly?"

"Yes. Who's this?"

"It's Robin. . . ."

"Robin?"

"Steve's daughter."

"Oh! Sorry. Didn't recognize your voice."

"Yeah, well. It's me all right, ha-ha! May I talk to Dad?"

"You just missed him. There a message?"

"Yeah. I'm supposed to come to your place today—"

"What? Steve didn't tell me that! He's on the road! I don't know what you'd do here all alone with me—"

"Kelly?"

"—I'm teaching yoga! I'm purging! I've got to take Bruno to the vet! I'm—"

"Kelly? . . . Kelly? . . . That's what I was calling about. Something's come up. I can't come after all."

"Oh . . . ah . . . . Really? Too bad."

"Yeah."

"Maybe we can set something up for another time, you know, one that's not so busy."

"Right. Sure. Well, tell Dad I said hi."

"I'll do that. Thanks for calling."

"No problem. See ya."

"Peace."

From: birdbrain76@airmail.com

To: gumdrop113@airmail.com

Subject: So there

Selena

Just so u know, I did get off my ass. I'm at the

airport. I'm on my way 2 Port Minton, Nova Scotia.

I'll send u a postcard when I find out who gave Mimi

the ring.

Don't work too hard,

Robin

Message 734

hey anita. i made it

c u in 3 weeks R

10

Saturday, 7 p.m.

***You, You and Mimi* (rerun)**

"Voyages of Discovery." Mimi interviews women
whose lives were irrevocably changed by a simple
road trip.

The bus driver pulls over to the side of the road and goes,
"Okay, little lady, this is it! Port Minton." He cranks open
the door.

I bend forward and look out the window. I go, "Where?"
MapQuest just showed a tiny dot for Port Minton, NS (as
in Nova Scotia), so I'm not expecting much—a little vil-
lage maybe, a store or two—but there's nothing here.

Like, I mean, *nothing*.

I'm talking a couple of shabby houses still sporting their

Christmas lights. A mobile home with a dog chained out front. An old boat leaning against a wharf. That's it.

The bus driver points across the highway and says, "See that road? Beautiful downtown Port Minton is right at the end."

The lady knitting in the front seat laughs, so I kind of laugh too and sit back down again. I figure he's joking. I guess the guy has to do something on these long trips to keep himself amused.

The bus driver looks at me through the rearview mirror. "Hey!" he goes. "Isn't this where you wanted to get off?"

"You're serious?" I say. "This is where I get off for Port Minton?" I put on my backpack and wheel my suitcase to the front of the bus.

Someone says, "Yup—what's left of it!" That gets a few chuckles.

The bus driver says, "You never been here before?"

I shake my head.

"You got people here?"

I shake my head again.

"Then Lord liftin', girl. What are you doing coming here?"

Good question. I don't know. I obviously wasn't thinking straight last night.

"Well. Um. I came to see the school," I say, because I sort of have to say something. "You know, Port Minton High."

Everyone's put down their knitting and word searches now. I'm clearly the most exciting thing that's happened on this bus route in some time.

A guy I thought was asleep goes, "That school's been closed for a good ten, twelve years!"

"Oh, more than that, Arch," someone says. "Seems to me it shut down right after the fish plant did."

"What's a fish plant?" I say.

This teenage kid snorts at me as if he's Selena's long-lost brother and goes, "You don't know what a fish plant is? What—you a Bister or something, girl?"

I don't know what a Bister is either, but I know better than to ask. The bus driver shuts the guy up pretty quick.

"Listen here, buddy, I'm not having that type of talk on my bus. Understood? This young lady's not from around here. My guess is she's from the city."

He looks at me with his eyebrows up and smiles. I nod. I'm not lying. New York's a city.

"No reason you should know what a fish plant is, then. But seeing as you asked . . . the fish plant's where they used to clean the cod the men caught. Not much cod around here any more so they shut down the plant. Most everybody had to move to find work. Port Minton pretty much died after that. The high school closed. Any kids still living around here—and there ain't many—go into Shelton, the town we passed a ways back. People put up a big fuss about it but the kids don't seem to mind. They like being where the action is."

The action. Like there's any action around here. I resist the urge to roll my eyes.

The bus driver pulls the door closed.

"Look, dear," he says. "You don't have to get off here if you don't want. If you can stand me for six more hours, I'll get you back to the airport. But you got to make up your mind. I got a schedule to keep. If I'm late into Cape Sable again, they'll skin me alive. So what'll it be? On or off?"

The bus driver's nice enough. He's not going to hurt me or anything but my heart starts pounding like crazy. I hate making decisions.

I stand there with this stunned look on my face.

The knitting lady takes pity on me. She says, "Irvine, the school's still here. Maybe she just wanted to see the building. For its—you know—architecture or something."

The bus driver perks up. "Oh. Is that it?" he says. "You just wanted to see the building?"

I blink him into focus. I nod. Sure. The architecture. That's it.

"Well then," he says. "That's easy enough!" He points out the window. "The school's just ten, fifteen minutes down that road over there. Can't miss it."

He opens the door again. "I'd take you down myself, but like I says, they'd skin me alive if I'm late into the Cape."

I thank him and bump my Louis Vuitton suitcase down the steps.

The knitting lady says, "I like your bag, dear. I bought myself a pink one just like it at the Sackville Flea Market last week."

The bus driver waves and pulls back onto the highway. I stand on the shoulder and look across at the sad little dirt road that leads to Port Minton.

I kick a paper coffee cup into the ditch. Only I could run away from home and end up in a place like this.

11

Saturday, 8 p.m.

Mini Mimi

In the first episode of her new teen talk show, Mimi interviews homecoming queens Alyssa Milobar and Erica Allan about navigating the perils of high school society.

Apparently, Monsieur Vuitton didn't design the wheels on my luggage for dirt roads. One of them is already jammed. I'm pretty much just dragging the suitcase now. It's getting all scratched to hell. Anita's going to kill me when she sees it.

Good. Put me out of my misery.

What was I thinking, just up and taking off like that? As if it was going to prove something to Selena. As if Mom ever would have set foot in a place like this. As if I even care where that stupid ring comes from. This has got to be the dumbest thing I've ever done in my life.

Next time I run away, I'm going to Paris. At least I know my way around there. At least there'd be *un bellhop* to carry *mon bagage*. At least the food is good.

Food.

That's my problem. That's why I'm such a wreck.

I'm starving. How long has it been since I ate? I didn't eat last night. I had too much to do. Even with Mapquest, it wasn't easy tracking down Port Minton, let alone figuring out how to get here. (Anita always handles my travel plans.)

I didn't eat this morning either. I couldn't. I was too nervous. I was sure Tony was going to realize something was up. He's usually standing by the limo for hours, all in a panic, waiting for me. This time, I wanted to go to the airport two hours earlier than scheduled! I've just got to pray he put it down to a sudden spurt of maturity.

I bought a chicken wrap on the plane. I ate a bit but then I had to stop. The woman next to me was watching *You, You and Mimi* on her video screen. I almost threw up. I couldn't hear what they were saying but it didn't matter. Just knowing Mimi was right beside me talking to Dr. Hannah Meeson—her "Happy Family Specialist"—was enough. Were they talking about me? About us? If not, why weren't they? (Is there a so-called family anywhere that needs help more than we do?)

Food was out of the question.

I was worried about missing the bus so I didn't get anything at the airport either. The counter where you buy your bus tickets had chips and candy and stuff like that. I was thinking about getting something there but when I handed the woman my credit card she said, "Robin Schwartz? You're not *the* Robin Schwartz, are you? Mimi's little girl?"

I went "No, no!"

You'd think the lady would be suspicious, the way I quasi-freaked and everything, but she started to laugh and said, "Just kidding! You must get that all the time. Guess you're glad your name's not Britney Spears, eh?"

I took my ticket and got out of there as fast as I could.

I was so relieved to be on the bus without any TV screens or people asking my name that I forgot about being hungry.

Until now. Now I remember. I'm starving.

We passed a gas station on the highway. They'd have food. How far back was that? Couldn't be too far.

I turn around, but then I think, *No*.

No. I've got to keep going. I've come this far. I'm not going to let anyone—i.e., Selena—say I didn't do it. (Why did I send her that stupid e-mail?)

I trudge on. It's July but up here I guess that doesn't mean much. It's getting cold. The fog just rolled in. Everything's so damp.

I go round a bend in the road and come to a drive-way with a chain across it. I look up and there it is. Port Minton High. Home of the Panthers.

I'd be willing to bet I'm the first person to come here for the architecture. The school is pretty much just a box—square, flat, white, wooden. The paint is peeling. The big wide steps are rotten right through and one of the railings is broken. Above the double doors, there's a white sign with hand-painted letters: Port Minton Rural Consolidated High School. (I guess they couldn't get all that on the ring.) The lawn is overgrown. The driveway is cracked and full of potholes. Bits of garbage dangle off the bushes out front.

I leave my suitcase on the lawn and walk up the steps. I lean over the good railing and look through the window.

It's your standard old-fashioned classroom, right out of some movie where girls wore big skirts and carried binders and boys got in trouble for tilting back in their chairs. It's got a green and black checkerboard floor. A chalkboard that goes all the way across one wall. A clock that's stopped at 12:22. And a big wooden desk for the teacher. If it weren't for the mess all around it, you'd practically expect to see an apple sitting on top.

There are still a few student desks but most of them are knocked over on their side. The place is dirty. There are broken beer bottles on the floor and gross drawings on the board. Someone wrote *John*—or maybe it's *Joan*—is *a Bister.* My guess is kids have been using the place as a hangout for quite a while. There's graffiti all over the walls.

I squint to see what else they've written. Nothing interesting—at least to me. No *Mimi Schwartz was here.*

It's not like I'm surprised. I checked Mom's website last night. It lists all the places she's toured since the show went global. Nova Scotia wasn't one of them. I told myself she might have come here on vacation, but I never seriously believed that either. (Mimi can't be that far away from her Versace supplier. She goes through jewel-encrusted bustiers at quite a clip.)

I'm not kidding myself. I know I didn't come to Port Minton because I had a burning desire to find out what Mom was doing with some grubby old ring. I just wanted an excuse to get away from my life.

I sit down on the steps. I get a little stab of guilt about not visiting Grandpa before I left. Poor guy. Stuck in that fancy home with everything he could ever want and all he does is sit around drooling. (We have a lot in common.) I should have gone to see him. He hasn't got a clue who I am but he seems to like it when I hold his hand and talk to him. As long as one of those nosy nurses isn't there, I can tell him anything.

How sad is that. My grandfather—the vegetable—is probably my best friend in the world.

I have one of those little laugh/cry moments, but I make myself stop. I can't think about stuff like that. I'm cold. I'm wet. I'm hungry. I've got to get out of here.

But I don't move. I can't. I'm suddenly exhausted. I look out across the road. I know the ocean's right there but it's so foggy I can barely see it. All I can hear is the waves hitting the shore. They're slow and heavy, like some cartoon giant clomping around in wet boots. The sound almost puts me into a trance. I think about those Arctic explorers who got so cold that they just kind of fell asleep and died. If you ask me, that doesn't sound like such a bad way to go.

Selena would love to hear me say that. She thinks I'm a lazy, unmotivated slob. The type of person who *would* just sit around and die because she couldn't be bothered doing anything else.

So what if I am? What business is it of hers? Who does she think she is, passing judgment on me like that?

I stand up and start walking.

It's raining now. Water's dripping down my face. My feet are wet. The suitcase keeps tipping over on its side and banging me in the ass or clipping me in the ankle. I don't even try to fix it.

Things get a little easier once I hit the highway. At least on the pavement my suitcase almost rolls. On the other hand, I've got so much water in my eyes now that I can barely see where I'm going.

I hear the swish of a car coming up behind me. I don't even think. My brain just goes, *I'm saved!* I turn around and wave and jump and scream.

An old brown van stops right beside me.

I open the door. The inside light doesn't come on. I just see this big, dark silhouette of a guy sitting at the wheel. That's when I realize what I've done.

Seventeen-year-old girl hitchhiking alone on a stormy night gets into a beat-up van. I've watched enough movies to know what happens next. Cue the creepy music. Cover your eyes.

12

Saturday, 9:30 p.m.
Radio Mimi

"Insight into Insights." Mimi interviews author
and scientist Nathan Allen about his fascinating
new book, *Flash: The Power and Glory of First
Impressions*.

The guy goes, "C'mon. Get in!" He reaches over and lifts
my suitcase up with one hand.

I can hardly say *Thanks but no thanks* now. I was the
one who flagged him down. What can I do? I climb in.

He doesn't even ask where I'm headed. He just pulls out
onto the road. That can't be good. It's obvious he doesn't
care where *I* want to go. He's got his own plans for me. My
teeth start to chatter.

"You cold?" he says.

I sort of nod. (Yeah, sure, I'm cold. Me shaking like this has got absolutely nothing to do with the fact that I'm hurtling along a deserted highway in some Psycho Murdermobile with a total stranger at the wheel.) I don't look at him. I just do up my seat belt and keep staring out the front window.

All of a sudden, I feel his hand graze my knee. I jump. I squeak like some giant mouse.

"Oops. Sorry," he says. "I was just turning on the heat for you."

Sure. Nice recovery.

I wipe my glasses off with my sleeve so I can at least see who's abducting me, but it only makes things worse. The smear of water turns the streetlights into big spinning stars.

The guy goes, "Here," and hands me a roll of rough blue paper towel. "Don't want you to miss anything."

What does he mean by that? *What kind of sick thing does he mean by that?* All I can think is *Anita, Anita, Anita, Anita.*

I sort of dweeble out, "Thanks." I wipe off my face and glasses.

Everything's clear again.

Too clear. I can see what I got myself into now.

A street lamp lights up the van for a couple of seconds. The inside is filthy. The floor is covered with food wrappers, old coffee cups, crumpled road maps. I wonder if this is where he lives, in the van. I bet he sleeps here all day, then spends his nights just driving the highway, looking for people like me. Lonely, defenceless, stupid people.

Nobody knows him. Nobody notices him. He's just another guy in a rusty van on the road to someplace else. He's long gone before anyone asks themselves about those screams.

The perfect set-up for the perfect crime. The guy's obviously smart. That's even scarier. I take a quick glance behind me—

For once in my life, I'm right. There are no seats in the back. Just my suitcase, a blanket, a chainsaw and some ropes.

Anita! Anita! Anita!

I suck in my breath. I try not to cry. I clamp my teeth together. I can't let myself fall apart. I've got to look strong, give him second thoughts about trying anything. Mimi did a show on self-defence once. That's what her experts said. Don't look like a victim. Act confident. Guys aren't going to do anything if they think they might lose.

I lift my head and push back my shoulders. This might be the first time ever that I'm happy to be big. For a second, I honestly believe I could take him.

Then I remember him pulling my suitcase into the van with one hand. My giant two-ton suitcase. He picked it up like it was a Happy Meal.

I haven't a hope.

The guy goes, "I don't run into many girls out here by themselves." He's got an accent. It sounds sort of like, "Oi doane run inta . . ."

"I'm not by myself," I say. I remember that from the show too. Pretend you're with someone.

"Oh yeah?" he says. "Who you with?"

Is he laughing at me?

"My boyfriend," I say. "He went on ahead."

"Nice guy! Leaving you on the side of the road in the pouring rain . . ."

I don't let that get me. "He had an appointment," I say. "He had to go. He's waiting for me. He'll be worried if I don't get there soon."

"Where?"

"Where what?"

"Get *where* soon?"

Where am I going? Think, think, think. What did the bus driver say? What was the name of that town?

"Sherbrooke," I say.

The guy goes, "Hunh?"

"I mean, Sherbet."

He sort of laughs. "Sherbet? No Sherbet around here. Isn't that something you eat?"

What's the matter with me? I'm getting abducted and all I can think about is food?

It's really dark now. Signs of civilization—what there were of them—have almost disappeared. Every so often we pass a house with a couple of lights on but that's about it. I'm on my own.

What if I just opened the door and jumped?

I look out the side window and see the guardrails whizzing past.

I'd die, that's what would happen. But at least it would be fast. Question is: would it be faster than the chainsaw?

"Do you mean Shelton?" the guy says.

"Yes!" I say. "Yes. Yes. Shelton. That's it. He's waiting for me in Shelton."

"Where in Shelton?"

Where? I don't know where! Anita, if you can hear me, tell me. Send me some sign: where would a boyfriend be waiting for me in Shelton?

The pause is getting suspiciously long. I have to say something. I go, "At the hotel." I know it's hopeless now but I don't give up. That's what they said on the show. Don't give up. It ain't over until it's over.

The guy starts laughing. "The hotel? The *hotel* in Shelton? You don't know where you're going, do you?"

"Yes I do!" I say. "Liam—that's his name—Liam Johnston is meeting me at the hotel! That's what he said!"

The guy goes, "Okay, okay. Sorry."

I can tell he doesn't believe me.

"Didn't mean to upset you. I think I know where to take you."

I bet he does.

He doesn't say anything else. He just keeps driving into the dark.

Should I bargain with him? I could give him money. I've got lots of money. What would he take? I have no idea what kidnappers ask for these days. If it's more than a couple of hundred, I'd have to give him a cheque. Would he take a cheque? Mimi didn't touch on any of that in the show.

And anyway, would that be tacky? I don't want to insult him. Maybe trying to buy myself out would just make him madder.

Or maybe he'd just take the money and kill me anyway. That would be like throwing it away! No use doing that. Anita hates it when I do stuff like that.

What's the matter with me? I'm sure Anita would make an exception, *just this once*, seeing as the guy's planning to kill me and everything.

I remember. The self-defence expert said I'm supposed to poke the guy in the eye with my keys.

Great.

Like I know where my keys are. I *never* know where my keys are! I bit my nails down to the quick last night so they're not going to be much good either.

Maybe it's just as well. If I poked him in the eye, we'd go off the road and I'd die anyway. Likewise if I kicked him in the groin.

And anyway, how would I even get my leg up over the steering wheel to kick him? It would be pretty awkward. I'm not that flexible at the best of times. Maybe I could just *punch* him in the groin. One quick jab—then while he's writing in agony, I grab the wheel and drive to safety.

Right. There's no way I could jab some guy I don't even know in the groin.

He puts on his blinker and turns down a road. A smaller, darker road.

I feel myself shrinking.

I try to make words come out my mouth but nothing happens. I'm doomed.

He turns into a driveway in front of this old ramshackle house. He stops the car. He says, "I think this is what you want," and leans his big body across mine.

I forget all about the show. I don't remember what they tell you to do at this point. All I know is that I'm not going to let anything happen. There's no way. My body knows that even better than my head does. It's like a reflex or something. I punch the guy as hard as I can right in the face. He goes flying back.

I shriek and shriek and shriek.

I've got to get out. My hands are shaking so much I can't undo my seat belt. Why did I put on a seat belt? Like that's what I'm worried about? Getting thrown from the car? I should be so lucky.

The guy's going, "What's the matter with you? What's the matter with you?"

I keep shrieking and tugging at the seat belt. It's slippery with spit and sweat and whatever else is oozing out of me.

The guy comes at me again. I hit him again. He swears. He's screaming at me to calm down.

And make it easy for him? No way. I'm going down fighting.

He leans toward me. I swing at him. He grabs both my hands and holds them with one of his. I'm flailing away with all my might but it doesn't help. I can't get loose.

"Enough!' he says. "Enough! Are you nuts?" He looks me right in the face like he's trying to hypnotize me or something. He does it until I stop screaming, and then he uses his other hand to unbuckle my seat belt.

It's all over. I know it.

All I can do now is appeal to his basic humanity. I say, "Don't hurt me. Please don't hurt me. I've got money."

He throws my hands into my lap.

He goes, "*Me?* Hurt *you?* What are you talking about! *You're* the one who just punched *me* in the face! I'm on my way home from work, minding my own business, when some nutcase flags me down and punches me in the face!"

Is he calling me a nutcase? Some guy in a dirty, gross, bottom-of-the-line van is calling me crazy? He has no right to talk to me like that. I was just doing what you're supposed to do in this sort of situation.

I go, "What did you expect me to do? Just let you—like"—I'm suddenly embarrassed; I'm not sure exactly how to say this—"have your way with me?"

His eye is starting to swell up where I hit him. He rubs his hand over his face. His whiskers make that sandy sound. He shakes his head.

"What are you talking about? Have my way with you? You mean, here? In the van? Just now?"

I nod. I'm getting scared again. Why did I even bring it up? Like he needed reminding.

He stretches his fingers out and opens his mouth into a big O. It's the classic *you gotta be kidding me* pose. He goes, "I was leaning over . . . *to open the door for you . . . to let you out . . . to get rid of you.*"

It's right about now that I realize—like, fully realize—what an idiot I am. He's telling the truth. Now that I'm actually looking at him, I see that immediately. Big, good-looking blond guys generally don't need to resort to abducting girls to have their way with them. I want to die.

(Now that's it's not an option, of course, I *want* to die.)

I try to smile at him but the best I can do is make my mouth into a wide, flat rectangle. It's the same face I used to give my orthodontist when he asked to check my bite. It no doubt makes things worse.

The guy looks at me and talks in this loud slow voice because by now he's figured out that I'm an idiot too. "Shelton doesn't have a hotel. This is the *hos*-tel. I figured that's what your boyfriend meant. That's why I brought you here. . . . I just hope for his sake he had the good sense to take off while he had the chance."

The guy's got very white teeth. They almost glow in the dark. I wish I'd noticed that before. I would have been a lot less likely to think he was a psychopath, had I seen those teeth. (My impression is that homicidal maniacs don't have a lot of time to spend on dental hygiene.)

"Look, um," I say. I've always been terrible at apologizing but this is the worst.

"Um," I say again.

There's a knock on the windshield. I scream.

The guy shakes his head at me, sighs, then rolls down the window. "Careful, Kay," he says. "I've got a wild one here for you."

This middle-aged lady with a bright orange raincoat pulled up over her yellow hair says, "Hey, Levi. It's you. Thought I heard something out here—What happened to your face?"

"Nothing. Banged it up when I was working at the wood-lot today."

"You're going to have quite a shiner!" she says. She wags her finger at him. "Oh, the girls are going to love that. They'll all be wanting to look after you now."

He goes, "Ha-ha."

I just look away.

"Got an empty bed for my friend here?" he says.

"Oh, you're teasing me now," she says. "I got too many—as usual." She waves at me to follow her. "C'mon in, dear. I'll put a fire on for you. You look like you've had a rough ride."

Levi lets a laugh out through his nose. "You don't know the half of it," he says. He passes me my suitcase and winks at me with his good eye. "Watch out for strangers now, girl."

Kay leans in the door and goes, "Listen. Don't suppose you'd clean my gutters for me sometime, would you, Levi? With this bad knee, I can't get up there myself any more."

He winks at her too. "When have I ever said no to you?"

As the van pulls out, Kay turns to me and goes, "That Levi Nauss. Don't you just love him?"

13

Saturday, Midnight
The Shopping Channel

Here's your exclusive opportunity to purchase silken pyjamas, luxurious Egyptian-cotton sheets and fail-proof sleep aides from Mimi Schwartz's glorious Sweet Dream Collection.

If I could just sleep, I'd be okay. My mind wouldn't be bouncing around like this. I wouldn't be thinking about Mom or Anita or Selena or even Dad. I'd completely forget about the whole—you know—"thing" in the van. Best of all, I wouldn't be hearing that German girl practising moose calls in her sleep any more. (I can't believe people actually pay to stay in a room full of strangers.)

Why can't I sleep? I'm exhausted. I was even too tired to finish the grilled cheese sandwich Kay made me.

Okay. That's not one-hundred percent true.

The real reason I went to bed is that I couldn't stand hearing her talk about Levi any more. Has she got a crush on him or something? Is she his mother? Or was she just trying to make me feel bad? "Oh, the girls all love Levi Nauss. Everyone loves Levi! So big and strong. A gentle giant! Give the shirt off his back to help somebody. And funny? That boy . . ."

Okay. Enough. I get it. I've just humiliated myself in front of Prince Levi of Shelton. How long before a juicy story like that makes it round a little place like this? My guess is it already has.

One more reason to catch the next plane—as in, bus—out of here.

Right. I've got to go to sleep. Tomorrow's a big day. I'm getting up early, getting home. I'll just tell Anita that Dad was away so I came back.

No. I can't say that. If she finds out he was on the road when I was supposed to visit, all hell will break loose. Mom's lawyer will contact his lawyer. Kelly will testify that I called to say I wasn't coming. No one will believe her, of course—I mean, she absolutely *swears* she hasn't had a boob job—but still. It's not going to make my next visit any better. Dad's a space cadet and everything, but I like him. In his own cheesy way, he's cool. He never bugs me about stuff. I can't go calling his girlfriend a liar. I need a place to escape to every so often.

I guess I have to tell Anita the truth.

Clearly I'm even more tired than I thought I was, because, for a second there, that actually sounds like an okay idea. I roll over to go to sleep.

My eyes pop back open.

Tell Anita the truth? Admit that I took off? Am I insane? She'd cut off my Visa. She'd be on me like a stalker. Life would be even worse than it is now—especially since she'd finally have a legitimate reason for torturing me.

And she'd tell Mom about it too, that's for sure. She doesn't tell her everything—Anita doesn't like to "disturb" Mimi unless she has to—but I can never get away with the big stuff. It must be duly reported to the authorities.

Not that Mom would do anything about it. (That would be a lot to expect.) She might sigh and tell me how disappointed she is. If she's not too busy, she might explain how my inconsiderate actions hurt "those who love me" and ask for a written apology. More likely, she'd just pull her lips together and look at me over her reading glasses before going back to her production schedule for the next day. Big deal. I can handle that.

Then why does it make me feel sick, the thought of Mom finding out?

I stare at the moon shadow the trees make on the wall. The rain must have stopped—they're not moving.

Because she'd know I was in her room. She'd know I'd found out about her little hiding spot. Why else would I go to a place like Port Minton?

No. No. No. I'm not thinking straight. I figured this out already. Port Minton would mean nothing to Mimi. She's never even been to Nova Scotia! And anyway, there's no way she'd ever own a ring like that. Some fan probably just sent it to her and . . .

Goosebumps start behind my ears and crawl all the way down my back. I suddenly *know* the ring is hers. Every inch of her room gets cleaned every day. The ring couldn't have just fallen on the floor. It wasn't from a fan either. Gifts from fans are opened at the office and donated to charities. Mimi never even sees them.

The ring was in the chair with that picture of Mom when she was a kid. She hid them there.

Why?

I totally give up on the idea of sleep.

I don't understand her. She's told the entire world about her nose job, her tummy tuck, her bad relationships, her jujube addiction. So why would she hide some old ring?

Okay, the ring I can sort of see. Maybe there's some romantic attachment to it. Maybe she was—is?—involved with the guy who owns it.

Yeah. So? Who cares? You can't pick up a magazine without seeing her "linked" to some new man. Old, young, single, married, funny, boring. It's always someone—even when it isn't.

I used to be in the paper a lot too when I was little, when I was cute. I got big and Mimi made a "plea for privacy." Since I never got around to snorting coke or running off with my tennis instructor or doing anything scandalous like that, the media kind of backed off. The paparazzi haven't bugged me since Mom spent a wad on that twelfth birthday party for me at the Russian Circus. As far as they're concerned, I don't exist any more. I'm not worth the effort. Nobody knows me.

In fact, I probably could have told Kay my real name and it wouldn't have made a bit of difference. It's not like there's only one Robin Schwartz in the world. It's not like Kay'd look at me and immediately see that cute little red-headed kid in the chef's hat. Even the lady at the ticket counter was only joking about my name.

But Kay had the *Enquirer* spread out on the kitchen table with a big picture of Mom on the cover. ("Oh, Mimi, Oh My! Did you buy yourself some new cleavage?") She folded up the paper to make room for me and went, "Sorry. Here I've been babbling away and I didn't even ask your name."

No way I could say Robin Schwartz then. Who knows what they were talking about in the article? I panicked. I did this stuttery thing for a while, then I said, "Opal." That's my middle name. I've always hated it. It's ugly.

Most people think it's Oprah—like Mom was naming me after her hero or something—but Kay got it right away. "Opal. Really? Nice name. You have relatives around here?"

"No," I said. "No, uh, my family's from . . ." I was desperately trying to come up with some lie when the grilled cheese sandwich started smoking.

Kay jumped up to deal with it. When she sat back down, all she wanted to talk about was Levi again.

Every time she mentioned him, I pictured myself sucker-punching him in the face.

"Saving myself" from his advances. It makes me cringe. I think of me saying *have your way with me* as if I'm some dainty damsel-in-distress and I cringe even more. I'm so embarrassed.

Is Mom embarrassed? Is that it? Is that why she hid the stuff?

No. This is a woman who's had her Pap smear done live on-air. What could be more embarrassing than that?

Some blurry old photograph?

No way. She's had a picture of herself as a kid on her show. I saw the episode. Why would she hide it now? Hide it inside a *chair*! I mean, that's not like throwing it under your mattress or anything. That takes work.

It almost makes me laugh. Unless a camera's aimed at her, Mimi doesn't do anything for herself. I can't imagine her down on her knees with a hammer and nails—you know, *squirrelling* the picture away. It's so out-of-character. Like she's going to risk chipping her manicure for something like that?

So maybe Anita did it for her. Maybe Anita's in on the secret. Maybe that's why she went so berserk when I knocked the chair over.

I don't think so. Anita did go berserk, but that's, like,

normal for her. If I'd stumbled on to some secret treasure trove, she'd have cranked the volume up way more than that. All things considered, she was almost reasonable. (She didn't break a blood vessel like that time I got grape Kool-Aid on the guest towels.)

No. Anita doesn't know. This is Mimi's little secret.

The girl across the room is smacking her lips in her sleep. She's either having a food dream or a guy dream. Whatever. I wish she'd quit it. It's really annoying.

I've got to get out of here.

Where am I going to go?

Paris. I keep thinking of Paris. I could live off croque monsieurs and Orangina, stay at that little hotel Mimi featured in "France for Freeloaders." I could just hang out.

French TV is lousy. Doesn't matter. If I got really bored, I could go sightseeing. Climb the Eiffel Tower. Look at the paintings in the Louvre.

There's something else about that picture of Mimi too. I can't put my finger on it. What is it? It's definitely Mimi standing there, but there's something about her that doesn't look quite right. Maybe if I could find out who the other people are in the picture, I'd know. There are some names on the back. I wonder if I could track them down somehow.

Mimi did a show on finding long-lost friends. It's easy now with the Internet.

It's not going to help. I only have first names. My guess is there are quite a few Kathy W.'s and Lenore T.'s in the world.

The ring's a better lead. I wonder if Shelton has a public library. If it does, they might have some stuff there on Port Minton High. How many guys could have played football in a little place like that? It shouldn't be that hard to find out where the ring came from.

I'll just stay in Shelton long enough to check that one thing out, then I'll get going.

Where? Not France. I'd get too fat in France. I've got to go somewhere where the food is bad. Where there's *no* food.

I'll Google "famine" when I'm at the library tomorrow. I'll figure something out.

14

Sunday, 10 a.m.

You, You and Mimi **(rerun)**

Mimi interviews four dynamic, attractive women
on the joys of being "Alone and Happy."

It's the quiet that wakes me up. I open my eyes and look around. It's bright and sunny but totally silent. It's so weird. I feel like I'm in one of those movies where every person in the entire world has just up and died except me. I almost panic for a second there. Like, where am I? Where is everyone?

No German moose calls. No smacking lips. Everyone else must have slipped into their spandex bicycle gear and taken off for another glorious day of inhaling diesel fumes.

I stumble out of bed and look around. I go, "Kay? . . . Kay?" I stop at the top of the stairs and listen. Nothing.

I'm alone.

That's when something bizarre happens. I forget about panicking. I forget about the ring and Mom and everyone. My body, on its own, just decides to take a deep breath and start smiling. So *this* is what freedom feels like! It's not as good as a coma, but just about.

I go to the bathroom and splash water on my face. I take out my retainer. I don't think Kay will mind me using her towel. I borrow a little of her toothpaste too. I squeeze some on my finger and start to brush.

Jeez, I look gross. There's a little scab on my lip from the chair bashing. I went to bed with my hair wet, so I've got a major Albert Einstein thing happening. I've got bags under my eyes the shape and colour of prunes. My glasses are bent. (I must have done that in the van.)

Who cares?

I spit out the toothpaste. I wipe my mouth off on my T-shirt. I love the thought that Anita isn't here to bug me about it. I even kind of like the look of that big blick of toothpaste across my chest. A bold stroke of self-expression.

I go downstairs. The hall's dark but there's so much sunlight streaming into the kitchen it's practically glowing. I feel like I'm some puny earthling being drawn into the mother ship. There's a box of cornflakes and a bowl on the table. Kay's left me a note on the back of a bulletin for the Shelton Volunteer Fire Department Lobster Supper. Her handwriting is all neat and perfect.

Hi Opal,

    I didn't wake you up because you looked awful beat. I've gone to do some errands. Here's some cereal. There's tea over on the stove. If you want to go into town, there's a bike in the shed. Just turn right on the 109 and take Exit 17 into Shelton. It should take you about twenty minutes. Don't worry about locking up.

Have a nice day!
Kay

I smile at her note and pour myself a huge bowl of cornflakes. They're a bit stale but whatever. It's probably the best breakfast I ever had.

I put the kettle on for some tea. Grandpa likes tea. I pour myself another bowl of cornflakes. I wonder where Kay keeps the television. I look around. I glance past the window and see an old lawn chair sitting in the sun.

It's so not-me but I get this urge to go outside. I remember staying somewhere with Mom that had chairs like that—the bent metal ones with the woven plastic seats that leave criss-crosses on your thighs that make them look like uncooked danishes. Where would Mimi ever have gone that had junky stuff like that? I don't know. All I remember is a little cabin on a lake. It was dark and kind of smelly inside but not in a bad way. The furniture was old and squeaky. No one was around except Mom and me.

And Dad. Dad was there too. It must have been during one of their little reconciliations. I was about eight. We sat around on the deck, swatting mosquitoes and doing this huge jigsaw puzzle of some castle with swans out front. We were so happy.

We canoed. We sunbathed. We swam. We had to push Dad in every time because he said the water was too cold. It *was* cold, but Mom and I didn't mind. Skinny little Mimi didn't mind. We swam and swam and swam and then we made a fire in the big old stone fireplace.

And Mom cooked! I mean, nothing fancy, but it was better than that old "Eating Like a Birdie" stuff. She made tea biscuits and pea soup and these delicious molasses pancake things, too. What did she call them? She had some weird name for them. Lassie tootins. That was it. *Lassie*, like molasses. I don't know what *tootin* means but I'm pretty sure that's what she called them.

Am I making this up?

It almost seems too good to be true. Unless I'm totally nuts, I think we even sang songs around the fire. Funny songs. Back then, at the cabin, Mom was as funny in real life as she is on TV.

How did those songs go?

All I remember is something about "*underpants and my friend Hans.*"

Okay, it doesn't seem that hysterical now, but back then I was rolling on the floor, laughing and laughing and laughing. Mom had tears streaming down her face too and Dad kept adding these heavy metal guitar licks that were so totally wrong. It completely cracked us up.

I'm going outside.

I hike up my pyjama bottoms with my elbows, grab the bowl of cornflakes and the teacup and back out through the screen door. It's actually almost warm. Not Antigua warm or even Bermuda warm but nice. I feel good.

I put my cup on the ground. I stretch out in the chair so I can rest my bowl on my belly. I lean my face back into the sun.

That's when I notice Levi Nauss looking down at me from the top of a ladder.

15

Kay was wrong. It doesn't take twenty minutes to get to Shelton by bike. It takes at least forty minutes—even when you're pedalling like a maniac because all you can think about is escaping as fast as you can.

What's the matter with me? I've got to stop screaming every time I see that guy. He's going to think I'm emotionally unstable or something.

But it's his fault! He shouldn't have snuck up on me like that.

Okay. Fine. He didn't exactly sneak up on me, but he could have at least given me some warning he was there.

Instead he hides out at the top of a ladder with his shirt off, waiting until I'm stretched out in dirty pyjamas with my disgusting hair all over the place and a bowl full—I mean, *full*—of stale cornflakes on my belly. Of course I screamed. Who wouldn't scream?

And then, of course, I jumped.

I get cereal plastered all over my chest and milk dripping into my pants and this crystal-clear picture in my head of exactly how ridiculous I look and he's laughing and then apologizing and then laughing some more and then *actually coming down the ladder* as if he's going to help me or something and I just can't stand it.

I stick up my hand like I'm a traffic cop and go, "Stop!" He stops halfway down the ladder with this big dopey grin on his face. He starts to say something, but I don't listen. I run into the house, up the stairs. I throw on some clothes, run back down the stairs, hop on the bicycle and start pedalling. I pretend I can't hear him calling me.

I must have been on the road for about half an hour before my brain would let anything in other than *No, no, no, no, no.*

Now I'm okay. I'm thinking clearly again. Everything's not perfect but I can handle it. I don't need to tell Anita I went to Port Minton. I can say I took off to visit Garlande Haney, this girl from school. Anita will act mad for a while, of course, but I know she'll be kind of thrilled too. Not only did I get off my "sorry behind," I actually have a friend!

What difference does it make if Anita tells Mom I went to Garlande's? As long as it's not Port Minton, she won't know I was in her room. She won't care. I'll catch the bus back to the airport tomorrow. In a little while—after some intense psychological counselling—I'll have completely forgotten about Levi Aren't-I-Adorable Nauss.

I cross the little bridge into town. I guess the river—or whatever it is—is kind of pretty. It's all sparkly and there are red and white boats with names like *The Lorna Marie* and *My Mistake* bobbing away on it.

The rest of Shelton is, I don't know, just kind of blah. The houses are old but they're not all Martha Stewarty or anything. Most of them are plain white or grey or brown.

Every so often someone's done something crazy like paint the door pink or put a flowerpot out front, but that seems to be about it for home improvements around here.

Unless I'm missing something, there's only one main street. It's got a bank, a couple of little restaurants, a pharmacy and a few stores. Most of them seem to be of the Buck-or-Two variety. There's a newspaper office and a doctor's office and a so-called antique store too. The sign for the bowling alley is so retro it actually looks kind of cool. (Given what the rest of Shelton looks like, I'm presuming that's an accident.)

A full-grown lady wearing a pink sweatshirt with a kitten painted on it points me toward the public library. (No way I'm going back to the hostel until what's-his-face is gone.) She's not sure if I can get on the Internet there—by the look on her face she's not sure what the Internet *is*—but she figures someone can help me with the bus schedule.

The Enos Hiltz Memorial Library is in a large old blue house just off the main street. Once upon a time, it must have been quite the place. It's got all that gingerbread stuff around the windows and stained glass above a big wooden door. Someone went to the trouble of making it look nice. The window boxes are full of geraniums or pansies or something. I lean my bike up against the railing and go in.

They clearly blew all their renovation money on the outside. The library's got high ceilings and an old fireplace but there are no desks or study cubicles or anything like that. The place looks like the guy who owned it just moved out one day and the next day someone lined up a bunch of book shelves right in the middle of his living room. Posters for church sales and yard sales and babysitters are tacked onto a big bulletin board in the hall. There are a bunch of ratty chairs scattered around, and, over by the window, an old wooden table with a computer on it.

Score.

I look around. The place seems empty. Should I just start using it? Should I say something? Go, *Yoo-hoo! Anybody here?* I don't know what to do.

I'm standing there, staring helplessly at the computer, when somebody comes up behind me and says, "Can I help you?"

I swing around, all jittery and guilty.

A lady with wild kinky grey hair is smiling at me through her big red glasses.

"Oh, uh. Sorry," I say. "Am I allowed to use this?"

She says, "Why sure you are! That's what it's here for." She's wearing one of those tie-dyed sundresses you pick up in the same place you buy your incense. "Can I help you find something?"

"Um, sure. A couple things, I guess. I wanted to look up the bus schedule to the airport."

She waves her hand at me. "Oh, I can tell you that off the top of my head! It comes through here every Saturday around 11 p.m."

"It only comes once a week?" I sort of reel back from the shock. "How do people get out of here?"

She looks around, then whispers, "We dig tunnels. When the guards aren't looking, we make a break for it."

I give this weak laugh. I didn't mean to insult her but jeez. Saturday? I'll never survive until then. I wonder if I can rent a limo.

A limo. In Shelton. Right. Dream on.

The lady says, "What was the other thing you wanted?"

Nothing. As of right now, the only thing I want is to get out of here.

The lady smiles at me. "Are you researching something perhaps?"

She's really trying. She's got her hands clasped in front of her and she's leaning toward me like she's an undertaker or something.

I'm here. May as well.

"Port Minton High," I say.

She gives me one of those "go-on" looks.

"I'm interested in, um, what the school was like . . . you know, the extracurricular activities. The teams. Stuff like that. Whatever."

She makes this little *hmm* sound and lifts her eyebrows. "The school closed a long time ago. Now why would you be interested in that . . . ?"

I feel like I kind of disappointed her. As if I'm a lightweight or something. She clearly expected more from me. I'm a good girl. I do my best.

"Oh, not just that," I say. "I'm also interested in how the closing of the school affected the students . . . or how it—I guess—impacted the community. . . ."

Or what my mother's doing with somebody's football ring. You know. That kind of thing.

She looks happier. She pulls a pencil from somewhere inside that gigantic hairdo of hers and taps it against her chin. "Well . . . I doubt you'll find much about that on the

Internet—but I might be able to pull together some pho-
tographs, newspaper clippings, information of that nature.
Enough to get you started, I'd think. Come by Tuesday
afternoon and I should have something for you."

I go, "Tuesday?"

The lady shrugs. "We're a volunteer library, I'm afraid.
We're closed Monday. The rest of the week, we're only
open a few hours a day. In fact"—she looks up at the clock
on the wall—"I'm closing in about fifteen minutes. I'd stay
longer, dear, but I'm taking my mother to her card group.
You're welcome to stay until then. You could use the computer if you want."

I nod in this vague sort of way. What am I going to
do all day in Shelton? I can't go back to the hostel. How
long is it going to take that stupid Levi to clean the gutters? (What are gutters anyway? Who even has gutters?
I've never heard of anyone cleaning gutters. He's doing it
on purpose.)

My face must have gone funny. The lady's looking at me,
all worried.

She says, "You don't need to go just yet. Maybe you'd like
to check your e-mail. I know kids your age are always having to check their e-mail. You're all so popular nowadays!

I was never that much in demand." She smiles like she's trying to cheer me up.

Fine. I'll check my e-mail. Keep her happy. I'm not expecting a whole bunch. (I'm not much in demand either.) I sit down and key in my password. I've got ten messages waiting for me.

Nine are spam.

The tenth is from Selena.

From: gumdrop113@airmail.com

To: birdbrain76@airmail.com

Subject: The Great Escape

U r kidding me! Port minton? That's so wild. How does it compare 2 hong kong? Did u find mimi's football lover yet?

Did u join the port minton cheerleading squad? Those were some pretty hot moves u did the other day in mimi's room. lol

Keep me posted.

Selena ☺

From: birdbrain76@airmail.com

To: gumdrop113@airmail.com

Subject: Secret Lover

No secret lover yet but have been practising cheerleading moves. Did a couple of jumps for a guy here. Dont think he was 2 impressed.

Hong kong has better moo goo guy pan but u cant beat the cornflakes here.

Will write more l8r.

Robin

16

The lady says, "Good news?"

I hit close and say, "Yeah. Good news." Sometimes I
don't even know when my face is smiling.

She puts a bunch of papers on the table. "I found these
for you. They're church bulletins from the Port Minton
United Baptist Church. I know it's not the school per se
but the church was very active in trying to keep the community alive. There might be some crossover with your
research. The church is shut down now too—but I think a
lot of the names you'll see here will come up again in the

school closure issue. Something for you to look at anyway."

Church bulletins. Thrilling. Who needs *People* magazine when you've got a stack of *The Port Minton Semaphore* to keep you up-to-date on all the hot gossip? I say, "Thanks!" and flip through a few as if I just can't wait to dig into them. (I wish I could fake things half as well as Mimi can.)

The librarian gives me one of those smiley frowns and says, "Well, I hope they'll be helpful. But now, I'm afraid, I'm going to ask you to wrap things up. Mother doesn't like to keep the ladies waiting."

She looks up at the ceiling as if something just came to her. "You know what? I'll mention your little project to Mother. One of her friends is a Port Minton girl, very involved, would know the whole story. I'll try to arrange to get the two of you together sometime for a chat. She loves to chat. . . ."

"Thanks," I say again—but that's not what I'm thinking. I'm thinking this is turning into way more than I bargained for. I just want to find out about the ring. I don't want to get stuck "chatting" to some old lady from the Sunset Manor Gin Rummy Club. Especially since my guess is she's not going to have any juicy stories about the Port Minton football team.

The librarian finds a plastic grocery bag for the bulletins and we head for the door. Just as I'm about to leave, I see Mom staring at me from a paperback book rack. *It's All About Mimi: My Life Story.* When did she write that?

I grab it without thinking. "May I sign this out?"

The lady looks at her desk. She looks at the clock. She bites her lip. She looks at me. She whispers, "Can I trust you?"

I nod.

"Then take it. I don't have time to sign it out now. Just promise you'll bring it back Tuesday. It just came in and Muriel Faulkner is dying to read it."

I say goodbye and sort of saunter off down the main street. I don't even get on my bike. There's no reason to move any faster than I am. The whole point is to waste time. As Selena was so happy to point out, that's something I'm usually pretty good at.

I schlep along, check out the buildings, look in the store windows. Lots of fancy candles for sale. Who even buys candles?

Tourists, I guess.

Maybe this is a tourist town. Maybe Mom came here on a vacation when she was a kid. Or maybe she was at camp around here. Was that picture taken at camp?

Maybe she met a boy there. They had a little fling. He sent her his football ring. A summer romance. Happens all the time.

No. She was only about ten in the picture. That's too young to have a boyfriend, even for Mimi.

Fine. She just *met* him at camp. They kept in touch. Years later, he sent her the ring.

It makes perfect sense. Done.

Now get me out of here.

I pass a beauty salon. Hair's Looking at Ya! What a classic. The window's plastered with these faded photos of models with huge, spiky eyelashes and seriously scary haircuts. (One girl looks like she got her head caught in a panini press.) With that kind of advertising, no wonder the so-called stylist is sitting inside by herself.

I turn to leave. My reflection pops into focus. Whoa. The model at least had an excuse—it was the eighties. My hair is just *bad*.

I stare at myself for a second.

I think, *Why not?* It couldn't get any worse than it is. Besides, it's like two in the afternoon or something. I can't go back to the hostel yet.

I stick my head in the door. I go, "Are you open?"

The hairdresser looks up from the Harlequin she's reading and says, "No, sorry. I just needed to get out of the house for a while. The kids were driving me nuts." She looks like someone who could be selling jewellery on The Shopping Channel but she sounds like she's from around here. She's got one of those accents.

"That's okay," I say, and start to back out. "I just wanted a shampoo."

She jumps up and waves me back in. "Oh, what the heck. I may as well make some money while I'm here." She throws her book on the counter. "I know how it's going to end anyway. They all end the same way."

She whips a plastic cape around my neck as if she's trying to get a bull to charge, then leads me over to the sink. She finds out I'm in town doing research on Port Minton—I figure it's easiest to stick to one lie—and she's off and running.

"Really? I'm from Port Minton myself. . . . Sorry. That too hot? . . . I couldn't wait to leave the place. I prefer being in town, but Roy, he misses the quiet. I say if you miss the quiet, why d'you go getting me pregnant all the time? There's no quiet when you got four kids and a couple of half-crazy German shepherds too. But that's not the type of quiet he's talking about, I guess. . . .

"Your hair's some thick. Your natural colour? Really? Gorgeous. . . . Anyway, Roy, he's from a fishing family. He and his dad were out on the water by four every morning. Rain, wind, weather. Didn't matter. Sounds like hell to me only a whole lot colder—but he loved it. Be there still except the fish dried up. Nothing much he could do then. He had to go where the work was. He come here and got a job at the mill and a nice little bungalow in town.

"I couldn't a been happier, but that's because my dad wasn't a fisherman. While the cod were still around, the fishermen did okay. At least their kids never went hungry. But folks like us, it wasn't so good. My mother worked in the fish plant. My dad did too when he was sober. Can't get rich that way—especially when you got eight mouths to feed."

She shakes her head as if she's talking about some other poor sucker. She's distracted for a second by her reflection. She fluffs up her eyebrows with her finger, but doesn't miss a beat with her story.

"Dirt-poor, hungry and all of us stuffed into that leaky little house way out on the point! Can you imagine?

"I shouldn't complain. The Port wasn't that bad. When we was kids, it was fun. We ran around like wild animals. We swam at the beach all summer—though now I don't know how we did it. It's some wretched cold out there. The rest of the year, believe it or not, we all piled into a one-room schoolhouse.

"The high school was a lot bigger, of course. Kids from all over the county came. That's where me and Roy started dating. Mind if I use some conditioner? Your ends are some dried out. . . . Too bad I got hooked on Roy so young, because high school was fun. The problem is those boys who start fishing early get them big shoulders from all that hauling and lifting and it's hard to look at anyone else after you see that. I tell my girls to go for the ones who read. They don't look so hot with their shirts off but they get better jobs later. Make lots of money, and you can get yourself a gym membership any time—right, eh?

"You got a boyfriend? Oh, you will! What with those eyes and this hair and that va-va-va-voom figure. Get a little makeup onto you and a tight shirt and the boys will be banging down your door. Me? There was only ever just Roy. I don't regret it. Much. He doesn't talk a lot but he works hard. And in high school, like I said, he had them shoulders. He was captain of the hockey team too. That was worth something back then. That practically made me royalty. For a while there, Port Minton was all about its hockey team."

I'm still, like, reeling from that "va-va-va-voom figure" comment, but she takes a breath and I leap in anyway. Sounds like she might be more helpful than those church bulletins.

"Oh, yeah. And what was its football team like?"

She towels off my hair as if she's demonstrating some illegal hold she picked up on the professional wrestling circuit. I'm half expecting her to knee me in the nose and finish the job.

"Football team? There wasn't a football team. There's no field!"

Note to self: so it must be a hockey ring then. Whatever. I go to ask another question but I don't have time. The hairdresser's off and running again.

"The only reason there was a hockey team was that Mr. Hiltz donated the arena. Coldest jeezly place on earth. I guess he was too cheap to donate a heating system for the stands. I can't tell you how many weekends I spent freezing my tail off in that place. Which side do you part on?"

She turns on the blow-dryer and starts hollering over the noise. "I know people are sorry the Port died. But I can't say I cried many tears. I got my own business today and it does okay. That never would have happened if I was still stuck out there. In the Port, everybody knew who you were and where you belonged. Nobody would have wanted Kirby Wentzell's daughter doing their hair, that's for sure. Like I'm going to give them cooties because my dad's a drunk! In fact, Roy's mother wouldn't have anything to do with me for the longest time. She figured I was just something Roy was going to outgrow, like that acne he had on his back. Mrs. Hiltz was the one who made her come around. She gave me the money to take my aesthetician certification. I guess Myrna finally had to admit that if Debbie Wentzell is good enough for Mrs. Enos Hiltz, she's good enough for her Roy."

She gives this hard nod of her head like *I sure showed her.* I leap in while I have the chance.

"Who's this Enos Hiltz guy?" I say. "Same guy from the library? Was he really rich or something?"

"In a word, yes," Debbie says.

She's really going at me with the round brush now. I've got to hang onto the armrests to keep from being dragged to the floor.

"He owned the fish plant, the pulp mill, the gas station, the newspaper and who knows what else. Let's just say, he did all right. Not many people liked him—you're not going to be real fond of somebody who pays you slave wages—but everyone likes Mrs. Hiltz. She's a good person. She set up all these scholarships and camps and music groups for us kids. She looked out for her own. Still does. She comes here every Tuesday for her regular comb-out. She still insists on paying me—even though I owe her everything I got."

Debbie hands me a mirror and swings the chair around so I can look at the back.

"Whaddya think?"

"Good. . . . Nice," I say. It's a little pouffier than I'd normally go for but it's definitely an improvement. Clean hair usually is.

I wish it was as easy to do something with the rest of me.

17

Sunday, 3 p.m.

You, You and Mimi **(rerun)**

Mimi's continuing series on "The Modern Family."
Today celebrity etiquette expert Alanna Darling
turns up her pretty little nose at teen table
manners.

The hairdo killed about forty-five minutes. Only three
more hours or so before it's safe to go back to the hostel. I
don't even need to ask myself how I'm going to spend it. I
know.

I'm going to eat.

I'm starving. The only thing I've had today is cornflakes
and most of them ended up on my chest. Whatever I get
this time is going straight to my digestive tract.

There's something called The Dairy Treet on the corner. It seems like the type of place that sells greasy fries and droopy ice cream cones covered in rubberized "faux" chocolate.

That's exactly what I want.

The kid at the counter tells me the ice cream machine is broken. To ease the pain of my obvious disappointment, he throws in some extra fries and supersizes my Coke, free of charge. My instinct is to lunge at the fries as soon as the guy hands them to me but I don't. It would be too weird eating inside an empty restaurant with him staring at me. He might feel the need to talk. I'm better off to sit outside at the picnic table and take my chances with the seagulls. At least I can tell them to get lost without feeling bad about it.

I fill a bunch of those little paper cups with ketchup. (Does anything make ruder noises than ketchup pumps? I keep going, "Oops, sorry," like I'm the one doing it or something. The guy either thinks I'm nuts or have a serious stomach ailment.) I slip the bag of church bulletins over my wrist, balance the ketchup on top of the fries, pick up the Coke with my other hand and push the door open with my hip.

I turn around and run face-first into Levi Nauss coming through the door with some girl.

I scream.

And then, of course, I jump and spill ketchup and Coke all over my shirt.

Levi and the girl start laughing.

I'm so mad—mad at him, mad at me, mad at him catching me about to stuff my big fat face, mad at that girl and her skin-tight jeans—that I just lose it. I go, "Arrrgh! *You again!*" and throw my fries right at him.

The girl jumps back and gasps.

Levi goes, "Me! What did I do?"

I push past him. I feel him take a step toward me but he doesn't get any farther than that. The girl starts hissing at him. What's *her* problem? (They weren't her fries.)

I don't wait around to find out. I jump on my bike and get out of there.

18

Sunday, 3:30 p.m.

Radio Mimi

"My Heart Races." Mimi discusses emotional escapism with the world-class runner and international playboy named—believe it or not—Joffy Dastard.

I'm crying.

I'm trying not to but I can't help it. I keep telling myself things like "You're making this sound a lot worse than it is," which I'm not, and "Someday you'll laugh at this," which I won't.

This really *is* as bad as it sounds. I've made a fool of myself again. I want to go home. I want to see Anita. She knows what I'm like but she doesn't care. She loves me.

I keep pedalling and wiping my face on my sleeve and pedalling some more. I don't know how long I've been doing this. Clearly, not long enough. I can still think. I want to get so tired that my brain finally stops bugging me.

Something whizzes past and I almost lose my balance. A van pulls up in front of me. Levi's van.

The only thing I can hear is my heart. Can teenagers die of heart attacks? (If they want to badly enough, can they?)

What's the matter with this guy? Why does he keep following me? I want to run off into the woods and hide, but even I know how ridiculous that would look.

Instead I just get off my bike and stand there and hope my face hasn't gone all blotchy and that he can't hear my heart too.

He gets out of the van with his hands held out in front of him, like *I'm not going to hurt you*. He goes, "Opal . . ."

When did he learn my so-called name?

I say, "Leave me alone."

He goes, "Look. I'm sorry. I didn't mean to—"

I go, "Leave. Me. Alone."

I start to walk past him like I'm all indignant but something happens. My neck turns to rubber. My legs suddenly feel like they belong to someone else. I have to blink to make things stop spinning around.

He says, "Are you all right?"

I say, "Yes."

He says, "No," and grabs my bike just before it hits the ground.

I follow right behind it.

I'm down on my knees, one hand on the pavement. I say, "I'm okay, I'm okay."

He says "No, you aren't."

He helps me up—I hope my armpits aren't totally wet and disgusting—and half carries me into the front seat of the van. He does up my seat belt and says, "I'll take you back to Kay's."

He throws my bike in the back of the van and pulls out. I'm leaning against the headrest and my eyes are shut but I can still tell he's looking at me.

He goes, "Are you all right?"

I say, "Yes," as in *I already told you that.* "I'm just hungry. I haven't eaten in a long time."

"Oh, is that all?" he says. "Well, I can help you there."

I open my eyes and look at him.

He peels a limp fry off his shirt. "Dig in!" he says. "I've got plenty more where they came from."

19

Sunday, 5 p.m.
Promo

Scrap your family! Turn your photos into stunning family heirlooms. Join scrapbooking artist Kendra Salna Meltzer on *You, You and Mimi* tomorrow at 3.

Kay is feeding me another grilled cheese sandwich. She claims she's going to sit here until I "finish every last bite."

Luckily, Levi wasn't as concerned for my welfare. He just dropped me off at the hostel and left. Had to hurry back to his skinny girlfriend, I guess.

I don't care. I don't care if I made an idiot of myself again. I don't care if they're sitting around snickering about me. I'm just focused on getting the shaking to stop. I finish the sandwich and a piece of blueberry pie too. Kay looks almost proud of me. I suddenly understand why they call it comfort food.

She goes, "Well, what did you get up to today, Opal? I mean, other than collapsing on the side of the road, that is."

She smiles and her face wrinkles up. That sounds bad but it isn't—it's actually sort of mesmerizing. It's like watching time-lapse photography of a flower blooming. I wonder what Mom would look like if they ever unfroze her face.

Kay touches her hand to her cheek and turns away. I realize I've been staring at her. I've embarrassed her. On top of everything else, am I turning into one of those creepy staring people?

"So . . . your day?" she says again. "How'd it go?"

I pull myself together and start talking. It's the least I can do. I leave out all the Levi stuff. I tell Kay I went to the library, that I'm here doing research on how the school closure affected Port Minton. The lie keeps getting easier. In fact, this time I decide to let slip that I'm doing the research for a university degree. (I don't want people guessing I'm only seventeen, lumping me in the "teenage runaway" category. Someone could feel obliged to track down my parents.)

Kay says, "Really?" and puts another cube of sugar in

her cup. She's either impressed or she thinks I'm bragging. I can't tell which.

"For a university degree? Who'd have thought little old Port Minton was worth that much attention?" She shakes her head and stirs her tea.

I make up some garbage about Port Minton being representative of small communities everywhere and how I'd like to get a closer look at the actual town and . . .

I don't know what happens. One second I'm gleefully inventing crap, and the next, my mind totally blanks out on me. I'm looking right at her, my mouth is wide open, but nothing's coming out. I get this horrible vision of what it must be like to be Mimi.

I'm bracing myself for Kay to point at me and shout, *Impostor!*—but she just reaches out and pats my hand. She doesn't think I'm a liar. She probably just thinks I have some emotional problem or something. That's why I can't finish a sentence without going into a trance.

Her hand is really warm, but so rough and dry it reminds me of an old scuffed-up sneaker. Dad's old scuffed-up sneaker. He's got this big house with a theatre and a complete state-of-the-art recording studio and he's still wearing those stupid sneakers.

"No need to explain everything now, Opal," she says. Her eyes are this really light brown, almost like the butterscotch topping they put on sundaes. "I can tell you're beat. Do you have a big day tomorrow?"

"No. Uh. No," I say. "I don't have anything to do." I push some crumbs around on my plate with my fork.

"Good. You look like you could use some R and R." Her eyes suddenly kind of light up. "How about starting right now? Like to waste a little time in front of the TV with me?"

TV is tempting—until Kay winks and says, "Mimi's got a celebrity special on tonight. . . ."

Did she notice I flinched?

My mother is everywhere. I can't believe I used to like it. I guess when you think about it though, why wouldn't I have? It was the most natural thing in the world when I was little. I remember in kindergarten this girl crying because she missed her mother. I didn't get it. I put my arm around her like I was so much older and wiser and said, "Don't worry. That's all right. Just turn on the TV. You can see your mother then!" It was like having a magic mirror or a guardian angel or Santa's cell number or something. I could see my mother whenever I wanted.

I suddenly understand something. It sounds like a real hippie-religious-freak kind of thing to say but it makes so much sense. My mother is everywhere—and nowhere. I could probably walk into a store in Katmandu, Reykjavik, Lima, you name it—and pick up a magazine with her face on the cover. But when was the last time I saw her? Like, I mean, actually *saw* her? She's like a hologram or something. She's there but she's not.

I say no to TV, thank Kay for the food and head up to bed. I am pretty tired but I know I won't be able to sleep. I lie on my bunk, stare at the ceiling and try to picture Mom's face. All I see is that person on TV. I can't remember the real her. I can get the clothes right and the hair right but her face is either blank or just a cut-and-paste job from some promo shot. The more I look, the less I see. It makes me feel like I'm draining away.

I've got to stop thinking about this stuff. I need to take my mind off it before I go seriously crazy.

I look around for something to distract me. There's not much here. The other girls aren't back at the hostel yet. My iPod is dead. On the little shelf by my bed there's a mystery paperback with the first couple of chapters torn off, a cheesy romance novel that would only make me more depressed, and those church bulletins the librarian gave me. It's a sad commentary on my life that the bulletins actually interest me.

I start flipping through them. In the third or fourth one, something catches my eye. It's the picture of that group of kids. The same one I found in the chair. Here in *The Port Minton Semaphore*.

I freeze.

It's as if the picture suddenly blows up to a full-screen image. The rest of the room shrinks down to a little icon in the corner. I'm stunned. Until this very second, I didn't honestly believe Mimi had anything to do with Port Minton. Sure she had the ring, but—I don't know—I figured I'd find some totally reasonable explanation for that.

This is not reasonable.

I stare at the picture in the bulletin. It's Mimi. What would Mom, a kid from New York, be doing in a place like this? What would a Jewish kid be doing in a Baptist church bulletin?

There's a caption underneath the picture:

Spirits run high at the annual Port Minton United Baptist Church picnic. Celebrating their win in the egg-toss event are, left to right, Kathy Whynacht, Lenore Tanner, Tracy-Lynn Carter, Miss Swinamer and Rosie Ingram.

The other names look right but that's not Rosie Ingram at the end. That's Mimi. It must be a typo. I sort of laugh. This has to be the only time in Mimi's life that someone got her name wrong. It's like someone mistaking Brad Pitt for the mailman.

I turn the page.

There's another picture of Mimi, taken on the same day. She's holding a trophy this time. The caption says:

It's a hat trick! For the third year in a row, Rosie Ingram wins the Junior Crafters Award for her lovely hand-knit tea cozy. Congratulations, Rosie!

My insides shrink up tight. I can feel every individual goosebump pop up on my skin, one by one. Something's wrong.

I scan the article. There it is again. "A special thanks goes to Rosie Ingram for helping out in the nursery."

I swallow so hard my eyes bug out.

I try to tell myself it's just a mistake. Someone didn't know Mimi and got the name wrong. But I don't believe that. This is Port Minton. Little, tiny Port Minton. Everybody must have known one another. No one would get the name wrong.

I look at the pictures again. It's the same girl in both of them. Is it Rosie Ingram?

Or is it Mimi?

Or is it both?

20

Monday, 8 a.m.
Breakfast TV

Host Ruby Krimstein interviews Mimi Schwartz about her new self-help book, *Sorry Is the Hardest Word: The Art of Apology*.

Believe it or not, I slept. You'd think something like that would have kept me up all night again but it didn't. It took my breath away. It made my heart pound. And then it put me right to sleep.

Somehow I must have convinced myself that it was no big deal. Mimi Schwartz used to be called Rosie Ingram. So what? Show biz people change their names all the time.

I'm not so relaxed any more, what with the sun up and that girl across the room doing a really bad job of tiptoeing out.

Now I'm—I don't know—mad, I guess. Hurt. Insulted.

Like, I mean, I know you're busy and everything but in the last seventeen years, could you not have given me a moment of your precious time to explain that your name's not actually Mimi Schwartz? Was that too much to ask?

Call me crazy, oversensitive, whatever—but it seems reasonably important to me that a girl know what her mother's real name is.

I'm suddenly too hot. I zip open the sleeping bag, throw my leg out, let the cool air seep in.

Mimi used to be Rosie Ingram.

Is that true?

What does that mean?

Why did she become Mimi? *When* did she become Mimi? *How* did she become Mimi?

Why wouldn't she have told me?

Why wouldn't she have told anybody? (Did she?) Why didn't anybody notice? (Did they?) And what—more importantly—was she doing in Port Minton, of all places?

I stare at the bare light bulb hanging from the ceiling. The brown cord is dusty and kind of frayed. I wonder if it's safe. Mimi's whole house burned down when she was a kid because of an "electrical malfunction."

Or at least that's what she said. That might be a big lie too.

I should just call Mom. Show her the evidence. Ask her to explain.

No. If the tables were turned, *she* could do that. She could confront someone. She'd love it! It would make a great show. Lots of drama and everything. But there's no way I could do it. I'm too scared. How would she react? What would she do? For some weird reason, I picture the wicked stepmother in *Snow White* smashing the mirror. (Why? Mom's not wicked. I don't think she's wicked. But how would I know?)

I could call Anita. She'd tell me. If I came straight out and asked her, she'd tell me.

I rifle around in my bag and pull out my cell. Get this over with once and for all. Anita doesn't need to tell Mom that she told me. Nothing needs to change. Nobody needs to know. Mimi can have her secret. Anita and I can have ours.

I open the phone. I close it. I can't risk it. What if Anita *doesn't* know anything about the Rosie stuff? I don't want to, like, betray Mimi. I don't want to hurt her. She's still my mother.

I hurt her once before. I feel sick just thinking about it. I was pretty young, maybe twelve or something and we were watching TV together. Watching *her* on TV together. She was interviewing this singer from some boy band that I was all crazy for and she teased him about something. I don't even remember what. I slapped her on the arm and went, "I can't believe you said that! I'm so embarrassed! I'm ashamed to have you as my mother!"

That's just what kids are like. I didn't mean it. I just had a crush on the guy. I had some dumb fantasy that maybe we'd meet someday and he'd fall totally in love with me. I didn't want anything Mimi said to come between us. (As if there'd ever be an "us"! As if Stuart Allen was saving himself for some pudgy twelve-year-old girl.)

I wasn't embarrassed of *her*. I just said that. Mom was the most important thing in the world to me! I was old enough by then to realize she was the only reason I had friends. She was a whole lot more interesting than I was.

I guess she didn't know that. She kind of pushed me away and looked at me really hard. It scared me. She'd never looked at me like that before. She went, "You're embarrassed of me, are you?" She sounded like the meanest girl in school, the one who doesn't even have to raise her voice to make you cringe. She pulled the bracelet she'd just given me off my arm and said, "Well, I guess you're too embarrassed to wear this, then!" She opened the window and chucked it as far as she could. She stormed out of the room and slammed the door.

I was shocked. I was mad and I was scared and I felt really, really bad because I knew it was my fault. I went into her room a little while later to apologize, but when I said, "Mom . . ." she just went, "Yes. What?"

She wouldn't look at me. Maybe she'd been crying too. I should have said I was sorry then but I didn't.

I just said, "Nothing," and went back to my room.

The next day there was a new bracelet exactly like the old one left on my desk, but Mom didn't sit on the couch with me watching TV any more. It might just be a coincidence but I went to boarding school right after that.

I don't want to hurt her again. (I don't think she wants to hurt me either. Maybe that's why we avoid each other.)

I make a deal with myself. If I'm going to figure this out, I've got to do it on my own. I can't let anyone know what I'm up to. I might need to know who my mother really is, but the world doesn't.

I can't ask Anita. I can't ask Mom.

I look at my backpack. That's okay. Maybe I don't need to ask anyone. Maybe the answer's right here.

21

Monday, 9 a.m.

www.bestblogs.com

Mimi Schwartz's latest post reveals her tips for
reading facial expressions, body language, even
fashion choices to find the real person hidden
behind the facade.

I should have done this as soon as I noticed it in the library.
If the book really is "all about Mimi," Mom's bound to at
least mention Rosie Ingram.

I turn to the index at the back. Lots of entries for Nelson
Mandela, Tom Cruise, Taylor Swift—even the Indonesian
lady who does my mom's facial peels gets three refer-
ences—but there's no Rosie.

I feel stupidly disappointed. Ever since I found her little cache, I've known Mom's hiding something. Did I honestly think she was just going to blurt out the truth in her memoir?

Would I even *want* her to? She can't tell her own daughter but she doesn't mind confiding in the whole world? How bad would that make me feel?

I can't let myself follow that line of thinking. I shake it out of my head and get back to business.

Okay. So Mom doesn't mention Rosie. Doesn't mean there couldn't be something else in the book that would help.

I look up *Port Minton*—nothing.

Nova Scotia—nothing.

Tanner, Whynacht, Carter, Swinamer, hometown, high school—nothing.

The first hit I get is for *childhood*. She covers it in two pages, right at the front of the book.

> I don't know anything about my birth mother. That bothered me when I was in my teens but, hey, everything bothered me then. Now I see it as a blessing. I

wouldn't be where I am today if she hadn't given me up. So, thank you, Birth Mother, whoever you are—and sorry about the stretch marks. I hope your life has been as fulfilling as mine.

I was adopted as a newborn by an older couple, Harry and Dora Reiner. Harry had a small electrical business at the back of a depressing strip mall just outside Nowheresville, New Jersey. Dora was a homemaker. It wasn't an exciting life—but they weren't looking for excitement.

Harry and Dora were Holocaust survivors who'd lost everything in the war—their money, their home and, saddest of all, their three natural children. What they wanted now was peace.

And, believe me, they got it.

My childhood was nothing if not peaceful. I honestly don't remember anyone other than the occasional repairman ever coming to our home. It was always just Mom, Dad and me. I didn't even have any school friends to play with.

That's not because I was a nerd or a loner or a weirdo—although, of course, I was. It's because I didn't go to school. My parents were so worried about "bad influences" in the public system that Mom kept me home and taught me herself. She'd been a teacher in Poland before the war and never lost her passion for learning, so my education didn't suffer. I can't help wondering, though—would I have turned into the shameless attention-seeker I am today if I'd had some friends to hang out with back then.

Dad worked long hours. That's probably why I was the first to notice there was something the matter with Mom. She'd gotten clumsy and was slurring her words. She never complained, but by the time I was fourteen, it was clear she had full-blown ALS (Lou Gehrig's disease). Dad hired a lady to look after her but we couldn't afford that for long.

When I was fifteen, Mom stopped being my teacher. And I became her nurse.

Don't cry for me. My mother was the world's best patient. No matter how bad her day or how unpleasant her symptoms, she'd always dismiss them with a wave of her hand. "Ah!" she'd say with a chuckle. "I've been through worse!" I couldn't argue with her there. Her attitude, her gratitude—her will to truly live!—inspire me still.

The disease eventually robbed her of her conversational skills, but it never diminished her joy in literature. I read to her for hours. Austen, Fielding, Thackeray, the Brontës—I was exposed to more of the classics at her bedside than I ever would have been at school.

That's not the only education I got at home, of course. I also had to learn to cook, clean, pay the bills and do Mom's hair. As she got sicker, I had to learn to give her medicine, change her diapers, monitor her vitals.

And in the end, of course, I had to learn to live without her.

A couple months after she died, our house burned down. We lost almost everything. It could have been the final straw, I guess, and for a while it seemed like it was. Dad and I cried our eyes out. We cursed the world. And then, when we realized that wasn't getting us anywhere, we moved on. What else can you do? The insurance money was enough for a new little house for us—and a new little nose for me. We settled in. We got back to living.

It wasn't much of a life for a teenage girl perhaps, but I don't dwell on the dark side. I thank the heavens and all the gods and goddesses therein that they honoured me with that experience. So what if I never learned how to dance, never had a date! Big deal. I learned self-sufficiency. I learned life is what you make it. And I learned every day is precious.

Nothing new there. Mom—or, more likely, her ghost-writer—stuck to the usual story. Like anybody else who's addicted to her show, I knew she'd been adopted. I knew my grandparents were Holocaust survivors. I knew their house burned down.

I sort of knew about Mom looking after my grand-mother too, although she never made that big a deal about it. I didn't really think of it as "nursing." I thought of it more as Mom plumping up Dora's pillows, getting her medicine, helping out with little things like that.

I flop back on the bed and try to remember what else Mom told me about her childhood.

Blue was her favourite colour.

She never had a pet.

She had lots of cavities.

She was skinny.

Now that I think about it, I'm not sure if she told me those things herself or if I picked them up watching the show.

I *must* know more than that about her childhood. When I was eight or nine, I went through a period where I positively bombarded her with questions. For some reason, I feel vaguely embarrassed even thinking about it. Why? All kids must do that.

Something comes back to me. This image of Mom in her room, getting dressed for some celebrity roast or Broadway opening. I was just little then. I sat on her bed, watching her try on different earrings, fuss with her hair, choose the right shoe. I was so happy, being alone there with her.

I asked her a question. Something harmless—what games she played as a kid, what her favourite dress looked like, I don't remember what exactly—and she went all Mimi on me. She rolled her eyes, gave this big fake sigh and said, "Why do you care so much about ancient history? Don't waste your time on that junk. Take it from me, darling. There's only one reason to ever look back and that's to see if your pants make your butt look big."

I laughed—mostly because at that point I was still shocked to hear my mother use a "bad word"—but I knew she wasn't just being funny. She wanted me to feel ashamed of even being interested in her past.

I must have got the hint because, eventually, I stopped asking.

Did I talk to Dad about his childhood? A bit, I guess. Enough to know that his first girlfriend's name was Charlene. That he was arrested for shoplifting at fourteen. That he never got along with his brother. That he stunk at school. (Considering all the drugs he must have done in his rocker days, I'm surprised he could remember that much to tell me.)

I pick up the book and start flipping through it again. I see myself poring over the pages and I have to laugh. I'm just another obsessive Mimi fan, needing her fix.

I come across a picture of Mom when she was a kid. It's not very good. It's blurrier than the photo I have, and her left side is sort of cut off. I wonder why she chose this one for her memoir.

Maybe the editor wanted to use a picture of her alone instead of with a group of kids. It makes sense. Mimi wouldn't have to explain where all those happy, smiling friends disappeared to.

Mimi looks a little older in this picture but that might be because of her haircut. The dorky pigtails are gone and she's wearing her hair in a bob now. I like the bangs.

I read the caption: "A rare day at the beach—and a rarer snapshot. A house fire when I was in my teens destroyed all my other childhood photos."

What's she talking about? There are other pictures of her. I know. I have one.

I'm almost mad. Why would she say that?

Because the picture I found doesn't belong to her perhaps?

No. I've already been down that road. Mom's room. Mom's chair. Mom's ring. Mom's picture.

So maybe she just forgot she had it.

I don't believe that either. Mom didn't go to the trouble to hide the picture and then just blank it out of her mind. That doesn't make sense.

It's her picture and she hid it. And I bet she hid it for exactly the same reason she didn't put it in the book.

I just don't know what that reason is.

I'm suddenly creeped out. There's something sort of horror-story about this whole *hidden picture, fake name, weird little ghost-town* thing. I get a shiver.

I'm just being stupid. There must be some explanation. Keep looking.

None of the other photos jump out at me as anything

special. There's a picture of Mom all bandaged up after her nose job. A picture of the house in Brooklyn. A bunch of photos of me as a baby, but only one of Dad. It's not even a family picture. It's that lame one off the cover of his first album, *Rock Hound*. (Did he actually wear his hair like that? Even Debbie would think twice before putting that picture in her window.)

Mimi devotes a whole chapter to her "Fashion Faux Pas," including the Jessica Simpson get-ups she wore after her divorce and tummy tuck. Nothing seems to embarrass her. If you didn't know any better, you'd swear she really would tell you anything.

Another chapter's called "My Brilliant Career." There's that famous photo of her in the ugly flowered dress with the puff sleeves and the tiny bow at the collar. That's when she was working at her first on-air job as a book reviewer for the public access station. They still called her Miriam then. A few years later, she moved into news for a while. You can tell she's in the news department because her suits are dark and her hair is plain brown.

After that, it's all Mimi. Her hair and clothes are changing faster than traffic lights now. There are a couple of pictures of me on set but most are of her and some famous person. Usually, they're both laughing. A few times, though, she's got this big sympathetic face on and there's a caption about some new charitable foundation she started. I stare at a photo of her, taken in a Pakistani orphanage. The kids are reaching up to touch her face. They all seem to know who she is—but I sure don't.

I close the book. I get up and go to the bathroom. I feel better once I've peed and splashed some water on my face, but "better," like they say, is relative. It's not necessarily good. This whole Rosie/Mimi mess is really getting to me.

If I'm right, Mom must have spent time here when she was young. Someone must have known her. Kay's quite a bit older than Mom, but maybe she could tell me something about her.

I look out the window. It's going to be a nice day.

No harm asking, I guess.

I'll bring the church bulletin down to the kitchen and "casually" flip through it while I'm eating breakfast. When I get to that picture, I'll say something like, "Hey, don't those kids look like they're having fun?" Then I'll sort of segue into whether Kay knows any of them or their families or whatever. I'll make it sound like it's all part of my research. It's not that crazy. I can get away with it.

22

Monday, 9:30 a.m.

The Shopping Channel

The worldwide debut of "Radiant," Mimi Schwartz's
line of morning moisturizers, glow crème and eye
dazzlers. Let your true beauty shine through. Be
Radiant.

I should have gotten dressed. I should have brushed my
teeth. I should have at least picked the crusty stuff out of
my eyes.

Instead I just jiggle into the kitchen in my skimpy pyjamas like I'm some Jell-O fertility goddess. It's too late by
the time I notice Levi the Stalker, sitting at the kitchen
table, looking right at me, smiling that stupid black-eyed
smile of his.

I completely forget about Rosie Ingram.

To my credit, I don't actually scream this time. I just suck in my breath and hold the church bulletin across my chest, hoping it's big enough to cover my boobs, and my armpits which I haven't shaved in, like—I'm serious—eons.

Kay goes, "Morning, Opal! Guess what?" She's practically singing. "Levi's got today off so he's going to take you to Port Minton!"

I do what any reasonable person would do under the circumstances. I gack like a cat spitting up a mouse carcass. In the time it takes Kay to get me a glass of water, I manage to pull myself together. This cannot happen. There is no way I'm getting back into a car with that guy.

I do that "No, no, I couldn't possibly" thing, but Kay won't hear of it.

She keeps going, "It's no trouble is it, Levi?" and then scrambling around getting a little "picnic lunch" ready for us. Whenever she turns away, I give Levi the evil eye, but he just puts up his hands like this is completely out of his control. He is so irritating.

Kay goes into full Anita mode. She's sort of pushing me to eat some cornflakes and telling me I should bring my bathing suit and then when I say I don't think I'm going to want to swim (i.e., expose my thighs), she totally ignores me and says that I should actually put my suit on here because she doubts there'll be a place I can change at the Port. It's really hard to get a spoon to my face without unleashing my armpits so I just take a couple mouthfuls, then dump the rest of the cereal out, clean my dish and head upstairs as if I'm going to get dressed or something.

I sit on my bed for a while and fume. I wonder if this is why the lip-smacking girl gets up and out so early? How come Levi doesn't bug *her*? I mean, okay. Thank you for the drive—"drives," whatever—and I'm sorry I punched you in the face and everything but will you please just leave me alone?

I'm going to say that to him. I may as well. I'll be gone soon. It's not like I'm going to be staying around here, eating at The Dairy Treet and staring at his stupid face for the rest of my life. I'm leaving just as soon as I find a few things out.

Maybe even before.

I mean, why am I hanging around here? Why don't I take off right now and just hire a detective? That's the type of thing they do. They'd get this Rosie/Mimi stuff cleared up in no time.

And then sell the story to the tabloids for millions.

Okay. I can't do that. I made myself a deal. I'm going to stick to it.

I put on some shorts and a T-shirt. I'm all ready to go downstairs but then I change my mind. Anita's the type who'd actually lift up my shirt to check what I was wearing underneath. I'm not saying Kay's that bad but I don't want to risk it. I put my swimsuit on and shave my pits too. I throw the shorts and T-shirt on over my bathing suit. Doesn't mean I'm going swimming.

I head downstairs. Kay's going, "Don't forget to show her this" and "Don't forget to show her that" and "Make sure she gets in for a swim" and warning Levi not to drive too fast and agonizing over whether four sandwiches will be enough and apologizing for running out of apple juice and throwing in a few more handfuls of fake Oreos "just in case."

Levi goes, "Oh, stop your worrying" and then, because he's a total suck-up, hugs her goodbye.

She beams at that. She pushes him away as if he's stealing a kiss or something and says, "Now, get going, the two of you. I want to wash this floor!"

I do my best to thank her but all I can think about is

getting stuck in the van with Levi. I keep remembering the way he and that girl laughed when they made me spill Coke and ketchup all over myself.

Levi opens the door to the van for me—such a gentleman!—and we take off. I keep waving at Kay until we're on the road, just so I won't have to look at him.

Levi goes, "So! Here we are. All alone again." Ear we ar. All lone agin.

"Yeah. Isn't that just great?" I say.

"No kidding!"

He's smiling. I can hear it in his voice. Does he not understand sarcasm or something? I go, "What's with you anyway?"

He does that "Me?" thing again. I wish he'd just drop the innocent act. It's getting seriously boring.

I say, "Yeah, you. What's with telling Kay you'd take me to Port Minton? Why are you doing this?"

He turns and looks at me.

I say, "Keep your eyes on the road, if you don't mind."

He goes, "Oops. Sorry. I find you distracting."

Please. I say, "Quit trying to be cute. Would you just answer my question?"

"I'm not trying to be cute. I just *am* cute." Oi jes am cute.

I'm not going to respond to that in any way, shape or form.

There's a pause while he realizes that he's not as charming as he thinks he is. He clears his throat. "Okay. Why am I doing this? Two reasons. One: Kay asked me to. She's running that hostel all by herself since Joey died. She needs all the help she can get. So when she wants me to do something, I do it."

I put my hand on my chest and say, "Well, she must be absolutely delighted to have a knight in shining armour like you to look out for her!"

I can tell I pissed him off. Good.

He says, "That's not what I meant."

I go, "Oh. Sorry. I guess it just sounded that way. And number two? What's your other reason?"

"I don't know." He shrugs. "I guess I like a challenge. Least I thought I did—until *you* came along. I mean, what's *your* problem?"

"*My* problem?" I can't believe this guy.

"Yes, *your* problem. I'm this normal nineteen-year-old male and every time you see me you scream like I'm some crazed perv just desperate to"—he wriggles his neck back and forth—"have his way with you."

I should have known he wouldn't be able to resist bringing that up again. Fine. I made a mistake. Score one for Levi.

"So what's that all about?" he says.

My lips go tight. My chest cramps up. He must think I'm delusional, like I'm under the impression guys can't resist me or something.

He goes, "Tick-tick-tick. Would you like to use a lifeline?"

Hilarious. He's putting me on the spot. He's making me feel bad. I don't want to talk any more.

"Hunh? What's that all about?" He says, "Come onnnnn!" like I'm a baby and he's trying to get me to toddle across the room.

I can't stand it any more. I blurt out, "I wouldn't scream at you if you didn't keep sneaking up on me all the time!"

He gets this look of total shock on his face. He sits there shaking his head, with his mouth hanging open, his eyes bulging. He looks like he should be put in a home and just taken out on weekends.

He says, "You're some big on yourself, girl. You think I'm spending my days tracking you down? That what you think? Can we please just review the facts? First time, *you* flagged me down. Second time, I'm up on some frigging jeezly ladder with my earphones in, minding my own business, when I hear this god-awful caterwauling. I didn't even know you were there until you started screeching! I was forty feet away! What could I possibly do to you? I can't even spit that far! Then the last time, I'm just walking into The Dairy Treet for a cone . . ."

"Oh, yeah? Really? The ice cream machine was broken!" I'm an idiot. Why did I say that?

He laughs. "What's that supposed to prove?"

That you make me uncomfortable. That you make me do stupid things.

"Nothing. I'm just saying."

"Fine. Mind if I go on? . . . So, even though, *unbeknownst to me,* the ice cream machine was broken, I walked into The Dairy Treet. . . ."

"With your *girlfriend* . . ."

Shut up, Robin! It's so obvious what you're thinking. Just shut up!

"Krystal's not my girlfriend! And what difference would it make to *you* if she was?"

He's glaring at me. That bruise probably makes his eyes look greener than they are. (Mimi's makeover guy always puts purple eye shadow on green-eyed people.)

"None," I say. "None whatsoever." I point at the road. "Now will you please just drive."

He laughs like I'm pathetic and goes, "Anyway . . . then you start screaming at me. . . ."

I go, "Because *you* made me spill ketchup and Coke all over myself!"

"Right. *I* made you spill everything. . . . And did I make you throw your french fries at me too?"

I should just shut up. I'm digging myself in deeper.

"Yes! Because you deserved it! You and your not-girl-friend were laughing at me! Then you stood around making fun of me! I could hear you."

"What are you talking about?"

"You know what I'm talking about." I'm not saying anything else no matter what he says.

"You're nuts," he says.

"*I'm* nuts? I should never have got in this van with you in the first place."

"No kidding! Well, finally, we've found something we can agree on."

"Yeah," I say. "Yeah. Right. Absolutely. One-hundred percent." I look out the window. I'm hopeless. Mimi did a show on "Social Ineptitude: The New Plague." I must have seen it ten times. Did I learn nothing?

There's this long silence.

He goes, "I'll take you to the Port just so we can tell Kay

we went there, then I'll take you back. I'll try to keep my hands off you until then."

Ha. Ha. "Thank you very much," I say.

"No problem," he says. "Believe me. It's no problem *at all.*"

Levi turns off the highway onto the same road I went down that first night. It looks different. It's not foggy today. I can actually see the ocean.

We drive a while in silence.

He says, "That over there used to be Port Minton High School." His voice is totally flat, like he's some lame cashier at the grocery store asking for a price check.

I'm glad I saw the school already. I don't have to look at it. I can act like I don't care what he says. He just keeps up his little tour-guide act.

"Most of the houses over there are empty now. Some are used for cottages. City people, you know. They like the view, I guess."

I just go, "Unh," and keep looking out at the water. It's so smooth and blue it's like an illustration in a picture book. I figure we'll probably be turning around pretty soon, but the road keeps going and he keeps pointing out more stuff.

When he says, "That used to be the rink," I can't help

but turn and look. This must be where the hockey team played.

He goes, "She's alive! She's alive!"

I sneer at him, then twist around to get a better view of the rink out the back window. It's made of that ripply metal stuff. It's red and peeling and kids have tagged it all over the place. You can still see the sign that says Malachi Hiltz Memorial Arena.

I say, "I thought his name was *Enos* Hiltz," before I remember I wasn't supposed to be talking to Levi.

"Malachi was Enos's father." You can tell Levi was just waiting for an opening to start yakking again. "Enos built it—though I bet his wife made him do it. I understand the guy was pretty tight with his dollars. . . . Hey! You want to know something funny about Mrs. Hiltz?"

"No, not really," I say.

He mutters something under his breath and then says, "Fine. Suit yourself."

We head down a hill and a little town comes into view. The word *town* might be a bit of an exaggeration. It's just a couple of streets down by the water. There's a great big old blue mansion on the hill that looks like something right out of *Beetlejuice*. Most of the other houses are small, white and boarded up. A lot have these ancient "For Sale" signs fading away on the front yard. Quite a few, though—four or five, say—still have cars in front. There are even some people walking around on the street. I'm kind of surprised.

I say, "I thought this was supposed to be a ghost town."

He goes, "You did, did you?" and then doesn't say anything else.

He knows I'm asking him a question. Why doesn't he just answer it? There's no way I'm going to beg him. I shake my head and look out the window again.

He does that little chuckle of his and goes, "As a special gift to Kay, I'll tell you that a number of people still live here. In fact, my family used to live here until a couple of years ago. Most of the people left are too old to move, too stubborn to move or both. Nobody actually works here any more except maybe Albert Ingram. He's a bit hard of hearing these days but he's still got a little store. Pretty much only sells milk, matches and . . ."

"Who?" I go because I can't help myself.

"Albert Ingram. You heard of him?"

This could be important. I swallow my pride.

I say, "Is he Rosie's father?"

"Rosie who?"

I go, "Rosie Ingram." I say the *who do you think?* part in my head.

He shrugs. "Could be. I don't know. He's, like, eighty or something. His kids would all be grown by now. . . . Who's this Rosie anyway?"

Good question. I try to work it out in my head. Rosie could be Albert's daughter, in which case she actually lived here. But if Albert's alive, why did Grandpa adopt her? Maybe Albert's her uncle. . . .

Levi says, "Hellooo? Who's Rosie?"

I shake my head. "No one. Just saw her name in something I was doing."

He goes, "What *are* you doing anyway?"

This is getting out of hand again. It's almost civilized.

I give him my standard answer. Research on the school. Blah-blah-blah. I throw the university thing in too, just to make him feel bad.

"*You* go to university?" he says. "Which one?"

"Harvard," I say. May as well really stick it to him.

"Oh, so you're a rich kid" He seems to find that funny.

I just squint at him like it's none of his business and let him make his own conclusions.

He smirks. "I figured as much. Well, I guess you come by it honestly, then."

I pick at my ear with my baby finger and look out the window. I think he can gather from that just exactly how much I value his opinion.

He pretends not to notice. He goes, "I'm at Dalhousie. Couldn't afford to go farther than that, but it's okay. I'm doing a combined major in sociology and marine sciences. . . ."

Oh crap. How was I supposed to know a big dolt like him could get into university? He's going to figure out I'm lying. I hate it when that happens.

He says, "I'm sort of interested in the impact of these dying communities myself. I guess that's why Kay asked me to take you. She thought we'd have something in common."

We both go, "Ha!" at exactly the same time. He laughs. I don't.

He's trying to be all pleasant again. He says, "What are you majoring in?"

I say, "I'd prefer not to discuss it, if you don't mind."

He sort of sings this little *la-di-da* thing under his breath. I stare straight out the window and hope that this is almost over.

23

Monday, 11 a.m.

You, You and Mimi

Today Mimi takes a good, long "Look at the Male Body." Sure to be a hit with her eighty-seven percent female audience.

The houses stop. The road gets smaller. We go around a corner and suddenly there, spread out in the distance, is this beautiful beach. It takes me by surprise. I say, "Wow" before I can help myself.

I've seen tons of beaches. I've been to the Riviera, to Hawaii, to most of the islands in the Caribbean. This is as good as any of them.

We're up high on a hill looking out at the ocean. The water is bright turquoise except where it splashes up against these giant boulders. They're kind of square and jagged as if they're made out of big, grey Lego pieces. The sand is really white. The beach seems to go on and on.

For some reason it makes me feel like crying.

Levi grabs the lunch bag and the towels. "C'mon," he says. "I have to take you swimming. I promised Kay that I'd immerse the Evil Screeching Troll into the magical waters of Port Minton Bay."

I do my best to ignore him. I get out of the van. The smell hits me. It's not that dead-fish-seaweed-fart smell you sometimes get from the ocean. It's the smell they must be thinking of when they name men's aftershave "Seaspray." It's fresh and, I don't know, sort of healthy or something.

Levi's already partway down the hill. He's waving at me and going, "C'mon!"

I can barely hear him over the wind. I take one last look at the view and follow him.

We cross a stream on this little boardwalk. Levi points to the right. He goes, "Those bogs over there are full of cranberries. People still come out here and pick them. They're not supposed to, now that this is a government park, but there's not much Dad can do about it."

I go, "Dad? *Your* dad? What? He the boss of everyone around here or something?"

Levi laughs. "Guess that sounded kind of dumb, didn't it? Dad's the park warden. I pretty much grew up here. It's one of the reasons I like it around here so much."

"Seriously?" I say. "You *like* living here?"

He pulls his face back and looks at me. I think he's trying to figure out if I'm joking or not.

"Seriously," I say.

"Yeah," he says. "It suits me. I like being outside. I like to kayak and fish trout. My brother and me are building a little camp up on the river—so I'm not bored . . . for now anyway. I'd probably go nuts if I stayed here forever. It's too small. There are times I think I'm going to lose it if I hear Alec Evans make the same bad joke or hear Krystal complain about her hair again."

There's this awkward pause when he says "Krystal" and we both sort of look away, then he just goes, "Yeah, whatever," and heads down the path. He grabs the back of his T-shirt and pulls it off over his head.

"Some hot," he says.

Not that hot, I think.

He's got those shoulders Debbie was talking about. I try not to look.

We get to the beach and I want to just stand there and

gawk at it, but Levi says, "No. Don't stop here. It's better farther along. Kay wants you to see the seals."

He pulls his sneakers off with his toes and leaves them on the beach. I do the same thing. The sand's so soft my foot twists with each step. It makes me walk with this huge wiggle, like I'm some cartoon hottie or something. I think about Debbie making that crack about my va-va-va-voom figure. I must look like I actually believe it.

We have to climb over this big boulder to get to the next part of the beach. Levi scrambles up like it's the easiest thing in the world. I grab onto a little notch and get one leg halfway up but then just keep sliding back down. I feel like the fat kid in gym class who can't get onto the second rung of the monkey bars.

Levi's standing on a ledge. He hunches down and sticks his hand out.

"Here," he says.

He gives me one good yank and I'm up on the rock and standing way too close to him. I can't move or I'll fall back down. I can smell his aftershave or his deodorant or whatever. I go, "Um . . ."

He goes, "Sorry," and steps back.

I don't think I've ever been that close to someone else's skin before. At least not like that.

We climb to the top of the boulder. There are these little pools where water must have splashed up. The boulder is kind of speckly grey and silver. The water's bright blue with rusty orange stuff around the sides. It makes me want to try painting again.

Levi says, "On windy days, the waves come up this high. They can pull you out to sea in a second. Lots of people have died that way."

I go, "Gee, thanks for taking me here."

"Don't worry. I'd save you." He winks. "Maybe."

I think about saying something like *I can take care of myself,* but that's just asking for it. He saw me trying to climb up that boulder.

He laughs. "We're okay. It's pretty calm today." He points, "Hey, look! Seals!"

I look. I see water. Rocks. Water splashing against rocks. And that's about all.

I say, "Where?"

"Over by those islands. See?"

I squint. I shake my head. It's a big ocean.

"Those black things. In the water. There! Can't you see them?"

I have no idea what he's talking about.

He gets behind me. He crouches down so his chin's leaning on my shoulder. I'm completely frozen. I feel like a mannequin in the plus-size department. He changes the angle of my body, then takes my right hand in his and points again.

He moves my finger around and goes, "One, two, three, four—do you see them now?"

"Yeah," I say. They look like scuba divers coming up for air. At another time, I might be interested, but right now all I can think about is my heart and Levi and my weird thumbnails that he's no doubt noticed and the scratch of his whiskers on my shoulder.

I say, "Thank you," then wiggle my hand out of his and step away.

We're both embarrassed now.

He says, "Okay, well, yeah, good. You saw your seals." He stands there nodding, with his hands on his hips.

I don't know what to do with my eyes.

After a while, he sort of mumbles, "O-kay . . ." then he turns and scrambles down the other side of the boulder. He jumps the last few feet onto the sand and holds his hand up to help me too.

I don't take it. I jump and pretend it doesn't hurt at all.

"The best swimming place is at the end of this beach," he says. "You get a warm current there."

I nod and keep walking. Neither of us says anything. Is this as awkward for him as it is for me?

These tiny sandpipers scurry along the water's edge on their little stick legs. Even in my stupor, I can see how cute they are. I can't believe Disney hasn't done an animated feature about sandpipers yet. I should suggest that to Mom. She knows the people at Disney.

Mom.

She might have walked here. Swum here. Maybe even come here with the "ring" boy.

I stop. I look around. I can't picture it. Beaches for Mimi have lounge chairs and waiters and access to the Internet. She's not the seal/sandpiper type at all. You'd think spending time in a place like this would do something to you. Would show.

It doesn't.

Levi goes, "Tired?"

"Uh, no," I say. "I was just, like, looking. It's nice."

He turns to the water. His face is all squinted up from the glare. "Yeah," he says. "It's pretty awesome. I never get tired of it."

He rubs his hands through his hair, then starts walking again. I follow a bit behind. We're alone. There's not a soul on the beach. I can't help looking at his back, his shoulders. He's like a triangle or rhombus or something. He's not all gross and bulgy like those Mr. Universe mutants. He's muscly but kind of slim too. I didn't think he'd be that slim. On the ladder he was just this scary blur.

I feel like one of those sick guys flipping through the dirty magazines at the back of the store. I try to look away but my eyes keep slipping back, taking another peek.

Yeah, okay. He's strong. So what? He's not perfect. There's this bony knob on the top of each of his shoulders. He's got tan lines from wearing a T-shirt all the time. There are a couple of chicken pox scars on his neck.

He swings a hand over his shoulder and scratches. One of his nails is purple as if he slammed it with a hammer. You can see big white half-moon cuticles on each of his fingers. The muscles in his other arm tense up when he finds the itchy part. I can see them all, like he's a picture in a biology text or something. How does someone get like that?

He turns around and catches me staring at the line that kind of swoops down the middle of his back.

I go, "Uh . . ."

He goes, "Yeah?"

I go, "Nothing."

"Nothing? You look like you were going to say something."

"Um . . . well, no. Not really."

He tilts his chin down and goes, "Just say it."

"I don't know. . . . I was just wondering what you do, I guess. I mean, like, for work. You know. When you're not at school. Kay said you had a day off so, like, I figure you must work." Why can't I just shut up?

"Our family's got a woodlot, so I work there." He keeps one hand on his chest while he talks. I don't look at it. "Other than that, I do handyman stuff for people. Nothing fancy. You know, joe jobs. Pushin', shovin', liftin'—that kind of thing."

I remember him pulling that suitcase of mine into the car and my stomach jumps.

"Oh," I say.

How stupid is that.

"I bet you'd be good at it."

He laughs. "That's me, all right. Strong body, weak mind." He makes a muscle and sticks his tongue out the side of his mouth. "Duh."

"I didn't mean that," I said. "I just meant . . ." There's no way out of this.

"Yesss . . ."

"I don't know what I meant." I turn away. "Are we almost there?"

He laughs again. "If you'd quit stopping we would be. You anxious to get there or something? I can take you the fast way if you want."

"Sure," I say.

He grabs my hand and starts running. Like, I mean, *burning* down the beach.

I'm screaming, "What are you doing? What are you doing?"

"You wanted to go the fast way!"

I can't breathe. I'm running too hard. My legs can barely keep up. They're flopping around behind me as if I'm one of those goofy albatross birds coming in for a landing. This is ridiculous. I'm trying to be mad but I can't. I start to laugh. I wish I'd worn my sports bra. I put one arm across my chest to keep my boobs from knocking me unconscious.

Just when I'm sure I'm going to trip and/or die, Levi throws himself down on the beach. I almost land right on top of him. I have to spit sand out of my mouth. I sit up and punch him on the shoulder a few times but he just laughs and laughs and laughs. I flop down on the beach. We both lie there with our eyes closed for a while, trying to catch our breath.

"Phew," he says. "Good thing I'm used to pulling heavy objects."

I, like, gasp. I can't believe he said that.

He goes, "Just kidding!" and gives me a little shove.

I don't laugh. He doesn't notice.

He sits up and claps his hands to get the sand off. "Okay," he says. "Time for our swim!"

"No," I say.

"What do you mean, no?"

"I'm not going swimming."

"Yes, you are."

"No, I'm not."

He's finally picking up the vibes. "Why?"

I don't say anything. I sit up. I look away. I want to go home.

He groans. "Oh, come on. You're not mad about that 'heavy object' joke, are you?"

"No."

"You are too!"

"Yeah, well, that's because it's not a joke."

"What are you talking about?"

I look right at him. I want to make him squirm. "Why would you make fun of a heavy person's weight?" He's not as nice as he thinks he is.

He goes, "At the risk of repeating myself, what are you talking about? Or should I say, *who* are you talking about?"

He knows who.

"Who's heavy around here?" he says.

I hate him.

He stands up. "You can't be serious. Please tell me you don't honestly think you're fat."

This is humiliating. Why do I always do this to myself? Running along the beach, I was almost liking him. I should have known this was coming.

He leans down until his face is right beside mine. I think he's going to whisper something in my ear. I'd swat him, only I'm afraid that would just encourage him.

He doesn't whisper in my ear. He takes my glasses off and puts them on the sand.

I go, "Hey!"

Before I can figure out what's happening, he puts one hand behind my back and the other under my knees and picks me up.

I can't help it. My arms go around his shoulders.

I say, "What are you doing?"

He's smiling. "Who are you talking about?" he says. He makes it sound like this is just a normal little chit-chat over cappuccinos.

I glare at him.

He goes, "O-kay, then. You leave me no choice. . . ." He throws me up in the air and catches me.

I squeal. I can't believe he did that! I grab onto his neck. That cracks him up. I take my arms away and cross them on my chest.

I say, "Will you please put me down?"

He goes, "Gladly—just as soon as you tell me who you're talking about."

I go, "Shut. Up."

He throws me up in the air again. He makes this big *Ooof* sound when he catches me. "Wow," he says. "You weigh a ton."

I try to look mad.

He goes, "Jeez . . . I don't know how many more times I can do this. Would you mind just telling me who you're talking about before my arms break off?"

I give him one of those *you're a jerk* smiles. He throws me up in the air again.

He goes, "Oh boy. I think I've had it. This is killing me."

"Good," I say, but I kind of don't mean it. "You can put me down, then."

He says, "I will," but he doesn't. He starts walking into the water.

"What are you doing?" I say.

"I'm putting you down."

"Where?"

"In the water."

"No! I'll get all wet!"

"No wonder you got into Harvard! You're a very smart girl. Not everyone immediately makes the connection between 'water' and 'wet.'"

I have to clench my teeth to keep from smiling. I can feel the cold hovering over the water. Where's this warm current he was talking about? I start making these stupid peeping sounds every time a wave laps up closer.

"Look," he says in this Mr. Reasonable voice. "I'm just trying to be helpful. You must be exhausted carrying this huge weight around all day. I mean, it's tiring *me* out and I've only had it for a couple of minutes. The water will make you feel lighter. It will ease your poor overburdened bones."

I laugh and then I hit him because I'm mad I laughed.

The waves splash up and soak my ass. I squeak and try

to lift myself out of the way. It's like I'm trying to scramble up onto his shoulder or something.

He's going, "Down, girl! Down, girl!" and laughing.

I'm laughing too. This whole thing is ridiculous.

Levi takes a few more steps and says, "Okay, my fat little friend, the time has come. You're going for a swim."

I go, "No!"

I clamp my lips together like a Muppet and shake my head. I practically crush his neck. He tries to pull my arms apart but I won't let him.

"Gee," he goes, "I thought it was all blubber but there must be some muscle in there too. You're strong."

"You're horrible," I say.

He looks me right in the eyes. "And you're stupid," he says. "You don't really think you're fat, do you?"

I don't know how to answer that. Why don't we just stick to the fun stuff?

He goes, "You do. I can tell. What? You want to look like a boy or something?" He pops his eyes out at me. "Good thing you're pretty, because you've got a serious mental problem. Luckily, I know the cure."

"Yeah, right," I say. "Okay, Dr. Freud, what do you prescribe?"

"It's called shock therapy."

I laugh. "Ooh . . . I don't like the sound of that."

"It's very effective," he says. "I'll show you."

Then, with me still in his arms, he falls backwards into the freezing water.

24

Monday, 1 p.m.

Mimi: The Magazine

The Summer Love Issue. It's hotter than ever out—
but it's not global warming. Love is in the air. Make
the most of it. Mimi shows you how!

I fly up out of the water with my mouth wide open and
my eyes bulging. I must look like that kid in *Home Alone*.
In my entire life, I've never been so surprised or so cold
or—so cold. That's all I am. One-hundred percent cold. I
start to run ashore. I can feel the arches of my feet curling
in on themselves like someone's pulling them closed with
a drawstring. Levi grabs me by the T-shirt.

"Ah-ah-ah. Not yet. I promised Kay you'd go swimming."

"I . . . I . . . did!"

"That's not swimming. That's dunking. There's a difference."

I don't have time to argue. A wave knocks me off my feet. I come up sputtering with hair all over my face. Levi laughs.

I push him as hard as I can. He goes under. I start to run ashore again.

He comes after me. I don't have a chance. He picks me up, runs back out and throws me in.

This time, I swim underwater as long as I can. When I come up, I see him looking around in a panic. He must think I drowned.

I go, "Yoo-hoo! Over here!" He gives me this *I'm going to murder you* look and starts dolphin-diving toward me. I take off. I'm a pretty good swimmer. By the time he catches me, we're both too tired to do anything except splash each other in the face a few times. We catch our breath and just sort of hover around for a while. His hair's all slicked back like he's an old-fashioned magician or Ralph Lauren model or something. It makes him look really grown-up. He has a very straight nose.

"You're shivering," he says.

"Surprise, surprise," I say. He takes my hand. I sort of float toward him.

He looks at me for a while, then says, "Your eyes are exactly the same colour as the water."

I don't know how to react. I let go of his hand. I turn away. I say, "Um. Do you want to go in now?"

There's a pause as if he's going to say something, then he just nods. "Yeah, okay. Sure. If that's what you want."

I don't answer. I catch the next wave. We bodysurf in to the beach. It's so much fun I drag him out to do it again.

25

Monday, 2 p.m.
You, You and Mimi

"Love in a Lunchbox." Guest chef and culinary historian Chris Filliter sheds new light on the humble sandwich. Is tuna fish on white really the food of love?

I peel off my wet T-shirt and shorts. Seeing me in my bathing suit might give him second thoughts about me not being fat but I'm so cold I don't care. It's the only way I can get warm. We sit on one towel. He puts the other one around my shoulders. He dries himself off with his shirt.

"Hungry?" he says.

I nod. He opens his mouth to say something. I go, "Don't even try."

He says, "What?"

"You were going to make a fat-girl joke."

He sighs and hands me a sandwich. "Am I really that predictable?"

"Yes." I take a bite. It's a classic old-lady tuna sandwich—squishy bread, crunchy lettuce, lots of Miracle Whip. I don't know what I'd think about it normally, but right now, it's delicious. I sit with my knees pulled up to my chest, eating, shivering, looking out at the ocean. My life is suddenly perfect. It's scary.

Levi rubs my back. "Cold?" he says.

I can't look at him. "Un-huh," I say. "Sorta." He rubs harder and edges a little closer to me. I lose the ability to eat. I'm either really cold now or really hot. I can't tell which.

He takes his hand away. I suck my breath in. Why did he do that? Did I do something? I look at him.

"Want another sandwich?" he says. He opens one of the waxed paper packages and peers inside. "I think it's chicken."

I shake my head. I've only managed to eat two bites of the one I've got.

He looks at my unfinished sandwich and lifts his eyebrows way up. He puts his hands on either side of my waist and squeezes.

He says, "I don't know how you manage to keep any meat on your bones. . . ."

All I can think of is how flubby I am. I go to push his hands away.

He says, "You eat like a bird!"

I've got one hand on his hand. I'm looking him in the face. I forget about how fat I may or may not be. Suddenly all I can think about is "Eat Like a Birdie." Should I tell him? Would he believe me? Would it ruin everything? People are never the same once they know I'm Mimi's kid.

He's looking at me too. He's waiting for me to say something.

I go, "Uh . . ." I'm not sure what comes next.

He lets go of my waist and moves back.

"Oops. Sorry," he says. "Was that a touchy subject? I didn't mean anything by it. Frankly, it was just another cheap excuse to get my hands on you. . . ." He pulls his head back and checks me out. "You've got a really small waist, you know."

I can't help myself. "You mean, compared to everything else."

"Yeah," he says.

I knew it was too good to last. "Gee, thanks," I say.

He leans back on his elbows. "That's *good*, Opal! Small waist. Big . . . other things." One side of his mouth smiles. "I hate to break it to you but that's the way the male mind works."

My heart makes one big thump as if it just ran headfirst into my chest bone. I have to turn away. Did he actually say that to me? I bite my mouth closed so I don't smile or laugh or, I don't know, squeal or something.

Then, out of the blue, my heart slams into my chest again.

I'm an idiot. Why am I falling for this? I know what's going to happen. He'll say what he needs to say. He'll act like he cares. He'll dump me. Same old, same old. Just a variation on the pattern I got used to with those girls at school, with Selena—with Mom, come to think of it.

I can still feel where he was touching me. Hot orange palm prints sort of throb away at my waist as if I'm a victim on *CSI*.

Neither of us talks for a long time. I don't feel happy any more, but after a while I don't feel particularly bad either. That's just the way things go. He probably didn't mean what he was saying anyway.

"Last chance," he says. He waves a waxed paper package in front of me. "Speak up or I'm eating it!"

I've been holding my sandwich so tight that my fingers have pinched through. I shake my head in the most neutral way I can. I'd like to get through this with some dignity.

"Oh-oh," Levi says. "Did I step over the line there?"

He's lying on his side, one hand propping up his head. The skin on the inside of his arm kind of sticks out where the muscle is. It's really white and smooth.

"Look, I'm sorry. I shouldn't have joked about that again."

"No," I say. "It's not that." I pick some grains of sand off my leg.

He sits up. "Then what is it?" He's sort of smiling at me, concerned, waiting.

I don't care what all those other people did or what they thought about me. I get this sudden urge to trust him. Wouldn't everything be perfect if I could trust him?

He puts his hand on my back again. "Is something wrong?"

"Um," I say.

I turn to tell him—tell him my real name, who my mother is, that stuff about the ring, everything—but his face is right there, just inches away. He could use a shave and he's got these little gold lines kind of radiating out from his pupils and there's still the purple ring from where I punched him and he goes, "What is it?"

I say, "I . . . I need to go to the bathroom."

26

Monday, 3 p.m.

You, You and Mimi **(rerun)**

"Surviving a Home Invasion." Hostess extraordinaire
Nicole Kelly shows Mimi how to deal with
unexpected, unwanted and even unwashed visitors.

I chickened out. Fine. Probably just as well. After all, I
promised myself I wasn't going to tell anyone about Mom.

But did I really have to say I needed to go to the
bathroom?

Could I not have come up with something else?
Anything else? *I've got a stomach ache. The Mob's after me.
I'm worried about money/global warming/my breath.*

Anything would have been better than providing
Levi with this nice mental image of me squatting, virtu-

ally naked, in the great outdoors like some big old cave woman giving birth or something. It's gross.

And speaking of squatting, what kind of park is this anyway? You'd think they'd have bathrooms around here—but he laughed at that too. It's a wilderness park. It's not fully functional yet. Washroom facilities come in Phase 2. Whatever. It all means the same thing. This is a toilet-free zone. Bend your knees.

He points to the back of the beach. "Just go behind the dunes," he says. "Don't worry. I won't look."

I trudge off with the towel around my waist. The dunes form a little trench. I'd probably be okay but there's no way I'm going to strip off right here in broad daylight. What if somebody else comes along?

I'm glad I didn't tell him. Not for Mom's sake—for mine. It would just make things weird. I'd be setting myself up again. I want him to like me because of who I am, not because of Mimi.

I turn and look at him. He's sitting there leaning against his knees, staring out at the water. I can see all those little bumpy things going down his spine.

I can't pee here. I'm too close.

I scramble up over the other side of the dunes, walk

through the beach grass and into the woods. The first part is scrubby. Bushes mostly. I squat down behind one and check. If he turned around, he wouldn't be able to see anything except my head, but still. I'd feel ridiculous. It would be so obvious what I'm doing.

He knows what I'm doing. Everyone does it. I'm normal. It's the people who don't pee who have the problem.

I know that but I still walk farther back into the woods. It must be the cold—I actually really need to go now. I keep sort of practice-squatting behind trees and looking out at the beach to check if Levi can see me.

He rubbed my back. He saw me in my bathing suit. He wasn't grossed out. He wanted another excuse to touch me. He *said* that. I'm out here all by myself, looking for a place to pee, smiling like an idiot.

I find a little pine tree. I peer out from behind it. He could probably still see me if he was really looking hard, but it doesn't matter. This is good enough.

I gather a bunch of dry leaves for toilet paper and make sure I position myself so that the pee runs away from my feet. I take another last look out at the beach. I start to pull my straps down. A shiver runs up my back.

I hear this raspy voice go, "What do you think you're doing, maid?"

In some part of my brain I know it can't be Levi because I saw him on the beach a second ago—but I guess I don't process that.

I swing around. I go, "Levi!"

There's a man standing there pointing a rifle at me.

27

Monday, 2:30 p.m.

Radio Mimi

In "A Rocky Start," Mimi looks at how to step back into relationships that got off on the wrong foot.

I cover myself with my hands as if he caught me naked. I start to shake even worse than when I was swimming.

The guy wags the gun at me and says, "Who are you?" He's got this dirty-old-man voice and an even stronger accent than Levi's. It almost sounds like he's saying "ye" or something.

I can't get my mouth to work. My brain is overloaded, taking him all in, dealing with dying, suddenly needing to pee more than I've ever needed to pee in my life.

I'm terrified. The guy looks like Rumpelstiltskin. An

armed Rumpelstiltskin. His face is unbelievably wrinkled. He's tiny—maybe five-two or five-three—and skinny. Like a little bird or baby rat before its fur's grown in. He's wearing boots and long pants and a winter jacket and one of those hunter's hats with the flaps turned up, but I can still see how skinny he is. His clothes must have been different colours at one time but they're so dirty now that they're all just variations on grey, as if someone took a charcoal pencil and shaded the whole picture in.

He says something that sounds like, "You durst not make me ask you again, maid. Who are you?" His voice is louder this time. He's missing all the teeth on his right side.

"Robin," I say because I'm not thinking. It comes out in a shaky little whisper.

"What? Louder!"

"OPAL," I say.

He turns his head and spits. "So yer one a those, are ya? It won't help you none here, maid. What yer doing on my land?"

He takes a step toward me. He's got a limp. His gun's pointed right at my belly button. Should I grab it? I'm way bigger than he is. I could take it. If I could move, that is. But I can't.

"I just needed . . . to go . . . like . . . to the bathroom . . . sir."

He jumps back at that. "You come here bold as brass to make yer water on another man's land? You people with yer high and mighty ways! You comport yourself like the Good Lord gave you dominion. . . ." He suddenly stops talking. He perks up his head like a hunting dog.

"Hey, Embree! What's up?" It's Levi.

The guy nods and says, "How do." He's not actually hiding his gun but he's sort of pretending that it's nothing to worry about.

Levi puts his arm around me. "I see you've met my friend Opal."

The guy rubs his scraggly beard. "I did."

Levi acts like he's introducing me to his grandmother. He says, "The two of you should have a talk one day. Opal's doing research on the area. I told her—you want to know something about Port Minton, Embree Bister's the man to go to! He knows it all."

I can tell the guy's not too pleased. He looks me up and down as if I'm the one with the filthy clothes and stringy hair.

He says, "I thank you for that, Levi, but I'll not be sharing my knowledge with the likes of her. I know her kind.

Making her water on my property! That's a slight I won't forget, Levi. As you rightly implied, I'm a man with a long memory."

Levi pauses like he's going to say something, then changes his mind. He smiles and says, "I never argue with a man holding a gun, Embree, so I think we'll just take off now. I'll tell my mother I saw you. I know she was hoping you'd come into the clinic and get that foot looked at. Take care of yourself now, Embree."

Embree has a little laugh at that. "You needn't be worrying about me." He pulls back his scrawny shoulders just to prove his point and says, "It's the others what got to worry."

We don't stay around to find out what that means.

28

Monday, 3 p.m.

See the World with *You, You and Mimi*!

Long-time Mimi associate Olivia Segsworth leads
a select group of adventurers on a tour of "places
that touched Mimi's heart."

Levi guides me out of the woods as if I'm a bomb victim or
something. He keeps saying, "It's okay. It's okay. That's just
Embree. He's not going to do anything. . . ."

We're back on the beach before I can manage to get any
words out. "Why didn't you *warn* me?" I say.

Levi's got this pained look on his face. "Sorry," he says.
"Sorry. I thought you were just going behind the dunes!
You'd have been fine there. Embree never comes out in the
open. I didn't even know he was in the woods these days.
He's usually on the Island."

I'm barely listening. I've got my head in my hands, trying to flush the sight of Embree out of my brain. Flush the stink of him out. When he came closer, I could smell him. Like dirty socks but kind of sweet too. Sugary. It's enough to make me throw up just thinking about it. Can Levi smell it on me?

"Good thing I went to find out why you were taking so long. I was worried you'd twisted your ankle or something. . . ." He puts this really serious look on his face. "Embree didn't actually catch you 'making yer water,' did he?"

Levi's trying to get me to laugh. I just glare at him.

"Then, come on, Opal. It wasn't that bad!" He rubs my arm like he's a dad and I'm a kid who just got cut from the soccer team.

I try to pull myself together and think straight. I've got too many questions—I don't know where to start. I just go, "He's a Bister?"

"Yup."

"Is that why people call each other Bisters around here?"

Levi clicks his tongue. "People shouldn't be saying that."

"Yeah, well, he shouldn't be pointing guns at people either! And he should take a bath occasionally too." I'm on a rant. "And what's with that cheesy pirate accent of his anyway? Like, what bad movie did he limp out of?"

Levi holds me at arm's length. I try not to look so mean. I know that was mean. The guy can't help being dirty. Or maybe he can. I don't know. What business is it of mine?

"Sorry," I say. "That was horrible. I'm just upset."

Levi picks up the towel and our wet clothes and stuffs them in the grocery bag.

He goes, "That's okay. You're right. He shouldn't be pointing guns at people. I imagine Embree's not your favourite guy in the world right now. . . . I doubt Embree's ever been *anybody's* favourite guy. . . ."

"Is he always doing stuff like that?" I say. "He must be pretty bad for people to be using his name as an insult."

Levi turns his head away from me and rubs his hands over his face. He's not joking around any more.

"It's not Embree's fault. He didn't start this whole thing."

"Start what whole thing?" I say.

Levi closes his eyes and goes, "Oh boy . . ."

"What?" I say.

"You're going to think we're so backward. . . ."

"Come on!" I say. "I just had the scare of my life. You got to tell me."

He pushes out his lips, he sighs, he nods. "Okay." He takes my hand and leads me back up the boulder.

"There was a feud," he says.

He's right. These people *are* backward.

"I don't know the whole story. I doubt anyone does any more. It happened, like, a hundred years ago or something. Anyway—see all those little islands out there? You wouldn't know it now but people used to live on them. The one way over to the left–with the tumbledown house on it? That's Bister Island. A long time ago, the people who lived there got really sick with some disease. They were quarantined— you know, kept separate from everyone else. That's how the feud started. I guess the Bisters felt that their neigh-bours were deserting them in their time of need. Everyone else figured it was the only way to keep the disease from spreading. Things got ugly."

"How ugly?"

"Don't really know. I've heard stories. Let's just say shots were fired on both sides. The Bisters kind of became out-casts after that. Everyone else left the islands and moved onto the mainland a good fifty years ago. The Bisters stayed."

I look at the little rocky island sticking out of the ocean. "How did they survive out there?"

Levi shrugs. "Fishing, I guess, though people around here claimed they couldn't live on that. I think that's how the rumour started that the Bisters were wreckers."

"Wreckers? What's that?"

"People who lure ships in to crash on the rocks so they can steal their cargo. . . ."

Is he making this stuff up? "Oh, come on. That sounds like something from a bad movie! No one would do that."

He pats me on the head. "Your innocence is charming, my dear. Of course people did that. Not just here. It wasn't a Port Minton thing. There are bad people all over the world. I just don't know if the Bisters did it. Everyone around here was always accusing the Bisters of something."

I go, "Yeah, well . . . maybe they deserved it. I mean, Embree's not the most law-abiding guy by the looks of things."

"True. He poaches deer. He makes moonshine. He spits in public. But he's not to blame for *everything*. When I was little, any time anything went missing, someone would say a Bister took it. It was as if no one in all of Shelton County ever did anything wrong except the Bisters. We didn't have bogeymen, we had Bisters. Kids didn't go out as tramps on Halloween, they went out as Bisters. You weren't an idiot, you were a Bister. Parents would threaten to wash their kids' mouths out with soap for saying such a thing, but you know what kids are like. They said it anyway. Some of the adults said it too. Still do."

He picks up a rock and pitches it into the water.

I say, "So do the Bisters still live out there?"

"No. Nobody does—except Embree, that is. About twenty years ago or something, the whole thing blew up. I don't know what happened exactly. There was some big scandal. The government stepped in and forced them all off the Island."

"So . . . why's Embree still there, then?"

"Dunno. You'd have to ask him, I guess."

I pull my face back in horror. Levi laughs.

"Just kidding. . . . I only know what Dad told me. I guess Embree used to live full-time on the Island until it looked like he was going to starve. Now he only lives there in the summer. He camps out here all winter. He claims it's his land. Claims it's belonged to the Bisters since the King gave it to them in 1605 or some damn thing. Who knows? He might be right. Embree's not stupid. And he's not crazy either. But you can see why the townspeople wouldn't want to have too much to do with him."

"So . . . how come you do?" I say.

Levi shakes his head. "I don't. Not really. When I was a kid, I was out here a lot with Dad. We'd always drop by Embree's camp, just to keep the wheels greased, you know. Embree's not the type of guy you can scare into doing what you want him to do. You got to kind of keep on his good side. It helps that Mum's a nurse too. She comes out every so often to check Embree over. He never does what she tells him to, but I think he appreciates that she's trying to help. That's why I knew he wouldn't shoot you."

"You knew that for sure?"

He rocks his hand back and forth. "Pretty sure. Good thing you didn't actually pee on his property, though. You'd have been dead meat then."

29

"Making the Best of a Bad Situation." Mimi discloses
how a potential disaster turned into one of her
most cherished moments.

The room is quiet. Lip-Smacking Girl left yesterday. Good
for me but bad for Kay. My twenty dollars a night isn't
going to go very far to keep this place running.

I look out the window. It's foggy and wet, but I don't
care about the weather. All I can think about is last night.
It keeps coming back to me in waves—big waves that
almost knock me over.

We were starving after being at the beach all day so
Levi took me to this sad little diner out on the highway. It

had a big sign that said World's Finest Fish and Chips. We sat on orange plastic chairs and looked out at the water while we waited for our order to come up. We talked a bit more about Embree and the Bisters but mostly we just goofed around. Levi told me funny stories about him and his brothers having jellyfish fights and sneaking into the liquor store dressed up as old ladies and tipping an outhouse over while his uncle was inside.

I told lame stories about being an only child. He didn't seem to notice how bad they were. He always laughed like I was a regular stand-up comedian. He kept nudging me in the side or wiping little bits of hair off my face or putting his arm around my shoulder and whispering things in my ear even though no one else was listening.

He asked about my parents. I told him my dad was a musician—true—and my mother was a relationship counsellor—more or less true. (I mean, that's what all the ads make out. "Want a happy marriage? Let your husband spend time with another woman. Mimi Schwartz! Weekdays at 3.") He thought it was funny—as in "peculiar"—that a relationship counsellor would be divorced, but I said it happens all the time. I think he felt sorry for me. You know, an only child, divorced parents and everything. It almost made me laugh. He's the one who lives in this little nothing town and has to do joe jobs to go to university!

But then I looked at those eyes of his and that smile he's always got plastered on his face and I thought, who's the happy one here?

The lady at the counter called out Levi's name. He went and picked up these huge orders of fish and chips. He poured vinegar over everything, then wolfed the whole plate down in about three minutes. I made it through about half of mine, which frankly was still pretty impressive. I would have eaten more but I felt too full. (I hate to sound corny but that's what looking at him did to me.)

It was just starting to get dark by the time we left. I said I was cold—I got too much sun, I guess—so he put his arm around me. We were walking out the door like that when this little blue car pulled into the parking lot and screeched to a halt right in front of us. I had to jump out of the way.

Krystal and one of her skinny friends got out. I felt sick.

Sick, fat, ugly, stupid and scared.

Krystal's nostrils were all flared up as if something didn't smell quite right. She went, "Hello, Levi," then gave me the once-over. "You run out of french fries to chuck at him or something?"

If she were in a movie, I would have laughed. She was right out of some teen comedy. The whole mean-girl-hand-on-the-hip thing. The big-eyed sidekick in the matching outfit. The little flip of her head.

I didn't laugh now.

I didn't say anything. I turned into this solid block of nothing. I saw myself exactly as she saw me. She was all perfect in her halter top and her little white shorts and her sunglasses pulled up on top of her shiny hair and there I was with my ugly bare arms and my wrinkled shirt and my belly all bulging from fish and chips.

Levi went, "Oh, come on, Krystal. Who'd go and chuck *Barb's* french fries? Speaking of which, you'd better hurry if you want some. She's closing in five minutes." He winked at her.

He talked to Krystal exactly the same way he talked to me. The same tone. The same sparkly eyes. The same little arm-rub at the end. I felt this sob kind of bunch up in the back of my throat. I looked away and swallowed.

He held the door open. Krystal's friend must have forgotten she was supposed to be mad because she said,

"Thanks, Levi!" in this chirpy voice. Krystal sauntered in after her as if she were America's Next Top Model. She turned and sneered at him in a way that somehow still made her look pretty.

Levi and I got into the van. He went, "Well, that hit the spot!" He said it as if nothing had happened. As if we hadn't run into them. As if things were just like they were before. Who did he think he was kidding?

I went, "Un-huh."

Levi didn't make fun of me or try to joke or change the subject or anything this time. He just pulled out and drove.

I stared straight ahead and thought of that episode of *You, You and Mimi* where Diane Chisholm, PhD (Doctor of Romance), talked about "Charming Billys." Apparently, these guys are all over the place. Charming Billys make you laugh, tell you what you want to hear, look you right in the eye. They say they're crazy about you and they mean it. That's what makes them so dangerous. They mean it when they say it to all the other girls they're hitting on too.

I knew that. I knew about "Rogues" and "Panty-Removers" and "Heart Specialists" too. I watched enough daytime TV to know to stay away from them. But here I was in a rusty van with the worst kind of all. I didn't know whether to hate him or to hate myself for *not* hating him.

I'm better by myself. I should just forget about other people.

He finally said, "I guess you're wondering what's up with Krystal and me."

I was going to keep my mouth shut but I figured that would just make me look like I cared. I went, "Sort of," but I shrugged when I said it.

"I'm not going out with her if that's what you think. I haven't gone out with her in two years! Honestly. We went out for a few months one summer. That's it. It wasn't even very serious."

I didn't say anything.

He went, "Nobody's heart got broken or anything. It wasn't like that."

I heard him tap his fingers on the steering wheel, then he sighed and said, "I don't know why she's acting like that. . . . She goes out with other guys and it doesn't bother me . . . but, like, every so often she sees me with someone else and she gets all hissy. I just try to see past it."

I could feel him look over at me. I didn't look back.

He said, "Sorry she took it out on you."

I said, "No problem. I don't care."

"You don't care about her getting mad? Or you don't care whether or not I'm going out with her?"

He was grinning at me. I could feel it. It was like he had a heat lamp aimed at me. I did my best to ignore it. I kept trying to make myself think *Charming Billy, Charming Billy.*

I closed my eyes. I shrugged again.

"What does that mean?" he said.

Another shrug.

He poked me in the ribs.

I had to bite my lip to keep from smiling. My face was all prickly inside.

"So?" he went. "Which is it?"

"Both," I said.

He pulled into Kay's driveway.

He leaned against his door and said, "I don't believe you."

I said, "Too bad. 'Cause it's true." I could keep my lips from smiling but my eyes were out of control.

"Oh well," he said. "I tried."

"Yup," I said. "You sure did."

He laughed at that. He didn't say anything else.

I looked at my hands, picked at my weird thumbnail. I wanted to look at Levi but I couldn't. After a while I went, "I guess I better get going."

He said, "Me too. I got a big day tomorrow." Then he put out his arm and leaned across me.

My lungs, my heart—everything—stopped at once as if someone had slammed down the off switch on some giant machine. *He's going to kiss me,* I thought. I could feel my hair and my skin and every little hair on my body tingling. I opened my mouth just a little and turned toward him.

But he didn't kiss me. He just pushed open my door and leaned back in his seat.

There I was with my eyes half open and my mouth half open and the horror of what I'd just done creeping up my neck.

"You okay?" he said.

I just nodded like a bobblehead doll and got out of the van as fast as I could. I started beetling back to the hostel. I don't know how I looked on the outside but inside, I was in agony. I was twisting up like a plastic toy dropped in a campfire.

Levi went, "Opal?"

When he says it, I don't even feel like a Robin any more.

I turned my head halfway around and said, "Un-huh?"

He was all stretched out so he could see me through the van window. He had this huge white smile on his face.

He said, "I was going to kiss you but I was scared you'd smack me in the eye again."

30

Tuesday, 10:30 a.m.

You, You and Mimi (rerun)

"The Look of Love." Mimi's personal stylist, Lucy Grant, gives desire-inducing fashion tips for the woman in love.

I get up. I wash my hair. I pop in my contacts and slap on a bit of mascara. I put on that turquoise shirt and those new jeans Anita got me. They fit perfectly. I love Anita.

I ride to the library in a daze. It's amazing I find my way there. I don't pay attention at all. I'm completely in my head, in yesterday, on the beach, in the van, with Levi. When I realize I'm talking to myself, I just laugh. Levi would laugh at me for doing something like that.

I lean my bike up against the railing, then try the library door. It's locked. The sign says, Open: 1–5. I've got half an hour to wait.

It doesn't bother me. The sun's managed to come out. It's almost warm. I flip through the church bulletins just to look like I'm doing something other than thinking about Levi. I try to remind myself that he's a Charming Billy but it doesn't do much good. I keep hearing him say, *I was going to kiss you . . .* , and I end up doing this full body smile.

I glance again at that picture of Mom as a kid. I think of the beach and the Ingrams and the Bisters, then I think of Mom and Dad and me together in that old cabin doing jigsaw puzzles. That makes me think of being on that plane with Mom when we played cribbage all the way to Buenos Aires as if she didn't have another thing in the world to do. Then I remember the time she bought me a book about bodily fluids that she thought was disgusting but was exactly what I wanted and how sweet she always is with Grandpa even when the nurses aren't around and I end up doing something I haven't done in ages.

I call her.

"Mimi Schwartz."

"Hi, Mom."

"Robin? Is something the matter?"

"No, no. I just thought I'd call. I didn't get a chance to say goodbye to you before I left."

"Oh, phew! Darling. You scared me. Well, I'm glad you're okay. Do you need money?"

"No, I'm fine. I'm great. How are you?"

"Me? Oh, you know. Busy. I've got to shoot a bunch of promos for next season. We're opening that Institute for Culturally Deprived Children tonight. On top of everything, the new James Bond stood us up for tomorrow's show. Honestly! Who does he think he is? His abs better be a whole heck of a lot better than the last guy's or he's not going to get away with stuff like that. I have no idea how we're going to fill his thirteen minutes. I could pull in Tom Hanks again but. . . . Oh, hold on, honey. . . . Yeah . . . okay . . . okay. In a sec . . . Birdie?"

"Yeah?"

"Sorry, gotta run. Ingrid's finally managed to get one of the victims of that big silicone scam on the line for me. Was there anything else you wanted?"

"Uh, well, no. I just thought that maybe when I'm back and everything we could talk about some stuff. . . ."

"Sure. Like what?"

"Um. Well, our family, I guess. I just realized I don't know anything about my, like, background, you know."

"Uh . . . okay. . . . Fine."

"You mind?"

"No, no, darling, of course not! Mimi mind? Please! I completely understand. Spending a couple of weeks with your dad would make anyone worry about their family background. . . . Just kidding! . . . Sorry . . . I'm coming! I'm coming! . . . Honey? I've really got to run. All the networks are trying to reach this woman. I've got to get her while I can!"

"That's okay."

"Bye, darling!"

"Bye, Mom."

I say, "I love you" too, but she's hung up by then.

31

Tuesday, 1 p.m.
Ego Altered **(film)**
Mimi Schwartz shines in her role as a displaced
person who tries to disguise her past at war's end.
A hit at Sundance.

I guess she must have had an audience. She was using
her "Mimi" voice. Doing all that "Darling!," "Please!" and
"Gotta run!" stuff.

That's okay. She's busy. I only feel sad for a second.

Levi's probably the reason. It's kind of hard to be sad
when he keeps flashing on my brain screen like some gorgeous computer pop-up.

I don't think it's just that, though. It's Mom too. I think
maybe I'm not sad because I understand her now—some-

thing *about* her now anyway. I know why she's not who she seems to be on TV, why she's not who she seems to be at home.

She's got a secret.

I don't know what it is, but there's definitely something going on here. There's something about her she doesn't want people to know. (The world might not believe it but Mimi Schwartz has secrets too.)

I take *It's All About Mimi* out of my backpack. I look at that picture of her on the cover with her crooked smile and her crossed arms and her raised eyebrow. She looks like she's exactly who people think she is. Funny. Confident. A little bit on the racy side. In other words—nothing like my mother at all.

I go through the book until I find that picture of her as a kid. It dawns on me that I might be able to recognize something in the background, now that I sort of know Port Minton.

I crouch over the page like I'm a scientist squinting at some little amoeba. I can't see much. The picture's really grainy, and there's hardly any background to identify anyway. For the first time, I notice part of someone's hand in the bottom of the frame. Mom wasn't by herself after all.

Someone had their arm around her waist.

Seeing that makes me think Mom's childhood might not have been as lonely as she claims. (It could just be my current frame of mind but that makes me feel happy.)

I get out the church bulletin to see if I can tell where the other photo was taken.

The faces of the kids are pretty blurry, but the area behind them is sharp. It's obvious it's Port Minton beach. In the background I can see the big boulder Levi and I climbed. (That makes me even happier.)

I study the picture some more, and suddenly, it's like I can't breathe. I open the book again. I line up the two pictures side by side on my lap. In the church bulletin, Rosie (or whatever you want to call her) is wearing a striped T-shirt and her hair is in pigtails. One of the other girls—Lenore, maybe—has her hand around Rosie's waist.

In the book, Mimi's wearing a button-up shirt. Her hair is cut to her chin and her bangs go straight across her forehead. There's a hand around Mimi's waist too.

Okay. So what? It's the classic snapshot pose. People line up with their arms around each other. The photographer takes the picture. Everyone moves apart.

But it's not just the same pose in both pictures. It's

exactly the same pose. The hand, the watch, the way the thumb kind of disappears—identical. The tilt of Rosie/Mimi's head, the slight curl of her lips, the jut of her elbow—it's a perfect copy.

My heart's pounding like a sound effect in a slasher movie. I root around in the side pocket of my backpack and get the envelope I tucked away. I take out the photo I found in Mom's chair. I put it beside the other two.

The one from the chair and the one from the church bulletin are identical. People, clothes, hair, background.

The one from Mimi's book would have been identical too—before someone Photoshopped it, that is. Photoshopped out the other kids, the striped T-shirt, the beach. Drew in a new shirt, restyled her hair and—now that I get a better look—did a little something to her nose too.

I turn the photo over in my lap. I can't look at it any more. I have to calm down.

I force myself to take some deep breaths. In through my nose, out through my mouth. In through my nose, out through my mouth. Things start to make sense. Now that I'm thinking straight again, I don't know why this would have scared me. Of course Mimi would cover her tracks like that! For some reason, she doesn't want anyone to recognize her as a kid. She *had* to retouch the photo for the book. Otherwise, someone would have seen it, would have made the connection, would have called *Entertainment Tonight.*

But why does Mimi still care so much after all this time? What's she got to hide? You'd think confessing to all the plastic surgery and men and those eighties dance outfits of hers would be way worse than this—whatever "this" is.

I'm trying to figure everything out when the librarian walks up the stairs. I shove the photo in the envelope, stick it in the backpack. She says, "Oh, I'm so glad you're here! I ran into Muriel Faulkner at the Save-Easy. She's coming in this afternoon to pick up that Mimi Schwartz book. I hope you brought it? . . . Good." She wrinkles up her nose and whispers, "I knew I could trust you."

She hands me the big box she's carrying and unlocks the door. "I'm very excited. I found lots of material for you. I hope it's helpful."

She turns on the lights and opens a couple of windows. "Ooh. Pee-yew! This place gets so stuffy when it's closed up for a few days. It's like I can smell old Enos here himself."

She bends her head and looks at me over her glasses. "Please don't tell anyone I said that. I should be shot. This library is a huge blessing for the town." Her voice gets all strained as she tries to pull open another window. "I'd just find it a whole lot easier to be grateful if I hadn't actually known the man."

She takes the box from me and puts it on a table. "Don't tell anyone I said that either. Especially Mrs. Hiltz. Which reminds me . . . she'd be delighted to have a little chat with you this afternoon."

I go, "Who? What?"

"Mrs. Hiltz. Mrs. *Enos* Hiltz. Remember I said a friend of my mother's was a Port Minton girl? That's her. She lives just around the corner. She naps from one to two but said she'll be home for the rest of the afternoon if you'd like to drop by."

I don't know what my face is doing but the librarian obviously figures out that I'm not thrilled at the idea.

"Don't worry," she says. "You'll enjoy it. She's a great old bird. Everything Enos wasn't. Cultured, down-to-earth, decent. She really worked hard for the underprivileged around here. Enos gouged the money out of people. *She* made sure most of it got back to them."

I say, "Sounds great."

She tucks in her chin and gives me this lame smile. I feel bad I'm not a better actress.

She says, "If you're worried about getting stuck there too long with her, arrive at about four. She'll be sure to hustle you out the door by five so she can pour herself a glass of sherry. . . . In the meantime, any questions and I'll be in the back. My name's Joan."

I thank her and sit down in front of the box. There's a pile of stuff here. I wonder if Rosie/Mimi's in any of it. I really need to find out what's going on. There's just something so creepy about that Photoshopped picture.

Minutes from town council meetings, letters to the mayor, newspaper clippings about the school closing, all the stuff that Joan no doubt worked so hard to find for me—I throw it aside. I find a bunch of photos in a big brown folder. Most aren't very interesting. Just people holding signs saying Save Our School or men in ties looking seriously at some official document.

And then there's the photo of the last Sunday school class of the Port Minton United Baptist Church.

The colours are faded but it's still sharp. There are only eleven kids, all lined up by height. I turn the photo over. Someone's written down their names and ages. *Rosie Ingram, 15,* is in the back row, third from the left. I flip the picture back over. It's her all right. She's older but it's definitely the same girl who was on the beach.

I feel sort of intensely calm, if you can be such a thing. I know what I have to do. I get out the church bulletins. I go through them all. Rosie Ingram is mentioned in three of them. Once at the church picnic. Once two years later for helping organize the little kids' Christmas pageant. And then again in the bulletin's final issue: "Congratulations go as well to Rosie Ingram for a perfect ten-year attendance record at our Sunday school."

A perfect ten-year attendance record.

It takes me a few seconds to understand exactly what those words mean. Mimi wasn't just in Port Minton for camp or to visit relatives. She grew up here. She wasn't home-schooled in Brooklyn. She wasn't some little fourteen-year-old stuck at home looking after her mother.

She was Rosie Ingram from Port Minton, Nova Scotia.

32

Tuesday, 2:30 p.m.
You, You and Mimi
"Birth-day Bloopers." Ten new mothers share their
horror stories from the maternity ward.

I'm not sure how long I just sit here, doing nothing, letting
it all seep in. It's like I'm at the dentist's, waiting for the
anaesthetic to kick in enough that I can get a tooth filled. I
have to wait until I'm numb enough to go on.

How did Rosie/Mimi/Whoever get from here to where
she is now?

There are a bunch of high school yearbooks in the box.
I take a deep breath and start there.

I do the math and figure that if Mom's forty-two now,
she probably finished high school about twenty-four years

ago. I find the right yearbook and turn to the graduation photos. There are lots of Ingrams but no Rosies. Nothing even close. I flip back to the photo in the church bulletin. The other girls' names are all listed there. I look them up in the yearbook. No Kathy Whynacht, Lenore Tanner or Tracy-Lynn Carter either.

Funny. Did they move away? Were they just church friends? Or did the school have a really high drop-out rate?

I kind of laugh when the obvious next question hits me: or did Mom just lie about her age?

Of course she lied about her age. She might have called herself Rosie, but she was still Mimi.

I scan through some older yearbooks. They're pretty much what you'd expect. Bad skin, thick bangs and glasses the size of ski goggles. There are Badminton Clubs, Debating Clubs and something called the Glee Club. (Is it only me—or is that kind of sad? How desperate do you have to be to join something called the Glee Club?) There's a boys curling team, a girls curling team and a co-ed curling team made up of all the same people as on the boys and girls teams. There's a pretty sorry-looking excuse for a basketball team.

And then there's the hockey team.

Year after year—a good ten pages of it. It's clearly the biggest show in town. There are endless pictures of kids getting trophies, scoring goals, piling up on each other after another big win. I wonder which one of those boys owned the ring.

I find a Roberta Ingram and for a second I think maybe Rosie is her nickname—but no. It couldn't be. I doubt they're even related. There's no resemblance at all. Roberta has shoulders that run off the edge of the page. That would be a physical impossibility for a little bird like Mimi. (There's only so much the plastic surgeon can do.) There are lots more Whynachts and Tanners and Carters too but not the ones I'm looking for.

What happened to all those girls?

I get out some more yearbooks. I've got this buzz in my head. I don't know what it's about but it's bugging me.

I absentmindedly turn pages. It's strange watching the styles change and people get almost more familiar or something. I see guys go from stick boys to captains of the hockey team, girls go from sort of nothing to prom queens.

There's hope for me yet.

That makes me think of Levi saying, *Good thing you're pretty* . . . I get a little stomach flip and for a few seconds I'm gone. I'm still turning the pages but I'm not here any more. I'm not concerned about Mom or Rosie any more. I'm back on the beach with Levi, reliving what happened, rewriting a bit, blushing.

That's why I'm amazed I even notice. I'm so totally lost in my own world I don't know how the words manage to get through, but they do. I turn a page and the name *Rosemary Miriam Ingram* just jumps right out at me.

Rosemary Ingram.

Miriam.

Mimi.

Levi disappears from my head. I stare at the page. There's a picture of Rosie. She's about eighteen in it but she hasn't changed much from the Sunday school photo. You can see it's the same kid despite the big glasses and the bad perm. This time, she's not smiling, not even a bit. You get the feeling she hates having her picture taken. (Who wouldn't with that perm?)

There's one of those stupid yearbook captions underneath the picture.

Being shy isn't all bad. Rosie's the only kid in Port Minton High who never got kept after school for talking in class! (Ha-ha!) Still waters run deep so we know Rosie's bound for great things! Good luck in the future, Rosie!

At first I think, *Mom's not shy!* But I know immediately that's wrong. Mimi might not be, but Mom is. She's always found it way easier to talk to a camera than to a real live person. (Or at least to her real live daughter.)

I flip through the rest of the yearbook. Kathy, Lenore and Tracy-Lynn are all there too—and having a fabulous time by the look of it. I even find Debbie the hairdresser and her big-shouldered Roy.

I close the book and, for the first time, notice the date.

The yearbook only came out eighteen years ago.

It couldn't be! There's something wrong here.

Mom was pregnant with me eighteen years ago.

33

Tuesday, 3 p.m.

You, You and Mimi

"Children Raising Children." Family physician and
author Michaela Meltzer-Gardner discusses the
alarming rate of teen pregnancies.

How could I be so dumb? Why am I even surprised? It's
the oldest story in the book. Rosie had to get out of town
because of an unwanted baby.

Me.

Unwanted.

My eyes fill with tears. It makes so much sense it hurts.

I open the book again. I stare at Rosie's picture until
I can really see her. Maybe that look on her face isn't

just about being shy. Maybe she's pregnant already. She's scared and she's worried and maybe she's ashamed too. That's why she's not smiling.

What gets me the most, though, is that she's actually pretty good-looking. I mean, she's not bad-looking or anything. Nothing a bit of makeup couldn't have helped. Mimi always made it sound like she was a real dog before her nose surgery.

Classic. What is it about girls? Why do we all think we're so ugly? Why do we always make such a big deal about nothing? I mean, I was expecting her to have some giant honker or something, but Rosie's nose is fine. Better than fine. Nice.

She added six years to her age, got rid of a perfectly good face and changed her name. How much do you have to hate yourself to do that?

Poor Rosie. I don't care what Mimi said in her book. She must have been miserable. I can't imagine being so ashamed of getting pregnant by some guy that I'd give up my whole life like that.

Some guy.

What am I talking about? Rosie didn't get pregnant by *some guy*. She got pregnant by Dad.

That means Rosie Ingram knew my dad. Dad lived in Port Minton too? This is getting freaky. It's like the pattern on the kaleidoscope just changed again.

He's three years younger than Mom—or is that three years older? Did he lie about his age too? He couldn't have been fifteen when he got her pregnant. Please, God, no. Now it's getting gross.

I flip through all the yearbooks looking for a Steve Schwartz. No Schwartzes. Nothing even close.

Who knows if that's even *his* real name? If he even went to Port Minton High? He could have been from anywhere. She could have met him at a dance or a friend's or at that fish-and-chips joint out on the highway. Maybe that lame band of his was just passing through one weekend.

No. It couldn't have happened that way. Mom and Dad got married. It didn't last long maybe, but it wasn't a one-night stand either.

I should just call him and ask. It's a bit hard to predict how Mom would react to something like that, but Dad wouldn't care.

Or would he? We don't really talk about personal stuff. That's probably why he's so easy to get along with.

Quit dithering. Just ask him. He's my father. He'd tell me. He loves me.

But . . . he hates my mother. Would I be betraying her by talking to him about it? Would I be giving him ammunition? Is he really like that?

I don't know what to do.

I stare at the wall. No. I made a deal. I promised myself I wouldn't tell anyone what I was doing. Anyone. *That means you, Dad.*

I go back to Rosie's yearbook. I look at every page, hoping I'll see something that makes sense. Kathy and Lenore are big into the Spirit Squad and there are a bunch of candid photos of Tracy-Lynn laughing and screaming and wearing one of those corny rainbow clown wigs—but Rosie only made it into the yearbook once, for her graduation shot. That's not much help.

There's the usual big section on the hockey team, but it's more interesting this year. The editor devoted a whole double-page spread to the hockey "Ring Ceremony."

The PMRCHS Student Council proudly raised $832.17 to purchase commemorative victory rings for each member of this year's Panthers. Our boys have made us super proud again! Student Council President, Colin Graham, presents Panther Captain, Roy Tanner, with this coveted souvenir. Thanks to Himmelman's Jewellers for giving us a price cut!

There were some bad photos of a "triumphant" march through downtown Port Minton but the rest were just of adoring fans hanging off various hockey players.

How would someone like Rosie—some little wallflower—ever have ended up with a "coveted" hockey ring?

And why?

None of the other yearbooks offer any clues. Rosie never shows up again. As the years go on, the hockey team seems to lose its edge. There's no more talk of championship rings—or "triumphant marches" for that matter. By the time the school closes down a few years later, the team is getting less coverage than the Debating Club.

The only other thing that catches my eye is that about a year or two before Rosie's graduation, some Bisters show up at the school. I notice a group picture with a Gershom and a Barnabas Bister. (Minerva Bister was "missing from photo.") I wonder if they're Embree's kids. They could be. The boys are skinny, with that same sour look to them. Gershom seems a little happier in the Friendship Club, but Barnabas still isn't smiling in the only other picture of him. He was one of four kids in the Literature Corner. (I'm sort of surprised they could even find that many.)

I look at the clock on the wall. It's quarter after four. I've got to go visit that old lady. I'm not dreading it any more. If she knows everything about Port Minton, she might actually be able to help me figure out how Rosie became Mimi.

I realize there's someone else who might be able to help me too. I turn on the computer.

From: birdbrain76@airmail.com
To: gumdrop113@airmail.com
Subject: Secret Lover
Hey Selena
I've got some really juicy stuff to tell u about a guy
I met but I need u 2 do me a favour now. It's really
important.
U have 2 go into mom's room. There's a folder
in the bottom left hand drawer of her desk. My
grandmother's obituary and mom's marriage

certificate r there. I need u 2 scan them and send them 2 me asap.

DON'T TELL ANYONE!!!!

I'll explain everything l8r.

U r the best,

Robin

34

Tuesday, 4 p.m.

Radio Mimi

"Fortune's Child." Others might credit her talent and looks but Mimi claims her success has more to do with good, old-fashioned luck.

Joan says I can leave the box of stuff at the library and come back for it tomorrow. She points me toward Mrs. Hiltz's house.

I thought she'd live in one of those big old mansions like you see in horror movies and decorator shows but she doesn't. She lives in a new brick house with a three-car garage, one of those U-shaped driveways and two perfect half-circles of flowers under the front windows. It would be no big deal anywhere else but in Shelton it looks like it's straight out of *Hollywood Homes*.

The doorbell makes this big *bong* sound. I almost expect some undead butler to miraculously appear, but it's Mrs. Hiltz herself who opens the door.

"Why, hello!" she says. She's all twinkly. "You must be the young lady Joan Chandler told me about. Come in! Come in!"

She steps back to let me pass and I get this little whiff of perfume.

Mrs. Hiltz looks as out of place in Shelton as her house does. She's tall—almost as big as me—and I guess the word is *elegant*. Her hair is really white and perfectly curled. (She was probably just in to see Debbie.) She's wearing a little eye shadow and some lipstick that's a shade or two darker than her pale pink suit. I don't know if it's the scarf she's wearing or the eye shadow but something really makes her blue eyes pop. Mimi's makeover guy might have suggested that she go a little easier on the hairspray but that's about it. She looks good. She makes me feel like a slob (and I got dressed up today . . .).

She tells me not to worry about my shoes and leads me into this huge sunny living room. The chairs are the old-fashioned kind with the claw feet. They look like they should be in a museum. A German shepherd is sleeping in a square of sunlight on the carpet. There's a shiny wooden coffee table with a silver teapot, some cups and a plate full of little-old-lady cookies.

She points to a chair and says, "Please. Make yourself comfortable." Then she puts her hand to her cheek like she's just done something terrible.

"You'll have to excuse me," she says. "I'm afraid I'm getting dotty in my old age. I didn't even introduce myself! I'm sorry. I'm Opal Hiltz. And who might you be?"

35

Tuesday, 4:15 p.m.

Mimi's Men

The only on-line dating service to offer prospective partners personally vetted by Mimi Schwartz's trained staff. Find love at www.mimismen.com.

Mrs. Hiltz is as surprised as I am when I tell her.

She says, "You're an Opal too? Really? Well, isn't that something! It's not a name you hear very often—especially nowadays. Are you originally from this area?"

I manage to say, "Uh, no," but that's all. I'm still trying to pull myself together from the shock.

"Are your parents?" she says.

I hesitate. For half a second I think I should come right out and ask her. The fact that we have the same name couldn't be random. Mimi must have known her—or at least known of her. Port Minton is a small place and she *is* Mrs. Enos Hiltz, after all. Mimi must have liked her too. She wouldn't have put Opal in my name if she didn't.

I bet if I told Mrs. Hiltz what I knew, she could fill in the blanks for me.

"Um," I say.

I think of the paparazzi and the tabloids and all the trouble Mom took to hide whatever it is she's hiding. I think of my deal.

"No," I say.

Mrs. Hiltz smiles. "You must be an October baby like me, then," she says. "Is it your birthstone?"

"No," I say again. For some reason that almost makes me feel guilty.

"Well, then it must just be a lovely coincidence!" She passes me the plate of cookies.

I help myself to a Fig Newton.

"Now," she says, "I understand from Joan that you're interested in the history of Port Minton. Well, you've come to the right place. I spent most of my life there. I didn't plan to, of course. I had a scholarship to university and was all set to head off, never to return. Unfortunately, my father died and Mother needed help supporting the younger children so that was the end of that. I found work at the fish plant. Horrible job—but I don't regret it for a minute. That's where I met my husband. Enos saw me on the line one day and must have liked something about the way I cut the head off that cod, because we were soon married. I've had a very happy life as a result."

She looks off in kind of a dreamy way but then catches herself. "Oh goodness. I do go on! You didn't come here to listen to me reminisce, did you."

I try to say something but my mouth is full of cookie. It's a little stale, and it sticks to my teeth. I guess she doesn't have many visitors.

Mrs. Hiltz says, "Here's some tea to wash that down with, dear. Help yourself to cream and sugar. I, unfortunately, have to take my tea clear—with a pill." She makes this big dramatic wave of her hand. "Heart problems. My doctor won't let me indulge myself any more. . . ." She pushes the plate of cookies toward me again. "But you eat up! Please. It will make me happy that at least *one* of us is enjoying herself."

She waits until I swallow, then asks me again. "So what exactly are you interested in?

The ring. My mother. Why she's lying.

I look at her but nothing comes out of my mouth. How do you bring something like that up?

"The feud," I say. At least that's sort of neutral.

Mrs. Hiltz's eyebrows shoot up. Either her tea's too hot or the feud's not that neutral after all. She puts her cup back on the table and smiles. False alarm.

"Oh, you've heard about that, have you? I guess I shouldn't be surprised."

She holds out the pot and says, "More tea?" I shake my head. "I presume you know the story, how it all began?"

"Not really."

She fills her cup. "Well, in the 1880s there was an outbreak of smallpox on Bister Island. At that time, quarantine was the only way to control a lot of diseases. Remember—there were no miracle drugs back then. All you could do was keep the epidemic from spreading. My guess is the Bisters would have demanded the people on Faulkner Island or Whynacht Island be quarantined too, had smallpox hit there instead—but the Bisters didn't see it that way. They took the quarantine order as a sign the community was turning its back on them. Maybe their anger at the time was natural—it must have been hard to see so many of their relatives die—but they never got over it. They

demonized the rest of Port Minton, which in turn demonized them. Things got worse and worse as the years went
on. The Bisters became more isolated and, not surprisingly,
more set in their ways. Port Minton people found them
strange and scary. The Bisters no doubt felt the same about
us. We avoided one another as much as possible. It was a
very sad situation. As a result, the Bisters never managed
to reintegrate themselves into society."

She takes a sip of tea, then smiles at me. She's ready for
another question.

"So was the feud the Bisters' fault?" I say. I consider
leaving it at that, but I tell myself to stop being a wimp.
"Or did other families—like, for instance, you know, the
Ingrams—have anything to do with it?"

"The Ingrams?" She frowns in sort of a confused way.
"No, I wouldn't say the Ingrams in particular had anything
to do with it. At least, no more than anyone else."

She turns and stares out the window for a second. She
moves her mouth around like she's smoothing her lipstick
or something, then she turns back to me. Her eyes have
lost their twinkle.

"The feud was an awful thing. The Bisters didn't behave
very well—but we mainlanders didn't do ourselves proud
either. I remember a group of Bisters coming ashore for

supplies once and the local men all getting out their rifles and sending them back.

"Now this was long, long after there was any threat of smallpox. People here just didn't like having Bisters around. I'm sure that was at least in part due to the fact that we were ashamed of ourselves. These ragtag people, half-starved, living out on that godforsaken Island? We all knew how terrible it was, but for a long time no one had the stomach to do anything about it."

I suddenly feel really sad. I think of all the stuff Mom does for the poor, the underdogs, the people most of us try not to even look at. I know all celebrities have their causes. You sort of have to, if you don't want to look like a complete selfish jerk. But Mom—I don't know—I don't think it's just a publicity stunt for her. I think cruelty or injustice or whatever you call it really bothers her.

I wonder if that's why she changed her name. Maybe it wasn't just the pregnancy. Was she ashamed of being a Ingram? Ashamed of even being connected to Port Minton because of what happened to the Bisters?

Mrs. Hiltz is looking at me funny. I must be doing that thing with my face again.

"This is petty, I know," she says, and smiles, "but I wonder how differently the story would have ended if the Bisters had only figured out how to keep themselves clean. You're too polite to laugh but it's true. People judge one another on the silliest criteria. Embree Bister—do you know who I mean?—he isn't the most charming man I've ever met but he's smart and well-read. If he ever sold Bister Island, he'd be rich too. I'd bet my bottom dollar that with a bath, a haircut and a new wardrobe, he'd have women lining up for him. . . ."

I try to give her one of those *you could be right* faces but it's hard. I get a flash of Embree cleaned up and out on a date. I feel my gag reflex kicking in. I presume Mrs. Hiltz forgot to mention a new set of teeth too—or just how desperate are the women around here? I can hardly wait to tell Levi about this. He'll die laughing.

The dog on the carpet suddenly lurches to life and trots over to the door.

Mrs. Hiltz says, "Casper? What is it, boy?" then stands up and looks out the window. She fluffs up her hair and checks her face in the reflection. The way she's primping, I half wonder if Embree is coming by to pick her up for a night on the town.

"Oh goodness, look who's here!" she says. I can hear the happiness in her voice. She's at the door before it opens.

A big bald middle-aged guy walks in. She tilts her head up and kisses him on the cheek. "Hello, dear," she says. "To what do I owe this pleasure?"

"Hi, Mum. I can't find my cufflinks for that nomination dinner. You wouldn't have an old pair of Dad's, would you?"

She shakes her head and laughs, the perfect adoring mother. "Oh, you're just saying that." She turns and sort of whispers to me, "He's always dropping in to make sure I'm still breathing. He treats me like I'm an old lady!" She starts wiping off his jacket and straightening his tie. "Let me just fix you up for a moment and then I'll introduce you to my new friend." She doesn't actually spit on a hankie and wipe his face but you can tell she's dying to.

"There. Now you're presentable." She turns him around to look at me. Too bad he's bald because otherwise he'd be pretty good-looking. He smiles like he actually means it.

"This young lady, believe it or not, is another Opal! Opal Schwartz—this is my son, Percy. He's running in the upcoming election."

Percy shakes his head. "Not quite, Mother. Only if I win the nomination."

She gives one of those *silly-boy!* looks. "Of course you'll win! And you'll win the seat too! Then all you'll have to do is provide me with a grandchild and I'll be perfectly happy!"

She's clearly enjoying teasing him. He looks up at the ceiling, like *spare me*. It makes me laugh.

I check my watch. It's almost five. I shouldn't have gone off on that tangent about the feud. I'd like to ask Mrs. Hiltz more about the Ingrams but she's not going to want me horning in on sherry time.

"Thanks, Mrs. Hiltz," I say. "I better get going. I've got to bike back to the hostel."

She makes this cartoony pout. I wonder if she was a flirt when she was young. "So soon?" she says. "I did so enjoy our little chat. Promise me you'll come again."

"Sure. I'd love to. I have lots more questions I'd like to ask you."

"Marvellous! Then it's a deal." She shakes my hand. "My . . . you have such large hands for a girl! I bet you'd be good at cleaning fish too!"

Great. Just what I want to hear. I try to look like that's a compliment. (Who knows? Maybe around here it is.)

All of a sudden, Mrs. Hiltz stops talking. She turns my

hand this way and that, as if she's mesmerized by it or something. It's really awkward.

Percy does this exaggerated eye-roll. "Mum! What are you doing to the poor girl?"

She looks up. She shakes her head as if she's coming out of a trance.

"Oh sorry, dear! I'm fine. I . . . I . . . well, I guess I was expecting to see an opal ring! All us Opals wear rings." She points at her own. "Someday, a nice man will buy you one. Just you wait."

Percy opens the door for me. "Don't listen to her." He says it like he's giving me some really, really serious advice. I can tell he's a bit of a joker. "Never expect anything from a man. It'll only get you into trouble."

I wave goodbye and wonder if he knows Levi.

36

Tuesday, 5 p.m.

You, You and Mimi

"Love Crazy—Part 1." Mimi gathers a group of her
celebrity friends to dish about the ill-advised
things they did for love.

My plan was just to get on my bike and ride home, but as
I'm cycling down Main Street I see a rusty brown van in
front of the hardware store.

The rusty brown van. It's not every girl's dream car but
it's mine.

I ride right past it because, I mean, what else can I do? I
can't just stop. I can't just go in and say, *Hi, Levi, I'm here!*
Krystal could pull it off maybe but not me.

I'm halfway over the bridge when I realize I can't go

back to the hostel. I have to turn around and bike past the hardware store again. I have to. *Treat opportunities like gift certificates to your favourite store. Cash them in before you lose them.* That's what Michael Davis—Mimi's life coach— always says. Normally I think he's full of it but now I see the wisdom. I wouldn't forgive myself if I just went home without even trying.

I smooth my hair, suck in my gut and ride really slowly past the hardware store. Maybe Levi will notice and call me over.

When he does, I'll pretend I don't hear him. Then when he calls again, I'll sort of jump and swing around with my hand on my chest. I'll say something like *Oh, you scared me. I didn't know you were here!*

Am I nuts? I can't even talk half the time Levi's around. Now I'm supposed to pull off some Oscar-winning performance?

I pick up speed and don't stop pedalling until I'm almost back at Mrs. Hiltz's. This is crazy. I better go home before I do something I regret.

But I don't. I can't blame it on Michael Davis any more either. It's me doing this now—but it's a me I barely recognize. I spend weeks of my life when I can't even get up off the couch, when I can't move. Now I *have* to move. It's like I'm obsessed or possessed or jet-propelled or something. I'm going back to the hardware store whether my brain thinks I should or not.

I ride back as fast as I can because it dawns on me that while I was sitting there wondering what I should do, Levi could have been driving away without me and I'd have missed my chance.

As soon as I see that his van's still parked out front, I slow down. I slow down so much that the bike wobbles. It's like I'm a kid out on a two-wheeler for the first time.

What if he's not in the van? What if he's in the store? I can't ride by *again*. I do have *some* pride.

I'll just go in. I'll buy something.

Buy what?

What difference does it make?

A hammer. Yes. I'll buy a hammer.

I pull up and lean my bike against the store window. I'm all klutzy. It slips down a couple of times before I can make it stay.

I look up just as Levi's coming out the door. My lungs inflate as if they're airbags and I just crashed into a brick wall. He's carrying a couple big grey sacks of cement.

"Hey! Opal!" he says with this huge smile. His black eye is mostly green now. He leans over and kisses me right on the mouth.

I jump back. The airbags inflate again. I can't believe he kissed me. My face goes blank but my mouth is buzzing like I overdosed on lip-plumping gel.

He laughs. "Did I surprise you—or did you just feel that spark of electricity go between us?"

I stand there doing this fish-gasping-for-air thing. He jerks his head at the van. "Get the back door for me, would you?"

I open it. He drops the bags on the floor with a big *thump.*

A guy in a store uniform comes up behind him carrying some tools and puts them in the van too. Something about him gives me the creeps.

Levi goes, "Thanks," and then puts his hand on my shoulder. "Gershom Bister, this is Opal Schwartz. She's here in town doing some research on Port Minton."

The guy looks straight at me for a couple of seconds, turns around and leaves. Levi watches him go into the store, then says, "Don't take offence. He's just shy. He's not a bad guy."

I manage to say, "That's okay."

I've got all these things I want to tell Levi, questions I want to ask him, but I'm too awkward. I don't know if it was the kiss or running into the Embree clone or just being this close to Levi again—but I'm totally messed up. I just stand there, looking away, dying.

"So," he says, "what are you doing here, all gussied up like that?"

He noticed. That just makes things worse.

"Oh. Um," I say, "I just came to—you know, like—buy a hammer."

He leans against the van with his legs apart and his arms folded across his chest. He says, "A hammer."

"Yeah," I say. "A hammer. They sell hammers here, don't they?" I try to look at him but I just can't. He's so cute and I'm such a bad liar.

"They do," he says. "It's a hardware store. They got lots of hammers." He seems to find that funny.

"So what's the big deal, then?" I try to sound all huffy.

"Nothing. I'm just wondering what you need a hammer for. Planning on building something?"

I go, "Yeah."

"Really?" he says. "What?"

"Well. Uh . . ." My brain sits there like a big lump of raw meat.

Levi starts laughing. His whole body's shaking. He reaches out and puts his hands on my shoulders. "You are so lame! I saw you riding back and forth. You didn't come for a hammer. You came to see *me*!"

I push him away. I go, "I did not!" I'm trying not to laugh.

He pulls me into a hug and rocks me back and forth. "You did so! C'mon! Admit it!" He nuzzles his face into my neck. He's all scratchy.

I'm laughing despite myself. "Okay, okay," I say. "Now would you quit it?" even though I don't want him to.

"No," he says. "Why should I?"

"Because everybody's looking!"

He keeps hanging onto me but he lifts his head and looks over my shoulder. "Like who, for instance?"

"That lady over there." I suddenly realize she *is* looking at us. I'm embarrassed.

He waves. "Hi, Mrs. Copps!" She waves back at him. "Don't worry about her. She's my old grade five teacher. She's used to me."

"She's used to you, is she? So you do this all the time?" I pull myself away.

"Now, now, that's not what I meant and you know it. Come here . . ." He pulls me back.

He's doing that thing against my neck again when this girl walks up and says, "Hi, Levi."

I jump away with my shoulders up and my arms straight at my sides as if some general just yelled, "Attention!" I'm terrified it's Krystal—but it's not. It's just that skinny friend of hers.

Levi goes, "Hi, Rachel."

No big deal. She gives him one of those twiddly-finger waves and keeps walking.

He takes me by the hand again but that's all. He can tell by the look on my face that he's not going to get away with nuzzling anymore.

He checks his watch. "Look. I got to help my uncle with a retaining wall tonight—but I got to eat first. Want to go down to the park and share a couple of sandwiches with me?" He sidles up to me again. "I don't usually offer to share my meal with anybody, but since I know you don't eat much. . . ."

I roll my eyes and try to look reluctant. "Yeah, okay. I don't have anything else to do right now so, like, I may as well. . . ."

He pulls his eyebrows way down like he's all concerned. "You sure? You don't have to clean your ears or clip your toenails or anything important like that?"

I stick my tongue out at him. He sticks his tongue out at me.

Next thing I know he throws my bike in the back of the van and we're heading down to a little park near the bridge. There's nobody there. Levi gets an old blanket out of the van. We put it on the ground and sit against a tree, our shoulders touching. The river's sparkly. There's a bit of a breeze. Levi takes out this big bag full of food.

I go, "That's all for *you*?"

"I said I'd share!" He hands me half a bologna sandwich. Before I can take a bite, he kisses me again. "I'm glad you came back," he says. "Gershom was taking so long at the cash, I was worried I was going to miss you."

I look at my sandwich and try not to implode. What am I supposed to say to that? Sometimes being too happy is as bad as being too sad.

He nudges me. "Eat up or I'm confiscating my sandwich."

We pass a carton of chocolate milk back and forth. We work our way through his food. Eventually we talk. I knew he'd laugh when I told him what Mrs. Hiltz said about all the women Embree could have if he just cleaned up his act.

"That's totally like Mrs. Hiltz." He doesn't say it in a nasty way. Everybody seems to like her.

"What do you mean?" I say.

"She's, just, you know, proper or something. She's not a snob or anything, but trust me—you'd never see her outside without lipstick on. She puts a lot of importance on that kind of thing. And you know, she probably has a point."

"About lipstick?"

"Nooo." He practically knocks me over with his elbow. "About the Bisters. People are stupid. We'd probably all rather spend time with a clean jerk than a dirty good person."

"That's not true," I say. "I'm happy here with you." I make this big deal about looking at his filthy T-shirt.

"Ha-ha," he says. "I could take it off if you want."

I go, "Keep your clothes on, if you don't mind," and look away so he doesn't know what I'm thinking.

After a while he says, "What are you thinking?"

I have to come up with something. I say, "Why didn't you tell me Mrs. Hiltz's name was Opal too?"

He makes this exasperated face.

"I *tried* to tell you on the way to Port Minton but you were all in your snobby *don't talk to me you lowly underling* mood. I said something like, 'Want to know something neat about Mrs. Hiltz?' and you went, 'No.' Remember?"

I'm embarrassed. I say, "Vaguely."

He goes, "You are *so* lucky I put up with you. The crap you dish out . . ."

He stands up, then pulls me up too. I can't help laughing at myself. He's right. I can be such a jerk. He puts his hands in my hair on either side of my head. I stop laughing. I freeze.

He says, "Do they call this auburn?"

I shrug. "Yeah. I guess."

"It's pretty. It's kind of red where the sun shines on it."

"Thank you," I say. I feel ridiculous. We just sort of stand there. I try not to look at him but he tilts my face back up. He's smiling.

"My damn uncle," he says. "Why'd I go and say I'd do this for him?"

He takes his hands out of my hair and rubs them down the sides of my arms. He leaves them on my hips. He closes his eyes, takes a big breath and shakes his head.

"We better go. I can't trust myself," he says. "You have no idea what you're doing to me."

I don't know what my reaction to that is but it makes him laugh.

"Again, Opal, that was a compliment. You don't have to look so horrified every time I compliment you."

He gets my bike out of the back of his van. "You better start home now. There's still a good hour or so before sunset but I wouldn't want you on the highway after that."

"Yes, Dad," I say. Sometimes I just can't help myself.

"Okay. Fine," he says. "Make fun of me all you want. I just want to be sure I can see you tomorrow."

He puts one hand on the handlebar and one on the seat, then leans over the bike and kisses me. It's just a little kiss. It doesn't seem like a Charming Billy kiss at all.

When it stops, I say, "Me too. I want to see you tomorrow too."

Finding that old ring suddenly seems like the best thing that ever happened to me. This probably sounds exactly like something Mimi would say but—I wonder if that's the reason fate sent me here.

37

Tuesday, 7:30 p.m.
You, You and Mimi
"Unsafe at Any Speed." Mimi adopts road safety
as her new cause—and not a moment too soon.
Eighty-four percent of her studio audience fails
the test on basic driving rules.

I do leave right away—just as soon as Levi's van disappears around the corner and there's no hope of me getting
another glimpse of him.

I head off down the highway. The sun's beginning to set
but it's not dark yet. There's no fog or rain or wind. There
aren't a whole bunch of cars on the road. It's like you'd
expect, pretty much deserted.

I'm a bit lost in my daydreams but I'm not totally out

of it. I manage to pull over onto the shoulder every time a car comes by. I always make sure there's lots of room to go around me. I want to see Levi again too.

I'm almost back at the hostel when I hear the sound of another engine coming up behind me. I pull over onto the shoulder. But this time, the car doesn't go around. The motor revs. I feel the air change somehow. There's this tiny moment when I kind of know something's going to happen. Maybe I sort of half turn my head to see what's going on. I don't know. I don't remember seeing anything. I just remember the shock when the car hits me.

There was this mean kid at my elementary school. He took this little girl's doll, threw it up in the air and then slammed it with a baseball bat. It went flying. Its head was bent back and its little arms and legs were spinning and the fluff was bursting out its belly. I figure I look just like that.

Everything has suddenly gone quiet, and slow too. I'm hurtling through the air but part of me is calmly thinking, *A car just hit me and I'm going to land in the ditch. I wonder if I'm going to die.*

Time starts up again really fast once I land and the noises pour in again. I hear a *thump* and a grinding sound and my own voice going "Ouf!" when the wind's knocked out of me. I don't know if I'm just lucky or if I actually manage to save myself somehow—but I don't hit headfirst. I skid with my arms out in front of me like I'm sliding into home plate.

It must be the shock that keeps me from feeling the pain for a while. I stand up thinking, *Well, that wasn't so bad.* I'm kind of expecting that whoever hit me is going to come scrambling down into the ditch any second, all worried and apologetic. I'll just say, *It's okay. I'm fine. I'm fine.*

But no one comes.

I'm standing there and I realize I must have slammed my ankle against a rock or something. Leaning on it makes the pain shoot up my leg like that red stuff in a thermometer. I get down on my hands and knees and start to crawl out of the ditch. That's when I notice that my palms are scraped raw and that the whole left side of my shirt is torn and that my new jeans—the only jeans that actually look halfway good on me—are all ripped to hell too. There's blood all over me—my fingers are sticky with it. The smell makes me feel sick.

If that stupid driver ever shows up now, he'd better be offering something more than an apology. I'm going to kill him.

Something clicks. Everything flips over. I hear that car revving again in my brain and I *know* this wasn't an accident.

No, I think, *he* was going to kill *me*.

Someone ran me off the road on purpose.

38

Tuesday, 8 p.m.
Radio Mimi
"Ain't No Mountain High Enough." How far would you go for your man? Mimi discusses her own personal limits.

The bike is toast. I leave it there. *I'm* toast. I need help. I wave and I scream but a lot of good it does me. There's no one around to hear me.

I grit my teeth and ease my backpack off as gently as I can. I'm looking for my cellphone, but I know right away it's not there. The zipper's wide open and the pocket's empty.

I try not to think about some crazy person coming after me to finish the job. I just pick up my backpack and hop like some dying bunny until I make it to the hostel.

Kay actually screams when she sees me. Before I know it, she's called a doctor and I'm propped up on the couch.

The doctor treats me as if I'm about six years old but otherwise he's pretty good. He says I don't have a concussion or any broken bones or any cut big enough for stitches. I just sprained my left wrist and my left ankle and "gave myself" a fat lip and a black eye. (*Gave myself.* Please.) He keeps saying, "Don't worry. You'll live!" and I keep wondering why someone doesn't want me to.

Who? Who would want to kill me? I don't even know anybody around here!

The whole time Kay's icing my ankle she's going, "I can't fathom someone clipping you with their car and not even stopping to see how you are. That's just not right. They shouldn't be allowed to get away with that. We should call the police!"

Police.

That's all I need. They'd find out I'm Mimi's kid, then next thing you know the media would be here, snooping around, taking pictures, figuring out the whole Port Minton–Rosie Ingram thing. Wouldn't be long before Mom's secret was plastered all over the Internet.

I start backpedalling like crazy. "What can the police

do? There were no witnesses. Even if somebody did hit me, they're not going to catch the guy now. And I'm not even sure he actually hit me. He might have just come close and I got spooked or something. . . ."

Kay is shaking her head and making these big angry sighs. I can tell she wants justice.

"Perhaps you're right but I *still* think we should—"

I cut her off. "Kay. I really just want to have a bath and go to bed. I couldn't face talking to the police right now." I try to sound as pathetic as possible. It works.

She stops sighing and just looks at me. Those butterscotch eyes of hers go all soft again.

She says, "All right. I can understand that, I guess."

She drapes my arm over her shoulder and helps me up the stairs. She's trying to take all my weight but I still wince at every step.

"Boy," she says, "I wish Levi were here right now."

"Yeah, me too" I say.

She winks and goes, "I bet you do."

I'm hoping my face is beat up enough that she can't see me blush.

She runs me a bath and tells me to holler if I need any help.

I say, "No, I'll be fine"—and I will be. Personally, I'd rather drown than let anyone help me in and out of the bath. I wouldn't even let Anita do that. . . .

I miss Anita. I want to talk to her. I want to tell her what happened. She wouldn't call the police. She'd track down whoever did this and kill them with her bare hands. Little Anita Martin, Vigilante Killer. That sort of makes me laugh, but my face hurts too much so I cry instead. Not big sobs or anything—I don't want Kay barging in—just tears. The salt stings my face. I look in the mirror. I cry some more. The only good thing in my life at the moment is Levi. He's not going to find me so pretty now.

It takes me forever to get my clothes off. Every time I move I find something new that hurts. I eventually manage to pull my jeans off the regular way, but in the end I have to cut myself out of the shirt with Kay's nail scissors. I cut off the label too. It's probably crazy but I don't want Kay finding out I wear Armani. Only rich kids wear shirts like this and I don't need one more reason for anybody to hate me.

I lower myself into the bath. The pain is terrible at first but it goes away. The water makes me hurt more where I'm cut but less where I'm bruised. It's a trade-off I'm willing to take.

I lean my head against the rim of the tub and try to chill. I wish I had some of that fancy bubble bath Mom got her perfume guy to make for me. (He called it "Birdie Bath" and put a little robin on the label, which even I had to admit was pretty cute.) Something about the smell of it could make me feel so good, even when I was feeling bad. It made my skin really soft too.

I think it's remembering the bubble bath that makes me feel better, but then I realize it's not. My brain hears "smell" and "skin" and "soft" and even though his skin isn't soft (at least on his hands where it's kind of beat-up), I'm thinking about Levi again. That's why I'm feeling good.

Then I remember my face and my big swollen lips and my black eye and I think of him looking at me, then turning away and running right back to that stupid, skinny, little Krystal. Just like that, my life sucks as bad as it ever did.

I only feel sorry for myself for a second because suddenly there's something else on my mind.

Krystal.

Who else hates me around here?

39

Wednesday, 1 a.m.

The Broken Doll **(film)**

Mimi Schwartz stars in this stinker of a film noir as
a broad with a strong attachment to a man and an
even stronger attachment to violence. No stars.

I toss and turn all night. There are two new people at the
hostel—two new weird sets of noises to get used to—but
that's not what's keeping me up.

It's not the pain either. I took a bunch of Advil, so I can
pretty much handle that. I keep the bottle beside me in
case I need more.

It's not even—*really*—that someone tried to kill me.

It's that I don't know what to do about it.

I know why Krystal did it. She's a jealous psycho. Rachel

saw Levi and me kissing in front of the hardware store. She acted all relaxed about it, like it was no big deal—but I bet she ran right off and ratted us out to Krystal.

I know how Krystal did it too. After she got the word from Rachel, she must have driven around until she found us. It's not that hard to track someone down in a little place like this. She must have seen us in the park. She hung around until Levi left, then followed me back. She waited until the time was right—no cars, no houses, no witnesses—and then just gunned her motor and went for it.

I know she's capable of it too. I still get the shivers when I remember her screeching to a halt at the fish-and-chips joint. She was about a nanometer away from me. She no doubt would have run me over then if she'd thought she could get away with it.

I should do something, but what? I can't call the police.

I can tell Kay. No. What good would that do? *She'd* just call the police.

I can confront Krystal, I guess. Tell her I know it was her. That could scare her off. But it could also backfire. It might make her even crazier than she already is. She'd kill me for sure then.

I can act like nothing happened.

No, I can't. It's not like she forgot to ask me to her birthday party. She ran me off the road. She could have killed me. This isn't one of those things where you just go, *Oh, well*, and, like, carry on. I'm always going to have to watch my back now.

I can go home. Krystal couldn't hurt me there—not with Anita baring her fangs and ready to lunge at any moment.

That's what I should do.

I go round and round and I always come back to the same conclusion: get out of here. But I just can't. I've come this far. I've done this much. I can't go now before I find out what's up with Mom.

That's what I tell myself, and it's sort of true.

Not as true, though, as the fact I can't go now because of Levi. I couldn't stand to leave him—or the "hope" of him at least. Part of me is still scared that he'll look at my face and go, "I'm out of here." But the other part of me wants to believe that he'll see my big, fat lip and say "ya pur girl" with that ridiculous accent of his, then he'll go out and track Krystal down and, I don't know, teach her a lesson or something. It's such a stupid, girly, "rescue-me" thing and I know I'm not supposed to think that way but I do, and it works. I relax. I snuggle into my pillow and I go to sleep and have the best dreams.

40

Wednesday, 9 a.m.

You, You and Mimi

"Instant Makeovers." Only got a couple of minutes to pull yourself together? Mimi and her "beauty brigade" show you how to go from ick to incredible in minutes.

I wake up. I feel like a junkie. That's how bad I need the Advil. I try to choke a pill down dry but it gets glued to the roof of my mouth. I hobble to the bathroom for a glass of water.

There's no glass.

I take a big breath and start down the stairs. It kills me to step on my bad foot but hopping down on my good one makes my face hurt.

Kay comes running out of the kitchen, waving her hands and going, "Oh my land, Opal! Stop! Stop!" She runs at me as if she's trying to keep me from hurling myself off a bridge or something. She gets her bony little shoulder under my armpit and practically carries me the rest of the way into the kitchen.

After some painkillers and some tea and a few spoon-fuls of mushy cornflakes, I feel a bit better. Kay sits at the table, looking at my face and shaking her head. She must be thinking, *What did I do to get stuck with this girl?* How many days have I been here? Three? Four? Whatever. This is the second time she's had to look after me. It's a lot to expect for twenty bucks a night.

"Listen, Opal," she says. "I got a call from Mrs. Hiltz this morning. She must have been talking to Dr. Ross, because she heard about your little 'accident.' She's offered to have you come and stay with her until you're better. She has a guest room on the main floor with a double bed and its own bathroom."

She must see my face sort of crumple at that because she goes, "I said no, of course—you'd be fine here. But now I'm not so sure. It's going to be hard for you, climbing those steps for the next week or so." Her eyes look really pained at the thought of it. She can't be too thrilled about having to get me upstairs again.

I should say something—I should let Kay off the hook—but then I'd have to stay with Mrs. Hiltz. She's nice and everything but, I mean, it would be so awkward. She'd probably want to talk all the time and I'd have to have dinners with her and there'd be nothing good to eat, just old lady stuff—creamed chicken and peas, things like that—and she'd fuss over me and I'd never have any time alone (i.e., with Levi). I'd rather just drop by some time and ask her a few questions.

Kay is looking over at the living room. She says, "You could sleep down here on that sofa maybe. . . . I don't know, though. You might be too tall. It might just be better to grit your teeth and take the stairs. . . ."

Her face gets all worried again. She chews on her thumbnail.

"I could try the sofa," I say. "I don't mind. For a couple of nights it wouldn't be so bad."

Kay almost smiles. She knows it's not going to work. "Okay, sure. Why don't we decide about that later? I told Levi what happened. He said he'd be by in about"—she looks at the clock—"oh dear, any minute I guess."

I jump up. The pain in my leg goes right into my teeth. It doesn't matter. It's nothing compared to the agony of letting Levi see me like this.

Kay goes, "Wait! Wait! Wait! Let me help you." She sets down her half-full teacup, gets out of her chair and starts helping me up the stairs.

41

Wednesday, 10 a.m.
Radio Mimi
"Talk a Good Fight." Dr. Morgan Wagner, world-renowned psychologist, introduces Mimi to her easy five-step process to winning arguments—and converts.

This look of horror passes over Levi's face when he sees me and I realize just how ugly I am. It feels so much worse than getting hit by that car. I can't help it—my eyes fill up with tears. Levi groans as if I just broke his heart, then puts his arms around me. That only makes me cry more, but at least now it's in a good way.

Levi goes into some shtick about trying to find a place he can kiss without causing more pain. He finally plants one on a spot just above my left eye. It doesn't hurt, but smiling when he kisses me does. I feel like I just flew back and forth to Europe on some supersonic jet or something. I've got emotional jet lag. I'm laughing. I'm crying. I'm happy. I'm sad. I'm a mess.

That's why he says I should stay with Mrs. Hiltz. It would be easier on me, he says. I'm not so sure. By the time he's talked me into it, he's got my bags packed and waiting downstairs for me. He comes up again, slings my backpack over his shoulder and gets me downstairs too.

I thought Kay would be relieved that I'm going but she looks worried. "I don't know if this is such a good idea. Mrs. Hiltz might not be able to look after you. She's quite elderly, you know. Levi, couldn't you take one of the beds downstairs for Opal? That wouldn't be much trouble. As far as the bathroom goes, I could find that old chamber pot—"

Levi cuts her off. "Kay . . . Kay . . . please. You're not seriously thinking of denying the girl a chance to stay at Hotel Hiltz, are you? When's she going to get another chance to sample the good life?"

I almost laugh at that. If he only knew. I'm going to the Hôtel du Cap Eden-Roc on the Riviera for the Labour Day weekend. It's a tad nicer than what I saw of Mrs. Hiltz's place.

There's this silence for a while. Kay opens her mouth to say something. Levi goes, "Yes?" but she just smiles and shakes her head.

"You're right. I'm being selfish. . . . I'd get myself knocked off the road too if I thought I could get a room there for a couple of nights."

Levi says, "Who wouldn't?" and hustles me out the door before Kay changes her mind.

He helps me into the truck and then climbs in. He pulls onto the road with this big grin on his face. I know he's up to something.

I go, "Why'd you talk Kay into that? Why do you care if I stay at Mrs. Hiltz's anyway?"

"I just think it would be better for you."

"Liar," I say.

"That's nice."

"Okay, you're not, like, a total liar. But there's something else too, isn't there?" I'm so loving this. I forget about the pain.

"Yeah, of course there is," he says. He does this sleazy Latin lover thing with his eyebrows. "Basic geography, my dear. You bill be close-air to mee."

This hot little fountain of something whooshes up inside my body. It feels so good it kind of hurts. I know this is gross but it does something to my spit glands too—I have to swallow. Is he doing this to me on purpose?

He says, "This thing at my uncle's is bigger than I thought it was going to be. I've got about a week's work there and it's just a few blocks from downtown. If you're at Mrs. Hiltz's, I can meet you for lunch, drop by the library, see you at my break. Why, heck, we could maybe even squeeze in a little hammer-shopping if you got the time. . . ."

I smile. It just about kills me but I keep smiling. I can't help it. Even my ears are smiling.

"There's another thing too," he says. "Frankly, I can't trust you getting back and forth to the hostel on your own any more."

I can't tell if he's joking. "What are you talking about?"

"Hmm. Let's see. One time, you head out in the hot sun with no food in your belly and practically pass out. Another time, you get run off the road. I'm serious, Opal. I've never seen anyone get in more trouble than you do."

He's making it sound like it's my fault. I'm not mad but I just have to tell him.

"Levi . . ."

"Yeah."

"This wasn't an accident."

"Whaddya mean?"

"I mean someone hit me on purpose."

He stares at me. He takes his eyes off the road so long I'm worried we're going to crash.

"Why? Who? Who would do that?"

He doesn't really believe me. I can tell. There's a moment when I don't think I can say it, then it just kind of spills out of me.

"Krystal," I say.

He almost loses control of the car. He goes, "Wait. Stop."

He pulls over on the shoulder and turns off the engine. He looks at me like I'm crazy.

"Krystal *Parker?*" One side of his face is all crunched up like tinfoil. "You mean, the girl I used to go out with?"

"Yeah," I say. "Her."

He pulls back his neck and shakes his head as if he can't believe what he's hearing. "Why would she do that?"

I say, "I don't know. I guess because she's jealous of me— like, I mean, us. You know."

"You saw her do it?"

"No," I say. "I didn't see anything. But that's because she hit me from behind. By the time I got up, she was gone."

"So how can you say it was her, then?" He sounds like he's taking her side.

"I just *know*. The person driving the car came at me on purpose. There was no reason to hit me otherwise. There was tons of room. It was light. The car even sped up right before it slammed into me!"

He leans his back against the door and stretches one arm across the dashboard. He taps a finger. He chews on the inside of his lip. He looks right at me the whole time.

He finally says, "Okay. All right. Say someone did do this to you on purpose. Nothing you've told me proves that it was Krystal. I mean, she can be a jerk but she's not insane or anything. It's a pretty serious thing you're accusing her of, you know."

"Well, who else would do it?" I'm getting mad now. He's supposed to support me.

"I don't know. Maybe a drunk? A bunch of stupid kids? An old guy who doesn't see so good any more? How about just some psychopathic maniac? You were all ready to believe the place was full of them before."

"No!" I say. "It was Krystal."

"No," he goes. "It was not. I know Krystal. I know why

you don't like her. And I'm sure she *is* jealous. But she wouldn't do this. She's just some silly kid, not a killer."

I won't look at him any more. I'm so mad. I'm so insulted! I want to cry. I want to run away but I can barely even walk.

"Opal," he says. He touches my arm.

I turn my head just a tiny bit but I don't look at him. I'm not stupid enough to do that.

"I'm not saying someone didn't do this to you. You were there, I wasn't. But you didn't actually see Krystal. It could have been someone else, couldn't it?"

He's sort of teasing me, sort of pleading with me. I can tell he just wants me to drop it. He takes my hand and looks at my palm. "Boy," he says. "You really got messed up. That's some major road rash there."

I can feel myself giving in. "She's the only one around here who has anything against me." I try to sound firm.

"Well, I don't know about that," he says. "I can think of *at least* one other person."

"Who?"

"Embree Bister wasn't so happy about you 'making your water' on his property."

I go, "Ha-ha. Very funny"—then my mouth flies open. I

turn and look at him. I can tell by his face that he was just doing that Levi thing again—trying to make me laugh—but it backfired, big-time.

"Embree," I say.

"Oh-oh. What? That was a joke, Opal."

"Embree could have done it."

Levi laughs. "Oh, please! Embree? For one thing, Embree can't even drive. I hate to admit it, Opal, but you were closer when you thought Krystal did it."

I don't know about that. I picture Embree with the gun, that look on his face. He's not a silly kid. He's crazy and he's dangerous and he doesn't like me either.

"What about Gershom?" I say. "Does he drive?"

"Yeah, so what?"

"What's he? Embree's son or something?"

"No. His nephew. That doesn't mean anything."

"They see each other?"

"I don't know. Probably. So what?"

"Gershom saw us together at the hardware store yesterday. He goes and tells Embree and . . ." I'm trying to figure this out.

Levi's shaking his head. "And then what? Embree says, you got to 'kill' this girl for me? . . . Why? Why would he do that? You can say a lot of things about Embree but I don't think he's the jealous type. And anyway, we only went out for a little while. I'm pretty sure he's over me by now."

I don't say anything. He shouldn't be joking around. Not about this.

"Sorry." He wipes the smile off his face. "I just don't understand why you think Embree would want to do something to you."

"I don't know! He's nuts, that's why! Remember . . . in the woods . . . he said something like, um, 'I've got a long memory'. . . . And then . . . when we were leaving, he went, 'It's the others that have to worry.' Something like that. You heard him. He was threatening me. That was a threat."

"He was just talking, Opal! Trying to sound big. It didn't mean anything—he just wanted to scare you."

"So maybe that's what he was trying to do last night! Scare me again. Maybe he told Gershom just to knock me over, rough me up a bit, you know. That's what happened, after all."

Levi's trying to look as if he's actually considering what I say. He's got his lips pushed together and he's nodding, but I'm not falling for it. He's just stalling.

He says, "Okay. Could be. But why? Why would he want to scare you? Believe me, there are a lot of people around here who've done way worse things to him than threaten to pee on his property."

I know what Levi's saying makes sense but the look on Embree's face makes a lot of sense to me too. The guy took an instant hate to me. Why?

"Maybe . . ." I say. "Maybe it's about me doing research on the area. You told him that's what I was doing." I'm not really sure where I'm going with this. "Maybe he, like, thinks I'm going to—you know—expose the Bisters or something. Open up that whole can of worms again. Embarrass them somehow."

Levi looks down at his knees and then back up at me. His voice is really calm. "Opal, I don't think you could possibly embarrass the Bisters any more than they've been embarrassed. Embree's way past that point."

He reaches out and puts his hand on my leg. I look at it and those big white cuticles and it totally takes all the fight out of me. I don't want to fight with him. Why am I fighting with him? I don't want him to go away. Who cares if somebody hit me? I lived. I'm here with him. He's got his hand on my leg. Just shut up, why don't I?

"Can I make a suggestion?" he says. "I think we should go to where the accident happened and take a look. I can't help thinking we're missing something here. Maybe there was an oil slick on the road or something. That could make a car swerve."

That wasn't what happened. I know that. But I don't like Levi thinking I'm crazy. I don't want him to give up on me. I just shrug, and let him take me there. I'll figure this out myself.

We drive along in silence until we get to the place where I went off the road. You can still see my tire tracks running straight along the shoulder, swerving, then suddenly ending. The bike is lying all twisted in the ditch like some mangled bug skeleton.

There's no oil slick.

Levi goes, "Hmm. There was a bit of rain last night. That could have washed it away."

"How come you can still see the bike tracks, then?" I say. I'm doing it again.

"Okay," he says. "Must have been something else."

"Like what?"

He opens his eyes really wide. "I don't know. Glare on

the guy's windshield, a bird, roadkill. Lots of things could have made him lose control."

"If it was just an accident, why didn't he stop to see if I was okay?"

He thinks about that for a second. "Maybe he didn't notice."

I turn and look right at him. Who wouldn't notice running someone off the road?

He puts his hands up in surrender. "Okay," he says. "I don't know, Opal. It's a mystery."

He wanders over and looks into the ditch. "Why don't I get the bike? See if I can fix it."

As if that piece of scrap metal can be fixed. He just wants to pretend this is nothing, forget about it, move on. I should too.

He slides down the embankment and comes back up with the bike over his shoulder. "Well, this looks like it's going to be a project I can really sink my teeth into!" he says, all cheesy Mr. Fix-It.

I try to smile but he's bugging me. It's like I'm a dog and he thinks he can just distract me with a new squeaky toy or something.

We get in the van and he goes, "Oh yeah. I found this beside the bike. It yours?"

I figure this is just another one of his little jokes. I turn and look at him like *Okay. Now what?* He hands me an old torn-up envelope. It's so dirty I don't recognize it at first. Then I see the corner of the picture sticking out and the lump of the ring.

I'm startled. How did that get here? Then I remember just stuffing it in the outside pocket of my backpack when Joan came up the library steps.

"Yeah," I go. "It's mine." I get this little panic attack. What would have happened if I'd lost it and Mom looked in the chair?

Has Mom looked in the chair yet?

Maybe she never looks in the chair. Maybe she's totally forgotten about the stuff she put there.

Maybe it's not even hers.

No. I know that much at least. It's hers.

"What's in it?" Levi says.

"Um," I say. "It's just a ring and an old photo from a church picnic." I want to tell him all about it—but I don't too. It's like I'm tiptoeing into a room I'm not sure I should be in.

"Oh yeah?" he says. "Can I see them?"

"Uh, sure." I hand them to him. There's nothing the matter

with that. I haven't said anything yet. I'll just see where it goes.

He looks at the photo. I can tell it doesn't mean much to him. It's just an old snapshot. His eyes, though, go a little bigger when he sees the ring.

"Hey. One of the famous hockey rings! Mum's cousin Donnie's got one. He was a left-winger on that team. . . . Who'd this one belong to?"

"Don't know," I say. "I just found it when I was doing my research." Will he ask where? How? My heart's making this hollow thumping sound.

No. He's turned the ring over and is squinting at the inside. There's something written there. Why didn't I notice that before?

He reads, "'For my secret love.'" He winks at me. "Oooh, baby. Port Minton must have been cooking back then. What do you think it means?"

I can't answer. I can't make words come out. It could mean anything. Everything. Was someone on the hockey team in love with Rosie? And if so, why was it a secret?

I just shrug for an answer.

Levi rubs the ring clean on his T-shirt. "I bet it wouldn't be that hard to find out who this belonged to—I mean, if you want. That championship was a big deal. I could ask Donnie. He might know."

"No," I say. "Don't do that. . . . Someone might want to keep it a secret." I've got to think about this a bit more. Maybe the fact that it's missing will mean something to people around here. Maybe it's missing because the guy is dead. Maybe he was murdered or something. Maybe my mother murdered him.

Maybe I'm losing my mind.

Seriously. There's no way Mimi murdered anyone.

I don't think. How would I know?

I must be pale or sweaty or flushed or something.

"Are you okay?" he says. "You look like you don't feel very well."

Of course I don't feel well. My body's bashed up and my head is spinning. I don't know who anybody is any more or why people are doing whatever it is they're doing to me. I want to tell Levi everything but I can't. I'm scared to trust him. I'm scared to let him see how crazy I might be.

Then Levi leans over and looks me in the eyes and says, "Really? I mean it. Are you okay?" He rubs his hands up my arms.

I say, "Yes," and I'm not lying. Right now, for this one little moment at least, I'm way better than okay.

42

Wednesday, 3 p.m.

You, You and Mimi

"Family Secrets." Mimi invites celebrity "heritage sleuth" Laura Buchkowsky to uncover the roots of the public's fascination with genealogy.

I tell Levi I've got stuff to do at the library. He helps me up the stairs and says he'll be back at five to take me to Mrs. Hiltz's.

Joan screams when she sees me too but not as loud as Kay did. (Maybe that's because Joan's a librarian.) I tell her the story—the part where I go flying, at least—and she *tut-tut-tuts* and shakes her head. She makes sure I'm okay, then goes back to her office.

As soon as she's gone, I check my e-mail.

Spam, spam, spam.

A notice from the school that final course selection must be made by August twelfth.

A reminder from Mom's assistant (cc'ed to Anita) of Grandpa's birthday party coming up in two weeks.

And a short note from Selena:

R u crazy? Go into her room? She'd kill me. Steal her personal stuff? She'd mutilate the body. Y dont u pay some professional criminal 2 do this 4 u? U got the cash.

Some friend. Fine. I'll do this myself. I go to Google and type in "Mimi Schwartz." Someone out there must know about her past. If not, at least it will take my mind off the car accident.

"Results: 1–10 of about 35,000,000 for Mimi Schwartz."

Thirty-five million results. I feel like they all just came crashing down on top of me. Where do I even start?

Forget her official site. I know I'm not going to get anything there. I check out Wikipedia. There seems to be some ongoing battle between contributors about what

Mimi's natural hair colour is, but other than that it's pretty much the standard stuff too.

I type in "Mimi Schwartz's family." Turns out that's the name of one of her biggest fan clubs. (Why do I find that sad?)

I scroll through some other sites. Lots of old photos of Grandpa and me. There are even some of Dad. None of them look like they were taken in Shelton County.

I try "Mimi Schwartz's birth mother," "Mimi Schwartz's family tree," "Mimi Schwartz's adopted family." Everything that turns up is stuff I've already seen or can't use. I need to find a site that isn't just a cut-and-paste copy of her bio.

I need dirt.

I have an idea. I type in "I hate Mimi Schwartz."

I get dirt. www.enoughaboutmimi.com is full of it.

Pictures of Mom without makeup, with her mascara smudged, with something between her teeth. Close-ups of blisters, warts and cellulite. (No way that's hers. Say what you want about Mimi but she doesn't have cellulite.) Rants about what a liar/hypocrite/"emotionally stunted Barbie Doll" she is. Whoever's behind this site really can't stand her. I wonder why. Is it just the usual anti-celebrity backlash or is there something else too?

I click on "The Truth Behind the Image." A full-length picture of Mimi appears. She's in the red strapless dress and full-length gloves she wore to the Academy Awards last year. She's laughing. She looks good. Before I know it, classic stripper music comes blaring out of the computer. I jump on the volume key as fast as I can. I don't want Joan thinking I'm up to something "inappropriate."

Someone's animated the image in that jerky *South Park* style. Mimi winks and starts doing a striptease. She peels off her gloves and you see that her hands are all hairy, with these long red claws. She throws off her shoes and she's got these little pig's feet underneath. She wiggles out of her dress. A big belly splops out. She turns around and waves her tail in this skanky way. Right at the end, she pulls off her face and you realize she's the devil.

It's weird. *I* can say the meanest things about my mother but I feel terrible when somebody else disses her. They don't even know her. How can they call her the devil?

I get a chill. Is there something I don't know?

I want to stop but instead I click on the "Mimi and Me" tab. Something called "Eyewitness Reports" comes up. I scan it. There are lots of entries about stuff like Mimi fart-ing in an elevator and blaming it on someone else (never would have happened) or pushing to the head of a line at a restaurant (could have, I suppose), but I scroll past those and go right to the important stuff.

I tried to tell her that "Eating Like a Birdie" was not a good name for a segment starring a chubby kid who obviously doesn't eat like a bird—but she wouldn't listen. She didn't care that it was her own daughter people would be making fun of. Everyone thinks she's so nice and open but, believe me, she's the most secretive person I ever met. The rest of the world might think she's their best friend but none of the staff do. They just keep their mouths shut and try to stay out of her way.

Darryl

Former head of wardrobe

You, You and Mimi

Mimi only talks about a fraction of the cosmetic sur-gery she's had. I used to work for her plastic surgeon.

Dr. Boileau basically rebuilt her from her toes right up to her hairline. Her own mother wouldn't recognize her if she saw her today.

Deena

Former receptionist

Pygmalion Enhancement Clinic

There's no way Robin is Mimi and Steve's daughter. It's genetically impossible. Everyone in the studio figures Robin is Beau Huxley's love child. Take a look at his interviews with Mimi when he was still playing for the NFL and you can see why. She was all over him. Don't tell me there was nothing going on there. He sure wasn't acting like a man with a wife and an evangelical ministry back home.

Aimee

Former line producer

You, You and Mimi

I knew Mimi when she was still Miriam. I was an intern at a public access TV station when she got the job hosting *Classic Book Talk*. She was sure nothing special back then. She was shy. She'd never been on-air. And she dressed like a middle-aged lady going to a PTA meeting. None of us could figure out why the job went to her. We found out later that her father basically bought it for her. It still pisses me off. If my father'd been rich enough to bribe someone, maybe I'd be a millionaire today too.

Sandra
Traffic reporter
CJCH

My colleagues and I at the National Institute for the Prevention of Security Breaches (NIPSB) have studied the syndicated talk show *You, You and Mimi* for the last twelve years. Lack of plausible life records— school certificates, photos, early work history—and changing facial structure first aroused our suspicions concerning the individual known as Mimi Schwartz. Over the course of our research, we have uncovered irrefutable proof that Ms. Schwartz is an enemy agent transmitting classified secrets to hostile states via her daily show. Seemingly innocent makeup choices such as the colour of eyeshadow or lipstick

are actually intricately calibrated codes designed to
alert alien nationals to the location of chlorine stock-
piles for our municipal water supplies. . . .

I doubt my mother is actually Satan or an alien agent
but I can't help thinking some of the other people are onto
something here. The "Eating Like a Birdie" stuff, the plasic
surgery—that all makes sense. Mom's first on-air job was
a free one for a community access channel—she admits
that in the book–so that story's not too far-fetched either.
I don't think Grandpa ever had much money, though. Of
course I might be wrong.

The Beau Huxley thing really hurts me. I'm insulted
that "everyone in the studio" assumed that my father
would have to be a linebacker, but I Google him anyway.
Beau's got the size, but I'm pretty sure he's not my father.
According to my math, Rosie was pregnant before she left
high school. Beau's website shows pictures of him leading
his team to victory at the Super Bowl that year. I somehow
doubt a big star of the NFL was dating the shyest girl at
Port Minton High.

I turn off the computer and look out the window. It's

like the more I find out, the less I know. How am I ever going to figure this out?

Get back to basics. Start at the beginning. Port Minton. I root through the box of stuff Joan got me. I find a magazine called *Travel Today*. It's got an article titled: "Port Minton: A Forgotten Jewel on the Picturesque South Shore."

Port Minton back then did look sort of quaint, I guess. The houses were painted up and there were boats in the harbour. Old guys in plaid shirts and big rubber boots sat around the dock apparently mending their nets. According to a sign, you could get an order of fish and chips for $1.75.

I almost flip right past the next page, until I notice the name Ingram. There's a photo of an old general store—no doubt the one Levi told me about. Mr. Ingram himself is standing behind the long wooden counter wearing one of those white aprons. He's even got little black bands on his arms to keep his sleeves out of the way. (Did he really dress like that or was this some costume the photographer dreamed up?)

I stare at the picture. Is this Rosie's dad?

If so, does that make him my grandfather?

I have no idea.

I realize the only thing I know for sure is that Mom's lying. She's lying all over the place. So what's true? Do I believe her—or do I believe enoughaboutmimi.com? Are they *both* lying? My brain creaks. This is like one of those Mindblower puzzles—and I hate that stupid game. There's always some catch that no normal person could possibly have figured out. Somehow—like, discreetly—I've got to find out more about Rosie. Somebody around here must know what happened to her.

I put down the magazine and stare into space. I'm thinking so hard I don't even notice when Levi walks in.

43

Wednesday, 5 p.m.

You, You and Mimi

"Best Guests." Storied socialite Rachel Allan reveals
her secret tips on how to be a perfect guest. They
must work. She's always invited back.

Levi picked me up at the library, goofed around for about
five minutes, then deserted me at Mrs. Hiltz's. He was all
sorry and kissy and everything but he couldn't do anything about it, he said. He has to get some work done on
his uncle's wall tonight. It's going to rain tomorrow.

Mrs. Hiltz seems almost too glad to have me. She makes
a big point of saying how she picked up some pop and
chips for me today. She makes me feel like such a "teen."
I'm surprised she didn't buy me a Hula Hoop too.

She gives me an old cane of her husband's and shows me to my room. Big bed. My own bathroom. A view of the garden. It's a lot nicer than my bunk at the hostel. She put little flowers on the table and fluffy towels by the tub and even had someone bring a TV into the room for me. That's the type of stuff Mom always makes sure Anita does before we have visitors.

Dinner is a mini pork chop, a scoop of practically liquid mashed potatoes and a pile of peas. Mrs. Hiltz cuts up my meat for me because of my sore arm, then starts asking me about my family and my background and my research. I have to keep coming up with bigger and bigger lies—I can't remember what I've told people already. I said Dad was a musician but did I give his real name? What did I say Mom does? A marriage counsellor or a psychologist? Mrs. Hiltz is just asking me where my mother did her training—and my insides are going all cold because I don't have a clue where people get trained for something like that—when Casper starts barking. The front door opens.

"Hey, Mum! You home?"

Mrs. Hiltz goes, "Hello?" She seems annoyed or something. She probably finds it rude to have her meal interrupted. (I guess old people care about stuff like that.) She excuses herself but doesn't have time to get up before Percy walks into the dining room. He's wearing shorts and a grey T-shirt soaked black with sweat. His knees are all dirty and bleeding. For a big bald guy, he's doing a pretty good imitation of a little kid.

I guess I must look even worse than he does, because he sucks in his breath and goes, "Geech. What happened to you?"

I give him the short version. He looks sympathetic, says something about campaigning to widen that stretch of the highway so accidents like this won't happen any more and sits down at the table.

Mrs. Hiltz isn't being very welcoming. She goes, "Eww! I don't know if you should stay, Percival. What were you *doing*?" She closes her eyes and turns her face away like he stinks or something. He doesn't smell that bad.

"It's Wednesday, Mum. Road hockey. I haven't missed a game in almost five years. I don't know why you look so surprised." He winks at me. "Poor dear. She's losing her memory." You can tell he loves tormenting her. (I wonder if Levi's going to be like that when he's old.)

Mrs. Hiltz says, "This is not 'surprise' you see on my face, dear. There's another name for it and we both know what it is."

"Yes, we do," he says. He's not the least bit offended. "Don't worry. I'm not staying long. I just wanted to know if you'd be my date for the constituency luncheon tomorrow."

Mrs. Hiltz's forehead wrinkles up like a sheet kicked down to the bottom of the bed. "Why? Where's Andrea? Why is she not going with you? I'm sure your constituents are more interested in speaking with your lovely young fiancée than with an old woman like me."

"Two things, Mother. Unless *you* popped the question, Andrea's not my fiancée. She's just a friend. You know that perfectly well. As for tomorrow, she's not coming because she's got her own meeting to go to. Not that it matters. . . . I'd prefer to take you anyway."

Mrs. Hiltz rolls her eyes but you can see a smile back there too.

"Well then, since you insist. . . . I'd love to, dear! Now why don't you get going? Pour yourself a nice bath."

"Yes, Mummy. And I'll be sure to wash behind my ears too." He stands up and leans over to kiss her goodbye.

She turns her face away in disgust.

He goes, "Ha! Fooled ya!" and steals her pork chop while she's not looking. He jumps out of her way before she can grab it back. He waves it by the bone, takes a big bite and, with his mouth still full, says to me, "So long, Junior. Don't let her bully you the way she bullies me!"

"I do apologize," Mrs. Hiltz says after the door closes behind him. "Now where were we before we were so rudely interrupted?"

I don't want to go back to talking about my family. It's too dangerous. I decide to focus on her favourite subject instead. I say, "So does Percy play a lot of hockey?"

"Some," she says.

I go, "Did he play in high school?" I'm getting an idea.

She's just put a small bite of mashed potatoes in her mouth so she only nods.

I say, "He wasn't on that team that won the big championship, was he?"

She swallows. "Uh . . . yes. I believe he was. . . . How do you know about that?"

"Oh, I just stumbled on it. Part of my research. I'd love to have a chance to talk to him about the team and, uh, life for young people in Port Minton back then. It must have been a big deal to be on that hockey team."

"Well. Yes. It was, I suppose, but that was a long time ago. Now what did you say your mother did again?"

I decide on marriage counsellor and just go with it. I

make some stuff up and then turn the conversation back to where I want it to go. I ask her if she knows Albert Ingram.

She smiles. "Of course. It would be impossible to live in Port Minton and not know Albert! What might your interest in him be?"

I've had enough of this. I just want to cut to the chase. "Well, to tell you the truth, I'm actually interested in Rosie Ingram. She's his daughter, isn't she?"

Mrs. Hiltz nods, then suddenly brings her hand up to her forehead. She's gone really pale. "I'm terribly sorry, dear, but I'm afraid I'm going to have to excuse myself. I'm having one of my little spells."

That kind of freaks me out. "Do you want me to call Percy?"

She waves that away. "No, no, no! I'm fine. It's nothing more than old age, dear. I just need to lie down. Leave the dishes. Velma will be by in the morning to look after them."

Within five minutes, we've both limped off to our own rooms.

I brush my teeth, looking at my puffy face as little as possible, and climb into bed, still thinking. Mrs. Hiltz knows the Ingrams. If she's feeling better tomorrow, I'll ask her about Rosie.

I've got the feeling I'm on to something.

44

Levi and I are swimming at the beach. It's a beautiful day. It's so warm out I don't even mind the freezing water. I actually kind of like it. My skin feels all tight and sort of tingly. It sounds corny but it makes me feel alive. This must be what those breath-freshener commercials are talking about.

I'm wearing a black bikini I saw in a store window. It's not really revealing or anything but it's better than that bright red bathing suit Anita packed for me. I've lost weight since I came here. My hips are still no doubt huge but my belly's flatter. I look all right. Levi seems to think so anyway.

He stands up in the water and slicks his hair back with both hands. He's really tanned but the undersides of his arms are white. He sees me over by the boulder and dives toward me. He's under so long I'm starting to worry about him. He finally pops up right in front of me. I jump. He laughs.

He puts his arms around me and says, "You have no idea what you do to me."

He closes his eyes and leans toward me—There's this huge smash and I wake up screaming.

I fly out of bed. My eyes dart around, looking for the robber, the bomb, the runaway vehicle, whatever. For a second I have no idea where I am—then I feel the pain shooting up my leg. I remember the accident and the doctor and, right before I stop screaming, Mrs. Hiltz.

I turn on the light and try to process what just happened. I feel a breeze. I pull back the drapes. Glass tinkles down. The window is totally smashed. All I can think is *I'm in so much trouble.* There's a brick on the floor with a piece of paper tied to it. My heart thuds. Someone's after me—again.

I'm kneeling beside the brick, too terrified to touch it, staring like it's some little alien spaceship, when Mrs. Hiltz runs in.

Her voice is all pinched and whispery. "Are you all right?" She looks like she had a worse shock than I did. She's out of breath and clutching her pale pink dressing gown.

I jump up. I can stand in front of the brick and hope she doesn't see it but I can't hide the window. I can't do anything about the look on my face. I'm screwed.

"What was that terrible noise?" she says. "Are you hurt?"

She puts her hands on my shoulder. They're so cold they make me flinch. She sees the broken window but doesn't seem to care about it.

"No. I'm okay," I say.

She looks down at the brick. She looks up at me. She goes, "Somebody threw that through the window?" She opens her mouth and just stays like that for a couple of seconds. "Who would do such a thing?"

I shake my head. What are the chances she'll just say, *Oh, well! No big deal*, and go back to bed?

She picks up the brick. "There's something tied to it,"

she says. She takes off the paper, puts the brick on the bed, reads the note to herself.

"Oh dear . . ." she says. She folds the note back up, holds it tight in her hand. "Oh dear," she says again, and gives this quivery little smile.

"What?" I say. It's like it's somebody else's voice talking. I'd never ask that. I don't want to know.

She gives her head the tiniest little shake. "Nothing, Opal. It's got nothing to do with you, I'm sure."

"What is it?"

"I don't want to upset you," she says.

"You won't. Really. What does it say?"

She looks away and then turns back to me. Her mouth has gone really small. You can see her sort of collect herself. "Oh dear. You're sure you want to know?"

I nod like I'm a little kid who's promising to be good.

She pauses, clicks her tongue, then says, "I guess I should tell you. You're the one who got the 'rude awakening,' after all. . . ." She takes a big breath. "Well—in a word—it's a threat."

I knew she was going to say something like that but it still takes the wind out of me. What have I done to make someone act so crazy?

Mrs. Hiltz holds up her hand and waves her palm at me. "No, no, dear. Don't worry. It's not the first threat I've had and probably not the last either."

She's had.

She thinks the threat's aimed at her!

It's too good to be true. I should just shut up, thank my lucky stars, but I can't help myself. I go, "What does it say?"

Mrs. Hiltz looks down at the paper as if it's got notes for her class presentation or something. "Well . . . there's some unpleasant profanity that doesn't really add much, but basically it says, 'I don't like your type. I'm going to kill you if you don't get your nose out of places it doesn't belong.'"

The word *kill* sort of vibrates through my whole body, like it's a hammer and I'm a gong. Whoever knocked me off my bike wasn't fooling around.

I should say something to Mrs. Hiltz. Tell her the threat was for me, not her. But how? I mean, what do I say?

I'm searching for words when Mrs. Hiltz goes, "I can't imagine who it would be from, though. . . . I'm not really rabble-rousing these days like I once did. Believe it or not, I used to be quite an activist."

She's got this half-smile on her face as if she's expecting me to have some suggestions.

"Maybe," I say, "it wasn't aimed at you. Maybe, um, it was aimed at me."

Mrs. Hiltz opens her eyes wide at that, then shakes her head and laughs. "You? You, dear? Who would have any reason to be angry at you?"

I could tell her my suspicions. Tell her Krystal's friend caught Levi and me kissing. Tell her how Embree caught me about to pee in the woods. Those are two places I wasn't supposed to be.

No, I can't.

There's no way I could say either of those things to Mrs. Hiltz. She'd be so grossed out. Kissing? Peeing? I can't imagine she's ever done either. I say, "I don't know. Maybe people don't like me doing research on Port Minton. Maybe they think I'm going to talk about something I shouldn't."

She looks me straight in the face for so long that I worry about her going off again—then she seems to come to. She smiles as if I just said something cute. "What could you possibly have found out that would upset people so much?"

I say, "I don't know." That's what makes me start to cry. I *don't* know. I wipe my eyes with the back of my hand. "I think I should go home. This was too scary. I just want to go home. I'll see how soon I can get a flight out."

Mrs. Hiltz's eyes get all sympathetic. "Oh dear," she says. "I feel terrible! I ask you to come here to get some much-needed rest and then this happens!" She puts her arm around me and squeezes. "I don't blame you for being scared. It must have been a terrible shock. I'd love you to stay with me as long as you'd like but I'd understand too if you feel you have to go. You've had such a difficult time. You might like your own mother to be looking after you now. . . ."

I nod but I'm not thinking of Mom. I'm thinking of Anita. I feel like I'm not going to stop shaking until I see her again.

"I guess I should call the police," Mrs. Hiltz says. She's saying it more to herself than to me but it freaks me out. I feel myself squeezing my hands into fists. If the police get involved, I'll have to talk.

Mrs. Hiltz lifts her chin, stares off into the distance for a second, then turns to me. "No," she says. "I am not going to call the police. Frankly, I'm the more likely target of this threat than you are, my dear. I can think of two thorny issues I was involved in recently. I've appealed the development of a strip mine in an ecologically sensitive area and I also began a petition to demand compensation for victims of abuse at the former orphanage. I wouldn't be surprised if this little package was from one of my opponents. Well, phooey on them! I'm not going to give whoever did this the satisfaction of thinking they scared me. I'm going to act like this never even happened."

She takes my hand and looks me in the eye. Her skin is smooth, like it's made of wax or something. She says, "I hate to put you in a position of perjuring yourself, dear, but would you mind not mentioning this little incident to anybody?"

"No. No," I say. "I won't tell anybody."

"Anybody at all? This is a small town. Word spreads like wildfire. Percy doesn't need to be worrying about something like this, right before an election."

I nod. I understand.

She says, "Thank you. I'll come up with some story about how the window got broken. I'll say a branch snapped off a tree and smashed it or . . ." She squints as she tries to come up with something better. "Or . . . I'll say I was playing catch with Casper and took a wild throw. Yes. That's what I'll say."

She looks at me like *Is that okay?*

I give this weak smile. I don't know how I managed to get off the hook so easy.

She says, "I'm old. I can get away with it. Percy will tease me mercilessly about my bad aim of course but it will be worth it. When the time's right, I'll tell him what really happened."

She turns to go. Her shoes crunch on the broken glass.

"Now watch your feet, dear. I'll find you a pair of slippers—then why don't you come and have a cup of cocoa with me? I think we could both use something to calm our nerves right about now."

She doesn't know the half of it.

45

Thursday, 10 a.m.

You, You and Mimi

"Taking a Stand." Mimi interviews Patricia McDermott, a courageous woman who faced her fears—and changed the world.

I sleep on the couch in the study that night. I wake up late the next morning to the sound of men replacing the glass. It's stupid but there's something about it that makes me feel better. I'm not so scared any more. It's like I hear them banging away and I think, *Stuff can be fixed. What's the big deal?* I didn't die. It was just a brick. An empty threat. Now that I've had some sleep, I realize it probably wasn't even aimed at me. I mean, Mrs. Hiltz seemed to have a couple of pretty good reasons to think she was the target. And anyway, who even knew I was staying here? Levi and Kay? *They* wouldn't be throwing bricks at me.

I decide right then that I'm not going to go home—not today, at least. I'm going to stay here and find out everything I can about Rosie Ingram. (While I'm here, I might even make an effort to get to know Levi a little better too. . . .)

I get up, brush my teeth, put my clothes on. My face isn't quite so puffy today. I do my best to cover up my black eye with some concealer. I put a bit of eyeliner and mascara on the other eye. I try out a couple of shades of lip gloss and end up going for a sort of rusty-coloured neutral. I braid my hair. I'll be okay.

Mrs. Hiltz is sitting in the living room, watching TV. She flicks it off when I walk in the room but not before I see Mimi get the audience all up on their feet for her patented "Powerful Woman Pose." Normally, all the "Fighting Female" stuff seems corny to me. Today, it seems like a sign.

Mrs. Hiltz says, "Oh, you caught me! I shouldn't waste my time in front of the television, but there's something about this Mimi woman I find absolutely intriguing!"

"Yeah," I say. "Me too." I get this urge to just come right out and tell her about Mom.

"Oh, good. Nice to know I'm not the only one who's fallen for her nonsense," she says.

So much for that.

Doesn't matter. Percy seems like a better bet anyway. He was at school with Rosie. He'd know where the ring came from. I'll see if I can arrange a meeting with him.

Mrs. Hiltz brings her hands together with a little clap. "So, dear, I've been thinking. If you *really* still want to leave, I'd like to drive you to the airport. If you can get a flight out, we could leave as early as this afternoon. I'd love to have the chance to get to know you a little better."

"Thanks," I say. "But I've decided not to go after all. At least not yet."

"Really?" She sort of chokes on her tea.

I pat her back. She seems so old and frail.

"I'm fine, dear. I'm fine. . . . That's marvellous news! I guess I'm going to have a chance to get acquainted with you after all. So what changed your mind?"

"You, I guess. You're right. I mean, I don't know if the brick was aimed at me. And even if it was, I shouldn't let people scare me— especially since I'm not finished here. There are still questions I need to get answered."

She puts a finger on her cheek. "Hmm. Anything I could help you with?"

"Actually, I was sort of hoping I could talk to Percy about it. Do you think he'd mind?"

I get the feeling I stepped over a line. Maybe she likes to be the expert around here. She fusses with her napkin, folds it up, tucks it under her saucer.

"Oh, well, dear, normally I'm sure Percy would love to help but he's just so busy these days. The election, you know. . . ." She gives me this embarrassed smile. "What are you interested in? Still the Bisters? The feud? The Ingrams? That sort of thing?"

She's looking at me so intently that it throws me. I hate all this lying. It makes my ears hot. I pour myself some orange juice from the jug she put out on the table, and try to sound nonchalant.

"Yeah, that's pretty much it. Just sort of what happened to everyone there . . ."

"Percy couldn't help you with that anyway, I'm afraid. He was away for a long time after high school. He lost contact with most Port Minton people. I wonder, though, if there's someone else who'd be a better resource for you. . . . Hmm . . . let me see who I can come up with."

"Thanks," I say. "That would be great. In the meantime, I think I'll go back and see what else there is on it at the library."

I pick up the cane and my backpack and get ready to go.

She gets up too. "Can I drive you over?"

"No thanks," I say. "A little walk won't kill me."

She tries to talk me into a "real" breakfast but I just want to get going. She shakes her head in this *young people today* way and holds the door open for me.

"You know," she says, "there *is* something I could help you with, come to think of it. Why don't you let me take you down to Port Minton this afternoon at about five? We had some grand plans a number of years ago to open a community museum in the old church. It didn't come to pass but I have a number of very interesting documents stored there, detailing the families of the area. I bet there'd be lots of information for you there. It's been ages since I was down to the Port and I would love to get a look at it again myself. Can I talk you into it?"

It might be just what I need.

"Sure," I say. "That sounds great."

"Wonderful. I'll pack us a picnic!"

46

Thursday, Noon

www.youyouandmimi.blogspot.com

Mimi complains how modern society is drowning in a sea of facts. What can we do to turn back the tide?

The library is cool and quiet. I head over to the table. The box is sitting there waiting for me.

I don't know why, but I see the box and this thing happens to me. I hear a clicking sound in my brain, as if someone's fiddling with the focus button. It's not like I'm hallucinating or anything but suddenly I realize everything's changed. The box used to be this big depressing, overwhelming, scary pile of papers. Now it's just a box. I can't even remember why it scared me. I feel my posture improve.

I might be a mess on the outside but inside I feel like I'm coming together. I got off the couch. I went to Port Minton. I'm gathering the clues. I'm figuring out who Mom is. I'm not running away. I'm falling in love.

I'm okay. I'm in charge. I'm normal. I'm good. (I sound like I'm watching too much *You, You and Mimi.*)

I sit down and pull the box toward me. I can do this. I get out Rosie's yearbook, just to see if I missed anything first time around.

An old *Canadian Geographic* magazine underneath catches my eye. I put down the yearbook and pick it up.

I'm stunned. Embree Bister is on the cover, looking just as mean, just as dirty and only a little bit younger than when I saw him a few days ago. There are a bunch of raggedy kids and a scared-looking woman in the background. The title's written in large white letters—"The Lost Tribe of the North Atlantic." Levi told me it was a big deal—but *that* big a deal?

I hold my breath and flip through the magazine until I find the article. There are lots of pictures of the Bisters. They all look like extras in a movie. Who else would be that dirty? I wonder if the photographer had to tell them not to smile— or were they all just as naturally charming as Embree?

The magazine's a good twenty years old but I can tell that even back then their clothes were out of date. One of the women is wearing a long dress—and it's pretty clear she's not heading off to the prom. Embree's wearing a suit with patches on the knees just like you'd see on some Halloween hobo. The kids must have just put on whatever they could find. One boy's shirt is torn up to his ribs. Another boy—who I'm pretty sure is Gershom—is wearing a jacket that was obviously meant for a very large man. Their hair is matted and long and sticking out all over the place. The snot under their noses is black and crusty. I can just imagine what they smelled like.

There's a picture of Embree sitting under a tree, reading an old book. The sidebar reads:

Highbrow Hillbilly. Despite no formal education, Embree Bister is a voracious reader. The shabby homes on the Island have little furniture and few amenities but are stocked with over seven hundred books, all dating from before the 1888 quarantine. Abednigo Bister, patriarch of the family at the time of the feud and Embree's great-grandfather, was an educated if eccentric man who'd sailed the world in his youth. His passion for learning continues in the family even to this day. Although woefully unaware of the world beyond Bister Island, the children have an almost encyclopedic knowledge of pre-twentieth-century art and history."

Another photo shows a guy in a white coat examining a kid's mouth.

The Bister diet is so impoverished that many people have lost all their teeth by their early twenties. Rickets and scurvy, although almost unknown today in the developed world, are also common afflictions of the clan. Many family members also have webbed toes and suffer from "the falling sickness" (epilepsy).

The worst picture, though, is of a girl holding a baby in her arms. I don't know why it bothers me so much. She's staring up at the photographer from a pit in the ground. She's dirty and kind of pointy-faced. She looks terrified— and sort of terrifying too. You wouldn't be surprised to hear she was possessed by an evil spirit or something.

Primitive Bunker. Minerva Bister and her 2-year-old brother, Cicero, were among several children found in an underground hideaway not far from the main residence. Their father, Embree, is a stern taskmaster who preached against the evils of the outside world to his flock of fourteen. Children were instructed to secrete themselves in this underground cellar at the first sign of an approaching boat. This may be why, until recently, government officials believed there to be only two children on the island, 16-year-old Gershom and 18-year-old Barnabas.

I feel sick, or I guess sickened. That's a better word. Imagine living your *whole* life on this tiny little island, in these nasty old shacks, with deerskins for windows and crates for chairs and a hole out back for a toilet. Imagine having to hide every time someone came over. (At least when I hide, it's in a comfortable room with a flat-screen TV.)

I skim the article some more for Ingrams but there's no sign of them. Mrs. Hiltz makes it into the magazine, though, lots of times. I recognized her picture right away.

Her hair was brown back then and she stood straighter than she does now, but otherwise she hasn't changed that much. Even on Bister Island, she was wearing lipstick.

I guess this is what she meant when she talked about rabble-rousing.

Despite her wealth, Opal Hiltz still considers herself a Port Minton girl. Widow of industrialist Enos Hiltz, she was the first to sound the alarm about the situation on Bister Island.

"I did it for two reasons," the well-known philanthropist says today. "I had a strong suspicion that there had to be other children on the Island. A young woman I once knew, Nettie Faulkner, had shocked the community years ago by running off with Embree Bister—and yet the only children anyone ever laid eyes on belonged to his brother, Disraeli."

Mrs. Hiltz attempted to ask after Nettie on Embree's occasional visits to town but the answers she received were, at best, evasive. She put this down to the Bisters' famous insistence on privacy, until a chance encounter made her believe that there was more at play.

She explains. "Last year at around this time, Embree

was in Port Minton with his nephew, Barnabas, picking up some molasses and flour. It happened to be our annual Spring Fair and I was manning the bakery table set up on Main Street. Barnabas was 17 at the time but so small for his age he could have passed for 12. I offered him a cookie. He gobbled it down like a starving man, and then, when Embree wasn't looking, asked if he might have a few more to bring back for his 'cousins.' I knew then that there were other children on the Island."

Early attempts by Mrs. Hiltz and other concerned citizens to bring resources to the Island were rebuffed with threats of violence. Finally, in desperation, Mrs. Hiltz brought in the provincial government. "I don't believe in forcing our way of life onto others but the welfare of the children took precedence over any qualms we had in that regard. We were worried that the youngsters were not receiving the medical care they might need."

Her concerns were justified. When a team of hospital personnel, social workers and government officials finally strong-armed their way onto the Island, they were shocked to find ten rail-thin children covered in sores and so filthy as to be almost unrecognizable.

Several of them reported they had lost siblings the previous winter due to starvation or to "the bloody flux" (dysentery). There was concern for the children's emotional health as well. Although polite and well-spoken, most of the children appeared as afraid of their adult relatives as they were of the strangers.

The children, the ill and the elderly were removed from the Island shortly after these photos were taken. Mrs. Hiltz shocked many by offering to foster one of the displaced children. Most others were adopted out of the area.

Mrs. Hiltz's childhood friend Nettie Faulkner was never found. Embrec claims she left him after the birth of their last child, but authorities believe that foul play may have been involved in her disappearance. The Bisters have never reported any deaths on the Island.

So much for not knowing anything about the Bisters. By the sounds of it, Mrs. Hiltz pretty much rescued those kids all by herself. I wonder why she didn't tell me. My guess: too humble. I can sort of understand now why Mom gave me the name Opal. Mrs. Hiltz is a pretty amazing—

I get a chill.

So you're one of those, are you?

I'm looking at this picture of Embree in front of his arsenal of old guns and that just pops into my head. He said, *What's your name?* I said, *Opal.* Then he said something like, *So you're one of those, are you?*

That's why he hates me. It's not just peeing on his property or my so-called research. It's the name. He must know Opal is Mrs. Hiltz's name too. She came in and broke up the Island, got all the kids off. Everyone else might think she's great but she must be pure evil to him. He probably figures I'm related to her somehow. Maybe he thinks she's up to her old tricks again. Maybe he thinks she wants to get him kicked out of the park or something. That might be enough for him to hate me too.

That might be enough for him to want to kill me.

I start feeling freaked out again. I throw the magazine back in the box. I try to calm down. I wish I could talk to Anita right now. Not about this. Just talk to her about anything. Hear her voice. That would make me feel better.

I can't call her. Doesn't matter what I talk about. She'd know by my voice that something's up. I can't fool her.

I get up and switch on the computer. I'll e-mail her. I'll

just say hello, tell her I'm okay. She'll e-mail back. That will have to do for now. I type in my password.

I've got mail.

From: gumdrop113@airmail.com
To: birdbrain76@airmail.com
Subject: Death-defying feat

U so o me! I went 2 the house yesterday cuz I got off work early. Mom ran out of Pledge & had 2 go 2 the store. She made me clean the baseboards while she was gone. She gave me hell for not finishing them by the time she got back but who cares? I got the file. U better tell me what this is all about when u get back. (U better tell me about this guy 2.)

Good old Selena. She was like this when she was a kid too. She tortured me but she always came through in the end.

I open my grandmother's obituary and there it is, plain as day, in the very first sentence. "Dora May Reiner (née Gotfrit), survived by her beloved husband, Harry, and chosen daughter, Miriam Ingram."

Miriam Ingram.

There it is. The proof. There's no "maybe" about it any more. Mimi used to be Rosie Ingram.

And "chosen daughter"—that obviously means adopted.

I check the date. Dora died just a month before I was born. She died in Brooklyn, just like Mom said in the book. Okay. That fits.

I open the other attachment, the marriage licence, and check the date there too. I was almost a year old at the time of the wedding. Why did they wait so long?

Maybe because of Dora? Maybe it didn't seem right to get married when she was sick—or so soon after she died. I shake my head. Who knows? Maybe Mimi couldn't find a dress she liked. Maybe she couldn't lose her baby weight. Maybe Jean-François couldn't fit her in for her eyebrow wax until then. Could be a thousand different reasons for it.

I think for a second. Okay. What do I know for sure? Mom definitely had left Port Minton by the time I was born and . . .

And that's about it. The sum total of my "research."

Where did she hook up with Dad, then?

I get out the yearbook again. I looked for Schwartzes

before but Dad might have changed his name too. I go to the hockey section. Maybe Dad was the manager or the water boy or something. Maybe they got rings too. I look at the team picture. There's a manager but it's a girl, and the stick boy is a fat little blond kid who bears a striking resemblance to the coach, and none at all to Dad.

I try to be systematic about this. I go row by row, look at each of the faces, check each of the names. Maybe I missed something before.

No one even rings a bell—until I get to Percy Hiltz. I didn't recognize him at first. By the look of the picture, he sweated just as much as he does now, but he was way skinnier then and had a whole head of thick red hair too.

I really wish I could talk to him. I bet he'd know. I just don't want to bother him while he's so busy.

I go back to the yearbook. I see the caption *Roy Tanner, Captain*. Debbie's Roy.

Maybe I don't need Percy after all.

I grab Rosie's yearbook. I'm going to get my hair done.

47

Thursday, 2 p.m.

You, You and Mimi

"Love Crazy—Part 2." Mimi's celebrity guests
continue to share more mortifying stories about
the things they did for love.

I know before I even see the van that Levi's near. I'm
not claiming to be psychic or anything like that but it's
true. I just know. I've got this little high-pitched hum
going all through my body. It's like the music in a movie
that tells you to brace yourself, something big's about to
happen.

I'm walking down Main Street to Debbie's salon. The
humming gets stronger. I look up and there he is, outside
the hardware store again. He smiles at me and it's like he

just pushed the fast-forward button on the remote. I'm a robot. I immediately start to hobble-jog over to him.

He starts singing, "*Go, Granny, go, go, go!*"

He makes me laugh. I can hardly wait to touch him, to tell him about the brick, the threat, everything.

Damn.

I stop. I can't. I promised Mrs. Hiltz.

He goes, "C'mon, Beulah! Don't give up now! You almost made it!"

Big deal. She'll never know. I'll make Levi promise not to tell too. I can trust him.

But that's what I thought about those girls at school too. I didn't worry about their little cellphone cameras.

I walk up to him. I swore I wouldn't tell a soul.

He looks at me funny. "Okay. What's the matter now?"

"Levi . . ." I say. A blue car pulls up into the parking lot. I recognize the screech of the tires. It's Krystal's car.

"Yeah?"

Do I need this now? What does she do? Keep driving up and down Main Street until she catches us together or something?

Levi gives my arm a little shake. "Yoo-hoo! What's up?"

I'm sick of her. I'm not going to take this any more.

Scaring me. Harassing me. Insulting me. He's mine. I feel like a dog, marking its territory or something.

I let the cane drop to the pavement, throw my arms around Levi's neck and kiss him. I kiss him for a long, long time. I rub my hands through his hair. I squirm. I wriggle. I moan. I do all the Hollywood make-out moves I can think of.

Get the message, Krystal?

I'm just starting to understand why they say that revenge is sweet when I hear this guy go, "You were supposed to be picking up some mortar, Levi, not some girl."

I jump back with my hands up in the air like a cop just pulled a gun on me. ("Robin Opal Schwartz, you are under arrest for impersonating a hot girl, moaning in public and unlawfully placing your big fat lips on an unsuspecting male victim.")

Levi doesn't seem the least bit embarrassed. He just laughs and goes, "Don't worry, Uncle Jimmy. Mortar's in the van. I'm on my way. Just saying goodbye to Opal here, that's all."

Jimmy shakes his head, slams the door of his blue car and heads into the store.

I groan—and not in that Hollywood babe way either.

I'm an idiot—and, as far as his uncle's concerned, a skank too.

Levi clicks his tongue. "Yowza! You're some hot-to-trot today, girl. What got into you?"

He sticks his neck right under my nose. "My new cologne, perhaps?" I shrug and move away. He moves in closer. "No. Seriously. Take a whiff. That it?"

I go, "No," and look away. I can't believe I did that. I've got to get out of here before Jimmy comes back.

Levi walks around in front of me. "What do you think it was, then?"

I'm too embarrassed to even glare at him.

"Hmm. I use their deodorant too." He lifts his arms and sniffs his pits. "It doesn't do much for me but . . . maybe the effect of the fragrance combined with the pheromones in my sweat was enough to send you into that—what would you call it?—frenzy? Yeah. That's the word. Frenzy of lust and desire." He starts moving his hips and making his lips go all rubbery like he's some sleazebag sexpot and I can't even pretend any more.

I go, "Shut! Up!"

That totally cracks him up.

"No, not yet! I have another theory too. Or . . . or . . ." I try to cover his mouth with my hands but he keeps swivel-ling his head away. "Or did you perhaps mistake Jimmy's car for Krystal's?"

I attack him like some crazed barbarian warrior.

He's killing himself laughing. "Bingo. Looks like we have a winner!" He puts on this tough-girl voice. "Back off, Krystal. Levi's mine! Smooch. Smooch. Ooh, baby."

I'm hitting him and I'm laughing and I'm practically crying because I've made such a fool of myself but some-how that only makes me laugh more.

He grabs both my hands and squeezes them against his chest, then clamps me into a bear hug. He says, "Oh, now I feel bad," and I think he's finally going to show me some mercy but instead he puts on this big pout and goes, "I was hoping for lust—but I'll take jealousy. Don't matter to me none. Heck, I wouldn't even mind if you were just feeling sorry for me."

Levi and I are still hanging onto each other, cracking up, when Jimmy comes back out of the store.

Levi wipes his face with the back of his hand and says, "Be right there, Jimmy." Then he waggles his eyebrows at me and whispers, "Hey. Why don't we see if we can make Krystal *really* jealous tonight?"

I squeeze my teeth together to keep my face from flying apart. I close my eyes.

He says, "I'll take that as a yes."

I nod, then I sigh and go, "No. I can't. I forgot. . . . Mrs. Hiltz is taking me for a picnic in Port Minton tonight."

Levi slumps against the van. He twirls his finger around like *ooh, whoopee, lucky you.*

I say, "It won't be very late. Mrs. Hiltz was in bed by eight last night. Maybe we could, like—you know—get together then?"

Levi pulls me toward him. "Sure. Eight, nine, midnight, whatever. I'll be waiting."

The sky suddenly gets darker. He looks up. A big black cloud is blocking the sun. "Oh-oh," he says. "I better get out of here. Jimmy'll kill me if it starts raining before I get this done."

He kisses me, gets in the van and waves. I never noticed before that his ears move when he smiles. (His ears, my heart.)

I forget about the brick. I forget about Krystal. I forget about Jimmy and all the stuff he's probably thinking about me. Who cares? There's only room in my head for Levi.

48

Thursday, 3 p.m.

Radio Mimi

"The Right Place at the Right Time." Author Tracy Hamilton discusses the chance encounter that changed her life and inspired her *New York Times* best-seller, *It Can't Be You*.

Debbie's just finishing up someone's highlights when I get to the salon. She takes one look at my black eye, squawks like some chain-smoking chicken and sends foils flying all over the floor. I try to help pick them up but she won't let me. She sits me down and makes me tell her the whole "accident" story again.

She and her customer cluck away about the decline of Western civilization for a while but eventually have to get back to deciding whether to go with ash blond again or try chestnut for a change. While I wait, I browse through the latest *Us Magazine* and daydream about Levi. I'm thoroughly enjoying myself until I see a sidebar about Mom ("Mimi's Got Man Trouble! Her Ex's Ex Tells All.") I know it's just garbage but it hurts. She's my mother. She's a human being. Why don't they just leave her alone? I toss the magazine back onto the coffee table and wait my turn.

Luckily Debbie takes my injuries to heart. She's way gentler this time when she scrubs my head. She's so nice I actually let her straighten my hair too. While she's at it, I take out the yearbook. I tell her I've decided to focus my research on her graduating class. I ask if she could tell me a little about each person.

It's like asking Anita if she'd mind reorganizing my drawers. I've created a monster.

She *tut-tuts* about the poor Bisters and makes some *wink-wink* comment about how she wished she got her claws into Percy Hiltz before he took off to see the world, but most of the stuff she talks about means nothing to me. I have to sit through these long stories about Janet who ran off with her best friend's fiancé and Darville who died in the terrible car crash and poor Angie who has that environmental illness where she's allergic to everything, including her husband, but who wouldn't be, with a guy like Gerry? (Debbie gets hives just looking at him. She can't imagine having his babies.)

I realize I've got to come up with a way of hurrying Debbie along.

I go, "Un-huh . . . un-huh . . . yup . . . yup," until she takes a breath, then I point at Rosie's picture and go, "And what about her? Where did she end up?"

"Rosie Ingram? She didn't go far. She lives just around the corner."

I go, "What?" My head jerks around so hard I hear my neck bones crack.

She says, "Sorry, honey. Did I burn you?"

I rub my head and act like, yeah, that's the problem. I have to keep calm. "Are you sure? Rosemary Ingram?" I point at the picture in the book again. "She lives here?"

"Yup. Well, she's not Rosemary Ingram any more, of course. She's Rosemary Crouse. But she definitely lives here. I don't know why, but she does. She won some lottery a couple of years ago, and what does she go and do? Fly to Jamaica? Move to Hawaii? No. She starts up a daycare centre in Shelton. Shelton! Can you believe that?

Thank God she did. I mean, me with four screamers. She definitely saved my life—and theirs too, for that matter. But seriously. Is that what you'd do if you'd won a pile of money? Look after somebody else's brats? In *Shelton*?"

I say, "No. I don't think so," but the truth is I'm not thinking at all. It's like I was hit by some power surge that blew out all the memory on my personal computer. The screen's gone black and there's smoke billowing out the sides.

If Rosemary still lives here, who's Mimi?

Debbie takes a hunk of hair and pulls it straight. (I wish someone would do the same thing with the mess *inside* my head.) She says, "Why are you so interested in Rosie anyway?"

"Um, I . . . I just heard people talk about her, I guess."

"You did? That's funny. What would people be saying about Rosie? She's not the kind of person people usually talk about. She's just this sweet, quiet girl, you know. Pretty ordinary."

Rosie's more than that. I don't know what—but she's got to be more than that.

I swallow. "Do you think there's any way I could meet her? I'd kind of like to, you know, interview her."

Debbie takes both hands and smoothes the front of my hair into matching swoops. "Sure, that's easy enough. What time is it?"

I check my watch. "Quarter to four."

"She'll still be at the daycare. You want to see her now? I could call her and ask if it would be okay."

I give this little tiny nod of my head. That's all I can do. I'm practically paralyzed. Would I be better knowing or not knowing who Rosie Ingram really is? I feel like one of those fancy show horses that skid to a stop right before the jump.

Debbie goes, "Oh, hey. What's your name? I never thought to ask before. I've got to say who's coming."

"Opal Schwartz."

Debbie goes, "Your name's Opal? No kidding!" and heads to the phone.

I get out of the chair and take off the cape. I have to lean against the counter for support. If Rosemary Miriam Ingram isn't Mimi, then nothing makes sense. I'm back to zero.

"It's a go," Debbie says when she returns. "Rosie was a bit shy at the idea of being interviewed but I said you were nice. I warned her about your accident too, so you don't have to go all through that again. Don't expect too much from her, though. She'll probably just want to talk about some kid's tooth falling out. Hope that's okay."

I do my best to smile, and give her a twenty-dollar tip. She tries to hand it back but I won't let her.

One way or another the tip she just gave me has to be worth way more than that.

49

Thursday, 4 p.m.

You, You and Mimi—BFF Special

Mimi celebrates the joy of friendship with twenty
of her best—and most famous—friends.

I stand outside the daycare for a long time and just stare.
Some lady comes out with her little girl and says, "Can I
help you?" but she doesn't mean it. She means, *What type
of nervous, sweaty creep hangs around outside a daycare
centre? Whose child are you planning to abduct?* She no
doubt saw Mimi's special, "Pervert-Proof your Kids!"

I tell her, "No. Thanks. I'm just here to see Rosie."

She smiles at me but hangs around watching until I go in.

I poke my head in the door just as kids are getting ready
to be picked up. A little bell rings. A lady with beige curly

hair and sort of see-through skin looks up and I know immediately. This is the real Rosemary Ingram.

Who was Mom trying to fool? The glasses are different from the ones in the yearbook but the nose is the same and so is the look in her eyes. (Our biology teacher told us shyness is genetic. You understand that right away when you see Rosie. It's pretty obvious she was born that way.)

She notices me and lifts her hand in a little wave. She gives the kid she's holding to another lady then starts moving toward me. She's hesitant. It's like she's walking down the aisle but she's not totally convinced she wants to marry the guy at the other end.

She says, "You must be Opal. Opal Schwartz, is it?" You can tell she's from Port Minton by her accent.

I say, "Yes. Hello." She's got a sad little smile on her face. She's standing in this mousey way but she's staring right at me. It's freaking me out.

She goes, "Why don't you come and sit down here where it's quiet and you can ask me your questions?" It sounds like, "Wo-i don ya come and sit down he-yah . . ."

I have to concentrate to understand her. How come Mrs. Hiltz doesn't have an accent like that? She's a Port Minton girl too.

Rosie leads me into a neon yellow room with a string of letters dangling from the ceiling. The place is full of Duplo sets and giant stuffed animals and tiny little kids' furniture. We sit on a bright blue sofa that's about six inches off the ground. I feel like Will Ferrell in *Elf* but Rosie's right at home. She's not much bigger than a child herself.

"Now what would you like to know?" she says.

Let's just get this over with.

"Tell me about yourself," I say.

She blushes so fiercely I worry I might have blown it. She starts glancing around, as if she's searching for an escape route. It makes me feel sorry for her. I don't want her to bolt on me.

I say, "For instance, high school. What was high school like?"

"Oh," she says. She seems to relax. "I thought you meant . . ." She shakes her head and stops. "High school . . ." She thinks for a second, then turns back to me. "Well. There were lots of dances and hockey games and things to do if you wanted to do them, I guess."

I make my voice all sweet. "Did *you* want to do them?"

"Want to? Me? . . . Maybe, a little. Sometimes. But I never did. I've never been much for, I guess you'd say, socializing and that, eh? I'm timid. That's why I like it here. With the little children. They take you for what you are. No one expects me to be much of a talker."

She looks at me again and smiles. Her eyes go back and forth across my face. It's too intense. It's like something a mother would do.

The thing that I've been trying not to think barges into my head.

We're both staring at each other now. I can hear little kids screaming and laughing in the other room but somehow I get the feeling we're all alone.

I swallow. It's like my head is full of reporters, all shouting out questions I should ask, but can't.

I do my best. I say, "Did you have any . . . friends on the hockey team?" I put a little pause in there, hoping she'll pick up on it, understand what I'm after.

"Any . . . friends?" she says. She pulls at a thread sticking out of the arm of the couch. She shakes her head and laughs a quiet, little laugh. "No," she says. "I didn't have any 'friends' on the hockey team. I wasn't exactly in their league." She puts her hand up to her mouth. "Oh!" she goes. "I made a joke. 'Not in their league.' Hockey league. Get it?"

She blushes again. I try to chuckle.

I say, "But did you *know* the guys on the team?"

"Oh yes," she says. "Sure I did. I knew the guys. Everybody knew them. I can't imagine any of them would have thought of themselves as my friend, though."

This isn't going anywhere. Mimi's the one who had the ring. Is it just a fluke I found it with Rosie's picture?

She says, "In fact, I only really had one friend . . . one *true* friend, I guess you'd say."

Then she stares at me. She stares at me so hard I feel like she's trying to mind-meld me or something.

I say, "Who was that?"

This look travels across her face. I don't know if it's surprise or confusion or worry or what. It doesn't stay long enough for me to figure it out. It's like lights from a car driving past. It's there then it's gone.

"Minerva . . ." she says. She sort of smiles but her eyes have gone all glittery. "Minerva Bister was my best friend."

I'm starting to understand something but I don't know exactly what. My imagination is whispering things to me that are too scary even to think about.

"Oh," I say. "How did you meet her?"

"In the washroom at school." She almost whispers, as

if it's too shocking to say out loud. "It was just after the people come in and busted up Bister Island. I'd got some glue on my hands and I went to clean them off. Minerva was standing in the middle of the washroom, looking at the stalls. I could tell she didn't know what to do. Poor thing. She didn't know how to use the toilet. She didn't even know how to ask."

Rosie laughs as if she's going to tell me a secret.

"I'm timid, but next to Minerva, I was like the class clown. She could barely get her mouth open. Didn't help she talked funny and called things by the wrong names. Old fashioned names. I remember she used to call the kitchen the 'scullery.' Sounded scary to me but that's what she called it. . . ."

For someone so shy, Rosie's having no trouble talking now. It's like she can't stop herself. She says, "Anyway, somehow I managed to figure out what the problem was. I showed her how to flush the toilet and how to pump soap out of the dispenser and how to tear off a bit of paper towel without the whole roll barrelling out—and we were friends from then on!"

"That was nice of you," I say.

Rosie shakes her head. "No, I wasn't being nice. I liked

Minerva right off. We understood each other. We weren't like the other kids. They flirted in the cafeteria and talked back to the teachers. They were always showing off, acting big. That wasn't us. We were quiet. We liked to sit around and knit, do our handicrafts, stuff like that. I wasn't real keen on books, but Minerva was. I'd wait until she'd finish, then make her tell me the whole story. *Wuthering Heights*, that was my favourite! Do you know that one?"

I nod. Yes, I know that one. Mom reads it every year. She's had it on her Book Club at least two or three times, enough to turn it into a bestseller again.

Rosie goes, "Wasn't it exciting? Heathcliff and Catherine and everybody marrying the wrong people! I just loved it—especially the way Minerva read it. She used to do voices for the different characters. You'd never think someone that shy could act—but she could. It was better than the movies. . . . I was some sad when she stopped coming to school."

"She did?" I say. "Why?"

Rosie shrugs as if the answer's obvious. "Couldn't take the looks from the other kids, the snickering and all that. Her cousins stuck it out. They acted like they didn't even hear it. But it was too much for Minerva. Too shaming.

She stopped going to school one day and never come back. Mrs. Hiltz learned her after that."

"Mrs. *Hiltz* taught her?" Why wouldn't Mrs. Hiltz have told me that herself when we were talking about the Bisters?

"'Taught her,' that's right. I should know better than saying 'learned her'. . . . Yup, Mrs. Hiltz was fostering her and she took it on herself to do the teaching too. Did you ever see that movie *My Fair Lady*? That's just what it was like. When she come here, Minerva didn't have the first clue about manners or hygiene or eating with a knife and fork. Nothing like that. Mrs. Hiltz taught her all that stuff. Taught her to talk like a city person too. Suddenly, it was us kids who grew up in the Port that had the funny accent and the bad manners, not Minerva."

Rosie laughs again in that embarrassed way and then whispers to me. "At first, my mum didn't like Minerva coming over to visit. She was a Bister and all, eh? After a while, though, Mum was begging her to stay so she could teach us youngsters some 'etiquette'!"

Funny to hear her say such a fancy word. It makes me think of that English lady who came on the show. She was big into etiquette too. She taught Mom and me which forks to use, how to get stuff out from between your teeth without anyone noticing, how to butter your bread. I hated that segment. It was so fake. Mom knew all that stuff already. She was a real stickler for it.

Rosie's smiling but I get the feeling that something's made her sad. She hangs her head and stares at the floor.

There's a pause, then she says, "Oh, would you look at these shoes!" Her toes have poked right through the top of her dirty pink sneakers. She's trying to be cheery, change the subject. "Minerva would be mortified to see me wearing these."

She puts her hand on the side of her face like she's pretending to be appalled.

"*Mortified*, that was her word. I don't know if she picked it up from Mrs. Hiltz or it come from one of her old-fashioned books but she was always in danger of being 'mortified.' I don't think they even had a mirror on Bister Island. The girl had no idea what she looked like when she arrived in Port Minton—and she didn't care. Then Mrs. Hiltz got Minerva's teeth fixed, fattened her up a bit, bought her some new clothes and, suddenly, Minerva couldn't bear to have a hair out of place! You could see that one day she was going to be a good-looking woman. Mrs. Hiltz was some proud of her."

Suddenly I feel like panicking. That thing she said about Minerva's hair, not being able to bear having it out of place. It gives me a stitch in my side, like I've been running too hard. I just have to keep breathing. I tell myself it doesn't necessarily mean anything. Lots of people like *Wuthering Heights,* like to be neat, polite.

I wipe my mouth and say, "What happened to Minerva?"

Rosie pulls her shoulders together as if she's got a pain in her chest and says, "I don't know." She shakes her head. "For two years, we spent all our free time together, then one day, she up and disappeared. Just like that. She didn't warn me. She didn't call. She didn't leave a note. Nothing. I asked Mrs. Hiltz about her but she didn't know where Minerva was either. I was worried something terrible had happened—that she'd gotten lost or killed or her dad had come and taken her back. I was some scared."

Rosie rubs her fingers up and down her forehead. It's as if Minerva just went missing yesterday.

She swallows and takes a deep breath. "Mrs. Hiltz called the police, but when she found out some of her valuables were missing she just let it drop. She figured Minerva must have stolen the stuff and taken off with it. As far as Mrs. Hiltz was concerned, there was no point in making a stink about it. She didn't want to get Minerva in trouble over 'trinkets.' Other than that, what could she do? Like she said, Minerva was eighteen by then. She was old enough to go where she wanted."

I say, "Was she angry, Mrs. Hiltz?" Maybe that's why she didn't tell me about the Bisters.

"No. More like disappointed, I'd say. I think Mrs. Hiltz always wanted a daughter. She loved all the buying dresses and the primping and the making yourself look nice. She put a lot of herself into helping Minerva. . . . It must have broken Mrs. Hiltz's heart when Minerva took off like that."

Rosie shakes her head the way people do when something is too sad even to talk about, then she says, "You know, I walked by the old Hiltz mansion down in the Port every day after school. I'd see Mrs. Hiltz out front, having a cup of tea or cutting flowers. She'd always say hello and ask after my mother—but she never mentioned Minerva. Not once. I couldn't understand it then but I guess that was just Mrs. Hiltz's way. She had to put things behind her and carry on."

"What about you?" I say. I'm not sure if I should be asking. "How did you feel?"

It's a long time before she answers. She fiddles with

her sleeve. When she finally speaks, her voice is sort of strangely happy. It makes me realize how bad she feels.

She goes, "My heart was broken too. People think you need to have some big romance to break your heart but you don't. Losing a best friend is almost as painful as losing a husband. I know. I've done both. When Minerva left, I cried and cried. My parents helped me look for her at first—we even took a boat ride out to Bister Island—but after a while they gave up. They found out my wallet had disappeared around the time Minerva left and that was that. 'Typical Bister,' they said. 'Can't trust 'em as far as you can throw 'em.' They forgot all about her good manners. As far as they were concerned, she was just as bad as the rest."

She looks at me. "Sorry," she says.

Why is she saying sorry to me?

"Did *you* think she took your wallet?" I have to know.

Rosie hesitates. "Sure," she says. "I knew it was her. I kept it in my jewellery box. She was the only one who knew. I was hurt at first that she'd steal from me. Then I was mad. Eight dollars was a lot of money to me back then, but I could have stood that. What I couldn't understand was why she had to go and take my whole wallet! I lost my birth certificate and my student card and all my photos too. There was a picture of my baby cousin and one of my dog and one of my favourite Sunday school teacher and me at the church picnic. I couldn't replace those. . . ."

I have to struggle to keep listening, to keep breathing. I feel like my blood's turned to Perrier water. It's cold and it's fizzy and it's freezing my whole body from the inside out. Rosie looks at me to make sure it's okay, then goes on.

"I got over it, though. I knew Minerva. I knew she wouldn't have taken my wallet if she didn't really need it. Something had been bothering her in the last few weeks. I tried to ask her what it was but she always said, 'Nothing.' She didn't want to talk about it. I just hope that wherever she is now, she's happy."

Rosie is crying now. Not sobbing or anything but there are tears streaming down her cheeks. I should put my arm around her—ask if she's okay—but I can't. I just sit there, stupid.

Stupefied.

I'll never talk again. You hear about that happening. People have this terrible shock and they never say another word for the rest of their lives.

Rosie wipes her face, blows her nose then stuffs the Kleenex up her sleeve. She's trying to smile.

"We had a lot of fun together, Minerva and me. We used to talk about all the things we wanted to do when we grew up. I'd never been able to do that with anyone before. She knew how to bring me out of myself, I guess you'd say. I told her I wanted to have a daycare centre. I did—and I never really changed my mind. Minerva, though, had a new idea every week. It was like once she realized there was a big wide world beyond Bister Island, she couldn't get enough of it. She saw a bus for the first time, she wanted to be a bus driver. She got her teeth fixed, she wanted to be a dentist. She went to the gas station, she wanted to be the person who cleaned the windshields. The funniest one, though, was when we took her out to get fish and chips. She decided she wanted to be a cook! That slayed us! The girl couldn't cook for beans. The only decent thing Minerva could make were these old-fashioned molasses pancakes. Now what did she call them? She had some funny name for them."

I remember Mom and Dad and me at that cabin we rented. We sang songs, we played board games and Mom cooked. It was the only time I remember her cooking. I remember laughing so hard when she told me what those pancakes were called.

"Lassie tootins?" I say. It's funny—those were just non-sense words before. They didn't mean anything. Now they mean everything.

Rosie looks at me and nods.

She says, "I knew it as soon as you walked in. You have her eyes."

50

Thursday, 6 p.m.

You, You and Mimi

"Old Dogs and New Tricks." Gerontologist Dr. Jonathan Allen looks at some of the amazing things octogenarians can teach today's youth.

We're almost at Port Minton and I still haven't told Mrs. Hiltz yet. The rain has just started. She's driving this enormous old Mercedes and chatting away about the first settlers in the area and various sailing ships that landed here and the impact of the terrible winter of 1818 and I'm going, "Oh, yes" like I'm actually following but all I'm doing is waiting for the right time to say something.

When is the right time to say something like this?

She starts in on the early hunting practices of the native

population. I notice she moves her head as if she's outlining a square when she talks. She always uses complete sentences. She could be a television reporter. Mimi used to be a television reporter. Did Mrs. Hiltz teach her that too?

There's *never* going to be a right time to say something like this. I should just leap in right now. Get it over with.

Mrs. Hiltz might still be mad at Minerva. I don't want to open up old wounds or anything. How many valuables did she take off with? How much were they worth?

Mrs. Hiltz slows down until she's almost at a dead stop, then turns on to the Port Minton Road. The sky and water are grey. Rain is pinging off the hood. We'll be eating our picnic indoors by the look of things.

We're alone in the car. There are no distractions. Mimi could buy Mrs. Hiltz as many valuables as she wants now. She could make it up to her. Mrs. Hiltz should know the truth. There's nothing stopping me.

"Mrs. Hiltz?" I say.

She turns and looks at me with her eyebrows raised like two perfect little white umbrellas. She's smiling. She's probably happy because she thinks I'm going to ask her some probing question about shipbuilding or pemmican-making or something.

I almost do—because I'm a chicken—but then I just blurt it out.

"Minerva Bister is my mother."

Mrs. Hiltz's eyebrows collapse and her lips go flat. She turns her head away from me as if she's a mechanical doll. She looks straight ahead. She moistens her lips and says, "Yes. I know."

"You do?"

"Of course I do," she says. "Why do you think we're going on this little outing? I knew it that first day, as soon as I saw your hands."

"My hands?"

"Yes. Your nails. That's what gave it away. And your hair too, of course. Your auburn hair."

I don't understand. My hands aren't like my mother's. My hair's not like my mother's. What's she talking about?

"Oh, and I guess it wasn't just that." Mrs. Hiltz is smiling again. "There are those cold blue eyes, of course. And your manner too. Asking me about Bister Island and Port Minton and the Ingrams as if this were just some innocent little history project you're working on!" She seems to find this funny.

"You're so like your mother. Really. All that lying, manipulating, sneaking around behind my back—"

"No!" I go. "That's not what I was doing. Honestly. I didn't know Minerva was my mother until today. Honestly!" How do I tell her that I was lying for a different reason entirely?

Mrs. Hiltz coughs out a laugh. She's driving faster now. Too fast for a twisty road. I put my hand on the dashboard as she screeches around a bend. The ocean's almost straight below me.

"Oh, really, dear." She puts on this squeaky voice. "'Honestly! . . . Honestly!'" She shakes her head. "Methinks the lady doth protest too much. You're a scheming tramp just like your mother. I clearly should have hit you harder when I had the chance."

It's as if somebody slipped a rope around my neck and yanked. I get it.

"*You* hit me?" I say. "In the car? That was you?" My skin shrinks.

"Yes." She sounds proud, as if I just complimented her on her prize-winning begonias.

A picture of Mrs. Hiltz in her nightie flashes into my head. Just like that, I understand something else too. The way she was out of breath. Her cold hands. Her shoes— her outdoor shoes—crunching through the glass on the floor. The fact that Casper didn't bark.

My screaming didn't wake her up last night. She'd been outside.

"You threw the brick too," I say.

"Yes, of course."

"*Why?*" My heart feels like it's trying to break out of my chest. This is crazy. Why would she do that? You'd have to hate a person to do something like that.

She laughs. "Because killing you on the road proved more difficult than I thought it was going to be. At the last minute, I held back. I was afraid to end up in the ditch myself. I didn't have the courage to try again. I decided another really good scare might be enough to stop you. It had to. I couldn't let you try to destroy us again."

"*Destroy you again?* What are you talking about?"

She sneers at me. "You know perfectly well what I'm talking about! I tried to be kind to you people! I gave my heart and soul to Minerva Bister! I invited her into my home. I taught her how to speak, how to dress, how to brush her rotten little teeth—which, by the way, I spent a small fortune to replace. And how does she repay me? . . . She seduces my son! She gets herself pregnant!"

My scalp goes all prickly before I even understand what the words mean.

Great big Percy.

The kid in the yearbook with the thick red hair.

Of course.

Percy Hiltz is my father.

Mrs. Hiltz is holding the steering wheel so tight her knuckles have gone white. For the first time, I notice her stubby thumbnail. It's shaped and filed and painted a pale pink but otherwise it's just like mine.

She takes short, loud breaths in through her nose. "Minerva duped dear, sweet Percy into believing they'd make the perfect family!"

The rain has made the pavement slippery. We hit the shoulder. Gravel goes flying. I grab the wheel and jerk us back onto the road.

I scream. "Slow down, Mrs. Hiltz! Please!"

She takes my hand—my sprained hand—and bends it back at the wrist. I don't know if it's the shock or the pain but it's like she zapped me with a Taser. I didn't expect an old lady to be so strong. I let go of the wheel. I fall back against the door, panting.

Mrs. Hiltz slows down.

"Excuse me. I apologize. I shouldn't let myself get so upset," she says. She sounds calm.

I breathe again. I rub my wrist and try to believe that this is just another scare.

"Now where was I? Oh yes. Minerva. She *said* she wanted to marry Percy and have the baby—but she changed her tune fast enough when I brought out my wallet. You see, my dear, everyone has their price. Minerva's was twenty-thousand dollars—a lot higher than most people's—but she was a lot smarter than most people too. Believe me, there were no flies on that girl—at least not once I'd given her a good bath!"

Mrs. Hiltz laughs at that. She has little white blobs of spit in the corners of her mouth and she doesn't even care.

I sit as still as I can, looking straight ahead, my back stiff. I don't want to do anything to upset her. Maybe this is like one of Anita's little fits. She'll blow up, get over it, apologize. I'll live. I'll go home.

Mrs. Hiltz is driving normally now. She's watching the road. She looks like the perfect grandmother, but her voice is hard. "I gave her the money and she promised I'd never see that despicable little face of hers again. It set my portfolio back a bit but, believe me, it was worth it. A Bister grandchild! I never would have been able to hold my head up in this town again."

I tell myself to ignore her. Hate her later. Don't move now. Stay alive.

"No," she says. "The money was well spent. Minerva Bister would have destroyed Percy. It took him years to get back on his feet again after what she did to him—then you come along to ruin him, just as his political career is finally taking off. You're not going to blackmail us!"

The woman's insane. I try to sound reasonable. I say, "That's not why I'm here, Mrs. Hiltz. Really. I don't want money. I'd never hurt Percy."

"You're right," she says. "You never will. Because I won't let you. I made the mistake before of thinking you Bisters could be trusted. I know better now. I'm not afraid of the ditch any more. I reminded myself this morning that a mother's job is to protect her children."

She looks right at me. She tries to put on her nice-old-lady face again. "Just relax, dear," she says. "It shouldn't hurt much if you relax."

She slams her foot to the floor and cranks the steering wheel to the right. We're heading straight for the ocean.

I can't just hope any more. I grab the wheel. Mrs. Hiltz lunges at me, slaps me, elbows me. I can't believe how fierce she is. I'm trying to control the car but I can barely see the road.

I'm terrified and frantic but suddenly I'm angry too. I scream at her, "Are you nuts? I don't need your money!"

She coughs out a laugh and I know that's just another way of telling me I'm a scheming tramp.

I think that's what gets me. Hearing her laugh like that. At me, at Mom.

Well, screw you. I don't care if you are Mrs. Enos Hiltz. As far as I'm concerned, you're nothing. Nothing compared to my mother, that's for sure.

I get this burst of something inside me. A doctor would probably say it was adrenalin but that's not what it feels like. Adrenalin's just a hormone or a chemical or an enzyme or something. This is bigger than that. It completely overwhelms me. I'm like a grizzly protecting her cub.

I grab Mrs. Hiltz's head so she can see me. I'm not even thinking about dying any more. I go, "Minerva is Mimi Schwartz! Do you understand? Minerva is Mimi!"

She gets this look of horror on her face, and I think I've gotten through to her—but I'll never know. She stops flailing. Her mouth opens. She makes a type of groan I've never heard before, and then her head clunks onto my shoulder.

I try to pull the wheel hard to the left but her body's in the way. I've got maybe a second to realize we're going to crash.

I scream, "Mom!" and my head snaps at the impact.

The next thing I remember is Embree Bister looking in the window and saying, "You all right, maid?"

51

Saturday, 1 p.m.
Radio Mimi

"Around the World with a Carry-on Bag." Mimi
shares some of her best tips for travelling light.

I see the cheap rental car parked near the beach. I ask Levi
to drop me off here. I'll walk the rest of the way by myself.

"No, you won't," he says. "I'm coming too."

I won't let him. She didn't want anyone to know yet. She
promised she'd give her PR people at least a day or two to
figure out how to spin things before the media get wind
of this.

He says, "I could be your bodyguard. C'mon. Please!"

He's trying to jolly me out of this. He's trying to see
what I'm up to. He knows nothing except that Mrs. Hiltz

had a heart attack, and there was a crash, and my mother is here to see me. He thinks it's strange she wants to meet at the beach, but there's nothing I can do about that. I'm not telling him anything else. Not yet.

"No," I say. "I can take care of myself, thank you very much."

"Right—" he says.

We both laugh. I've got fifteen stitches in my forehead to complement my black eye.

"Sure you can."

I start toward the beach even though he hasn't left yet. Despite everything that's happened in the last week, the first thing that goes through my head is, *I walk away and he's going to see my fat ass.*

It makes me laugh. I turn back. He *was* looking at my ass but, judging by the expression on his face, he didn't mind the view.

I motion, *Get out of here!* with my hands. He does this *Pleeease?* thing with his face. I shake my head. He pretends to pout but eventually backs away.

I head down the path. Mom and Percy were this age when they met. I wonder if they goofed around like that too, if he made her laugh, if he told her how pretty she was.

I think of Percy in the hospital room with his head in his hands and I'm pretty sure he did. It was something about the way he looked at me when he found out. The way his eyes filled up with tears when he tried to tell me how hard it's been all these years not knowing what happened to her, to their baby. The way he kept staring at me.

He must have loved her.

I cross the wobbly little boardwalk and I can't help asking myself, *But did she love him?*

We didn't talk about that on the phone the other night. She was too shocked. Me being in Port Minton, the accident, Mrs. Hiltz dying, all that stuff about the Bisters—it was a lot for me to dump on her at once.

She didn't try to hide, though. She admitted right out who she was. She said, "yeah" to being a Bister, to taking Rosie's identity, to getting money from Mrs. Hiltz, to everything in *Canadian Geographic,* to most of the stuff on enoughaboutmimi.com. Even *Us Magazine* apparently was onto something. Dad's ex-girlfriend was going around telling all these people that I wasn't his kid. Mimi knew everything would come out sooner or later, she said. She always meant to tell me. She just couldn't face it yet.

I went, "Why?"

She paused, then said, "We have to talk."

It was almost funny. It was such a Mimi thing to say. The studio guest makes some sort of vague comment about a new relationship and Mimi leans in close and goes, "Oooh, darling. We have to talk." The audience laughs. They cut to a commercial. Revelations to follow.

The tone was different now, though. She wasn't trying to get something out of me this time. *We have to talk* was a promise.

"I'll fly in tomorrow," she said.

I wanted to say, no, tell me everything now. I didn't want to give her time to come up with a new story. But, turns out, I'm glad we waited. It's given me a chance to get everything straight in my own head.

At first, it was the facts that were so big and scary. But now, they just sort of . . . are. Dad isn't my dad. Percy is. Grandpa isn't my grandpa. Embree is. Mom is my mom but she's not Mimi. She probably isn't Minerva or Rosie any more either.

Who is she really?

That's what I want to know now. Who cares about the facts?

52

Saturday, 3:30 p.m.
You, You and Mimi
"Mother–Child Reunion." Mimi and adoption-rights advocate Laura Jeha reunite seven adult children with their birth parents.

Anita would have run to me the moment she saw me. She'd have screamed and cried and kissed me all over my face.

Mom just sucks in her breath and starts walking toward me. She's got her sandals in her hand. She's barefoot. I can't remember the last time I saw her barefoot.

Her hair's a mess. There are grey circles under her eyes that she hasn't done anything to cover up. She's not even wearing lipstick. She didn't need to hide out here. No one would recognize her as Mimi Schwartz. *I barely recognize her.*

"Birdie," she says. "I'm really sorry."

She reaches up and touches my stitches but I don't think that's what she means. She hugs me. I hug her back. We're both awkward. We've never done a lot of hugging.

"Let's sit down," she says. "I'll tell you everything and then—if you want—I'll take you home."

Her face sags like a balloon four days after a birthday party. It makes me sad. She's interviewed the Queen of Jordan. She's talked to Mafia hit men. She's grilled big stars on-air about their alleged drug use, criminal records, impending divorces. But I can see she's scared to talk to me. Her own daughter.

I drop my cane and lower myself against a rock. She sits with her knees up and her feet digging into the sand. I notice her toes aren't webbed and I get this little shot of happiness. I think, *So she couldn't be a Bister, then!* but the happiness doesn't last long. It's like a firecracker that flies up in the air and then just fizzles back to earth. I know she's a Bister. I'm a Bister.

Do I care? I don't know.

Mom picks up a handful of sand and lets it run over her feet. "Ask me whatever you want," she says.

I've got so many questions but the first one is obvious. "Why didn't you tell me?" I don't say it in a mean way or an accusing way or anything. I just need to know.

Mom doesn't do any of her Mimi stuff. She doesn't nod her head or rub her chin or touch my knee. There are no reaction shots for the camera. She just looks straight ahead at the ocean and talks.

"Two reasons, I guess," she says. "I promised Mrs. Hiltz that I'd keep my mouth shut until she died—so I did. Despite everything, I figured I owed her that much."

She must know how crazy that sounds. "She *did* rescue me, Birdie. If it weren't for her, I'd still be out there. . . ." She points her chin at Bister Island. It's sort of a tough-guy thing to do, like a gang member picking a fight or something. Does she hate the Island, or hate Mrs. Hiltz?

She shakes her head, pauses, sighs. "The other reason was that . . . I don't know. I guess I was ashamed."

"Of what?" I say. "Blackmailing her?"

"Is that what Mrs. Hiltz told you?"

There's an edge to her voice and for a second I worry she's going to blow up at me—but then I realize I'm not the one she's angry at.

She says, "Please, tell me you don't believe that. She gave me the money! She *forced* it on me! I didn't even know what was in the envelope until I was long gone!"

Mom turns away from me. There's a long pause. When she finally speaks, she's calm again. "Look," she says. "This is what happened. Mrs. Hiltz took me in. I thank her for that. I still do. She cleaned me up, dressed me, taught be how to act like a lady. She was very kind to me. She expected Percy to be too. And he was.

"Neither of us meant to fall in love. I mean, I was terri-fied of him at first. He was so big and, you know, jolly. . . . I froze every time he came near me. But Mrs. Hiltz sort of pushed us together. I realize now she'd already envisioned his political career. She knew he needed to be able to deal with the underclasses."

A little smile floats across Mom's face. I think she's embarrassed.

"That's not why Percy was doing it. He was just kind. Way before there was anything between us, Percy took the time to teach me how to use the phone book, how to change the channel on the TV, how to open a milk carton, all that stuff I didn't know. He wanted to take me to parties too—but I wouldn't go. I was too shy. I wasn't ready.

"Somewhere along the line—I guess I'd been there about a year—we fell in love. There was nothing bad about it but somehow we both felt uncomfortable letting other people know. Maybe we knew some of them wouldn't approve of the match. I didn't even tell Rosie. We knew better than to let on to Mrs. Hiltz, of course—but mostly because if she found out, we knew we'd never be able to get any time alone. She'd be suspicious of us heading off on those long drives together. . . ."

She squeezes her lips to one side of her face and lifts her eyebrows. I guess she's telling me that I was conceived in the back of a car.

"Things changed when I realized I was pregnant. We were scared at first but we talked it over. We loved each other. Mrs. Hiltz had said she loved me. We were naive enough to believe she was going to be thrilled at the thought of us giving her a grandchild."

We both laugh. I mean, it's horrible and it's tragic but it's funny too. As if Mrs. Hiltz would be thrilled about a teen pregnancy, not to mention a Bister teen pregnancy.

"She looked surprised when we told her but kept that perfect smile on her face. She even congratulated us. It was all very pleasant. We talked about what we'd name the baby, where we'd live, what we'd do when Percy went off to university the next year. Then it was seven o'clock and Percy had to leave for hockey practice.

"The door had barely shut behind him before Mrs. Hiltz turned on me. She called me a tramp, a slut, a Bister! I'd betrayed her, ruined her son's life, destroyed her family's good name. She said she wanted me out. I said, no. I couldn't go. I couldn't break Percy's heart! She laughed at that. He'd just been using me, she said. He'd come to his senses soon enough and realize he wanted nothing to do with a low-life like me."

Mimi rubs her hands over her face. Even though she's upset, I notice that's she careful to rub up, not down. Dr. Boileau said it was better for her skin.

"It was terrible. In moments, I'd gone from the happiest I'd ever been to the saddest. It was like someone had baked me a great, big birthday cake, then the candles went and exploded in my face. I ran into my room, sobbing. I didn't know what to do, where to go. I just collapsed.

"Mrs. Hiltz knocked on my door a little while later. She handed me a big fat envelope and said, 'Take this and get out.' I did."

She lifts her chin and speaks in this really slow voice.

"That's what happened. I have nothing to be ashamed of as far as that goes."

"So then what *are* you ashamed of?"

She looks out at the water. I don't know if it's the glare that's making her squint or if she's trying not to cry.

"Myself," she says. "You can dye my hair, give me a new nose, put me in designer fashions—but it doesn't make any difference. I'm still a Bister. The lowest of the low. My whole life has been about trying to get over that. I kept my mouth shut all these years because I was embarrassed about who I was. I kept telling myself that one day I'd be good enough to deserve Percy—and then I could talk."

She reaches out like she's going to touch my hand but she doesn't. She picks up a pebble and rubs it in her fingers. "I thought the same thing about you. One day, I was going to be so good, so perfect, that I could tell you who I was and it wouldn't matter."

"But, Mom!" I go. "I wouldn't have cared! I wouldn't have . . ."

I want to push up close to her, put my arm through hers, put my head on her shoulder—but I don't. I know she doesn't want that. I'm not sure either of us could handle it. I'll save that type of thing for Anita.

"No. Maybe you wouldn't," she says, "but I couldn't risk it. All my life people have said it didn't matter—then acted like it did. You know, there was this big 'outrage' when *Canadian Geographic* did that story on us. Everyone around here made it sound like they were so shocked at the way we'd been living. But that was nonsense. Everybody here had known about us for years! Government people came by occasionally. Antique dealers rowed over to buy furniture off us for a tenth of what it was worth. Fishermen got their moonshine from us. Some minister even dragged Father and my uncles off to school for a while when they were boys. The minister's intentions might have been honourable but the experience turned the Bisters off civilization for good. Father vowed he would never expose his children to that type of ridicule. The locals were more than happy to let him have his way."

She gives this little "hmmph!" and shakes her head. "You can't tell me no one around here knew there were fourteen starving kids and a couple of dying old folks on that island. I mean, come on! How come nobody ever asked about what happened to my mother? The towns-people knew about Nettie Faulkner. It was a big scandal when she took up with a Bister. Once she was on the Island, though, it was like, 'So long, Nettie!' Nobody ever bothered to see how she was doing—whether she was even still alive! When the cancer took her, we just filled her pockets with rocks and buried her at sea."

Mom burying a body at sea. I've never even seen her make a cup of tea for herself. It's like she's morphing before my very eyes. She's not Mom. She's not Mimi. She's someone else entirely.

"Were you glad when the people came to get you?" I say.

She rubs her hands back and forth through the sand in a big arc. "We didn't know what to think, us kids. My little sister had died the winter before. Starvation. Something should have been done but the adults were too proud to go for help. Now here was help. You couldn't expect us to turn it away. It was scary to leave the only home we ever knew, but, hey—the new place had Popsicles! The new people didn't cane us when we were bad or lock us in cellars. They fed us when we were hungry. They gave us clothes that fit and warm baths and actual shoes. Who'd want to go back to Bister Island after that—even if we could?

"It wasn't until I went to school that I realized all this bounty came with a price. I was still just a Bister—at least as far as most people were concerned. I say 'most people' because it wasn't everyone. . . ." She turns and looks at me. "You met Rosie."

I nod. "I thought she was my mother."

"You might have been better off if she were."

I try to say "No!" but she won't let me.

"I mean it," she says. "She's a wonderful person. You know, I've done more shows than I can count on heroes. People who've jumped onto subway tracks to save a stranger or fought off an intruder or thrown themselves on a hand grenade. And every time I do one, I think of Rosie. We always make bravery out to be this big, flashy thing. It isn't always. Rosie Ingram is one of the bravest people I ever met. I mean it. I'm not saying everyone at high school was out-and-out mean or that some people didn't try to help. But Rosie was the only one brave enough to really get to know me. She didn't care if it looked bad on her. She liked me and she didn't try to pretend she didn't. That's real courage. Unfortunately, it's just not very good TV."

Mom smoothes down her hair but it doesn't help much. It's so weird to see her look such a mess that I get a sharp little pang. Did I really need to dig all this up? Who cares? Who's it helping?

Her, maybe. She just keeps talking and talking like she wants to get it all out of her system.

"It's funny. Mrs. Hiltz was the one who got all the glory for being brave. My cousins went and lived at the 'Home for Delinquent Boys.' Nobody else would have them. The really little kids were adopted into families who lived somewhere else. But me, I found a foster home with the richest person in town. People were *astounded* Mrs. Hiltz had taken in a Bister. She was a saint, a hero!"

We laugh a little at that. Some saint.

"I believed it too. Mrs. Hiltz was so kind and patient. She kept telling me how smart and pretty I was. I was in heaven. No one had ever praised me before. No one had ever proudly presented me to their friends!"

Mom's voice gets all tight and I know she's about to cry. I put my hand on her back but she goes stiff, so I take it away. She starts to talk again as if she's perfectly fine.

"I think of those ladies with their Betty Crocker hairdos and their little sandwiches saying, 'This is the Bister girl? Why, Opal, isn't she lovely!' and I realize the whole thing was about *her*. About what a good job *she* was doing. Rosie didn't have any reason to be nice to me. She just was."

"So why did you steal Rosie's wallet then?" She said I could ask her anything.

Mom puts her hand over her mouth and sort of hums or moans or something. "I didn't mean to *steal* it. I went to Rosie's after Mrs. Hiltz kicked me out. I only wanted to say goodbye but I couldn't get the words out. At some point, she went to the washroom. While she was gone, I took her wallet out of her jewellery box. I just wanted a picture of her so I'd have something to keep, but she came back too soon. I put the whole thing in my pocket and told her I had to get going. I hugged her goodbye. She must have wondered why there were tears in my eyes. I always felt bad about that."

"What did you do then, when you left Rosie's?"

"Got on the highway and hitchhiked into the city. I hung around there for a couple of days not knowing what to do. Percy had told me about New York once. I decided to go. Lucky for me I had that wallet. I got to the airport and found out I needed ID. I had Rosie's birth certificate and student card. That's how I became Rosemary Miriam Ingram. . . . That was another thing I wasn't planning on doing."

She pauses. "None of this was planned, Robin. I just did what I had to do. I want you to know that."

"Okay," I say. We've both been called scheming tramps. Doesn't mean we are.

She looks at me for a while, then says, "I got to New York and put the rest of the money in a bank account. I planned to send it back to Mrs. Hiltz as soon as I got a job. I saw a notice tacked up on a bulletin board. A man needed someone to look after his sick wife. Room and board included.

"That's how I met Grandpa. I'd looked after my mother when she was dying so I knew what to do with Dora. I read to her, I bathed her, I cleaned the house, even cooked a bit. I didn't tell Harry I was pregnant, but after a while it became obvious. I was worried he was going to throw me out, but he didn't. One day, he just said, 'You can stay here as long as you need to.' He never asked who the father was or what I was going to do when the baby came along. He just made sure I didn't work too hard and got to bed early.

"Dora died a few months later. I stayed on, cooking and cleaning for Harry. You were born. I named you Robin because I wanted you to be able to fly away if you ever needed to. And I named you Opal because . . . I guess back then I still believed Mrs. Hiltz was good and I was bad."

She shakes her head. "Anyway, you came along and Grandpa fell in love with you. I wasn't going anywhere then. We were a family."

Her face goes blotchy but she just sucks it up and keeps going. "That thing you read on enoughaboutmimi.com is right. That's more or less how I got my first job. Harry was doing some electrical work at the studio the day the *Book Talk* host up and quit two hours before the show. Harry lied and said I was twenty-five, told them I could do it, told them I had experience. They didn't go for it at first. Then he said, 'Give her a chance and I won't charge you for the work I did.' The station was a shoestring operation. They almost *had* to give me a try.

"Harry came home all excited. I told him there was no way I could do it. I was too shy. He wouldn't listen. He said I just had to ask a professor a couple of questions about Jane Austen. The professor would do all the work. I still said no. Then he said, 'You owe it to me.' He didn't mean it, of course. He only said that to make me do it. He bought me a dress, fixed my hair and basically pushed me onto the set. The only thing that saved me was that I'd read all Austen's books a million times. I practically knew them by heart. I asked my first question. The professor answered. I was so fascinated I almost forgot I was on TV. I'd found my calling. I became the regular host."

Her voice has changed. I can see her body loosening up. The words are just pouring out of her.

"One day, I met your dad—Steve, I mean—at the studio. It was just as his song was starting to get airplay. Around the same time, Harry saw an ad for a newsreader on a local station—a paying station—and he prodded me into applying for it. I got the job. Steve's song flew up the charts. He adored you in that *whatever goes* way of his. I thought we were in love. We got married."

She rolls her eyes at that. It obviously wasn't much of a love affair. No surprise there, I guess.

"It was all happening so fast. This time, though, I wasn't going to let things fall apart. I should have given more time to you but . . . but, I don't know. All I can say is, I really believed I was doing this for you. You were going to have a mother you could be proud of, a family you could be proud of, a good name . . . everything. That's why I hired Anita. She was warm and loving in a way that I couldn't be."

She turns and looks at me. Her eyebrows are squished together. "I'm sorry I couldn't give that kind of affection to you myself. But I couldn't give you something I never had. I hope you know I love you just the same."

I'm embarrassed. "Yeah," I say. "I do."

She nods—she's embarrassed too—then goes back to her story. "I never imagined that my career would take off the way it did but I understand how it happened. On TV, I didn't have to be myself. I could pretend to be whoever I wanted to be. It was the only place I felt completely comfortable. As you know, intimacy isn't my strong point."

She raises her hands up in a shrug. It's a Mimi move, sort of clowny. Something she'd do right before a station break or on a promo for her next show. I see what she's trying to tell me, though. There's nothing she can do about the way she is. That's not necessarily a bad thing.

She says, "I got a local talk show. I tarted up my wardrobe and changed my hair. I wasn't worried about anybody recognizing me then. I mean, the only people who knew I was a Bister were in Port Minton. They'd never see the show. Most of them wouldn't have recognized me even if they did. I'd been on the Island until I was sixteen. Even when I moved into town no one ever actually made eye contact with me—except, of course, Rosie and the Hiltzes, and they weren't around. So I didn't really *need* to change my appearance. I just wanted to update my look.

"Then the show went national. That made me a little nervous. Things were going so well—I didn't want to lose everything I'd worked so hard for. I had my first plastic surgery."

She turns and shows me her profile. "I had a bit taken off the end of my nose. Not much. Nobody thought anything of it. Everyone does it there. Each time we took on new stations, I'd get a little more afraid of being recognized. I'd plump up my lips, get new cheekbones, square off my chin."

She pulls her feet out of the sand. "I even got my toes fixed. Did you know I had webbed feet? They're actually not all that uncommon. But for me they were like the mark of Cain. Proof I was a Bister. When you were born, I was terrified your feet were going to be webbed too. It never crossed my mind that it would be your thumbnails that would give you away. That's a Mrs. Hiltz trademark— something to be proud of!" Her face says *yeah, right*. She shakes her head.

"You know, I always meant to—I guess—confess. Grandpa wanted me to. My analyst wanted me to. *I* wanted to. But I could never bring myself to do it. I'd lived with the lies for so long. And, let's face it, they worked for me. I was rich. I was famous. And—dare I say it—I was respected. That's what I wanted most of all—the respect. I was terrified of what would happen if I admitted I'd been lying all along. Would my fans reject me? Would *you* reject me?"

I start to say something but she puts her hand up to stop me.

"I don't know if you can understand this or not, but the fear of confessing was always so much worse for me than the anxiety of living as a fraud. I guess that's why I told my audience anything else they wanted to know. I figured if I was really, really frank about my plastic surgery and my bad eating habits and my acne outbreaks, they'd never suspect I was lying about the rest of my life.

"And to tell you the truth"—something about that phrase makes us both laugh—"before the Internet came along, lying wasn't that hard. Eighteen years ago, getting fake ID was a piece of cake. I've been a Bister, a Ingram, a Reiner and a Schwartz—and until now, I managed to do it all under the radar. As for my other lies, I kept them simple—the fire, the adoption"—she takes a big breath— "how you came to be. . . ."

She looks at me with a pained smile. I take it as an apology. I know she's sorry she didn't tell me the truth. I shake my head as if I'm okay with that. Her face loosens up. She pats my leg.

It's a couple of seconds before she continues. "I was lucky, I guess. Lord knows, Steve's got his share of faults but a lack of decency isn't one of them. I told him I got pregnant on a one-night stand with some guy I never saw again. He just shrugged—waved it off—and accepted you as his own.

"The photo was a bit more of a problem. I'd held on to it as a keepsake. I never planned to pass it off as being a picture of me. But the cable TV station needed a childhood photo for a Christmas fundraiser one year. All I had was that picture of Rosie. A little while later, someone asked me for a photo to use in a profile for the local TV guide. I used the same one. It seemed harmless enough.

"Then my career started charging ahead. The picture got used a few more times—I could hardly say no when someone asked—but now it was making me nervous. I was a public figure. Who knows who might stumble upon that picture? I got someone to touch it up for me—just enough so it believably looked like the same girl but not so much that anyone would immediately recognize it as Rosie. I relaxed. It became my official childhood photo. I should have thrown the original out—and the ring too—but they meant too much to me. Believe it or not, I've never been as happy as those two years I spent at Mrs. Hiltz's."

She sighs. She goes, "Well, there you have it!" She sounds like she's ready to cut to a commercial or introduce tomorrow's show, but then her face softens and she says, "Is there anything else you want to ask me?"

"Yes," I say. It seems so petty and self-centred but . . . hey, I'm seventeen. I'm allowed to be petty and self-centred sometimes.

"Why did you take me off the show? Because I got fat?"

Mom goes, "No! . . . No!" but I don't believe her. She says it in that fake *why would you ever think such a thing?* way.

I just look at her.

She turns away. "Okay. Not really."

At least she's being honest.

"Not the way you mean, anyway. You were definitely getting a little more than plump and you know what they say, the camera adds fifteen pounds. So, yes, that's why I took you off the air."

I try to smile, like, *oh well, who cares,* but I can feel tears burning behind my eyes.

Mimi rubs my knee and says, "Let me explain. *I* didn't care that you'd gained weight. Lots of girls do at puberty. It was natural. I knew you were going to be tall like your dad. So that wasn't it.

"I took you off because it bothered me that the whole world was going to be judging you by the ridiculous size 2 standards of prime-time TV. They'd ridicule you. They'd splash unflattering pictures of you in the tabloids. I couldn't do that to you. Any cut rate psychiatrist can figure out why I needed the public to love me after all I'd gone through. I wasn't going to do the same thing to you. I wasn't going to let you be 'shamed' that way. I wanted you to be who you were, become who you wanted to be without millions of people always pointing out what was wrong with you."

We're both crying now and neither of us has a Kleenex. Mimi wipes her nose with the back of her hand. Big rice-noodley strings of snot droop off her fingers. We both go, "Yuck!" She doesn't know what to do with it. She looks around and then just wipes her hand on her T-shirt. We're suddenly both laughing in that grossed-out, just-stepped-on-a-slug way.

Mimi goes, "Oh good Lord. Once a Bister, always a Bister, eh?"

My nose is running over everything now too. I wipe it off on my sleeve. "You and me both," I say.

Mom stops laughing. She shakes her head with a little smile. "No, you aren't, sweetheart. Being a Bister isn't a hereditary disease. It's not something you're born with. It's something you catch from other people. And you didn't catch it. In fact, I look at you and I don't see any Bister at all. What I see is Percy. To be honest, that's another reason I took you off the air. I knew after all the surgeries I'd had that no one was going to recognize me. But the older you got the more you looked like your dad. Tall and healthy and with that beautiful red hair. I was afraid you were going to blow my cover."

Suddenly she looks small and scared. I put my big arms around her and hug her. She hugs me back.

"Now I have a question for you, Birdie," she says into my shoulder.

I go, "Okay."

She pulls back and looks me in the face. "Where do we go from here?"

Where *do* we go from here? A few weeks ago, I would

have been terrified by that question but now it feels almost exciting. Just the idea that I'm *going* anywhere. I couldn't even move before. I couldn't get off my sorry behind. Now there are so many possibilities. I have a mother now. I have a couple of fathers. I have a boyfriend. I'll check my e-mail when I get back to see if I've still got a friend. (You never know with Selena. If not today, tomorrow.)

So where do we go from here? I don't know.

I smile and I shrug.

53

Saturday, 6 p.m.

You, You and Mimi

"Teenagers in Love." Parents may be terrified of young love but psychologist and author Eliza Richardson believes it's the key to future happiness.

We talk some more on the car ride back from the beach. It will be a while before I get the whole story, but bits and pieces are coming out.

Gershom knows everything. He was the first person Mom called after she talked to me Thursday night. Barnabas, her other cousin, took off in his early twenties. No one has heard from him since.

Anita doesn't know anything. Mom hid the picture and ring in the chair to make sure Anita wouldn't find out.

(The way Anita is about cleaning out drawers, Mom had to be careful.)

Mom never paid Mrs. Hiltz back. Instead, she sent an anonymous donation of twenty-thousand dollars (plus interest) to one of Mrs. Hiltz's favourite charities. That's as much as she could stomach. She knew if she sent the money to Mrs. Hiltz directly, she'd just assume Minerva had stolen it from someone else.

Rosie didn't win the lottery. Mom just made it look that way. It was her way of saying thank you.

Selena's university is paid for. Selena doesn't know it but Anita does. Anita just makes her work so she doesn't get spoiled. Typical Anita.

Mom's going to call Rosie soon.

She's not going to call Percy. Yet.

She doesn't want to talk about Embree. There's only so far she's willing to go.

She asks me to come home with her, but I can't. Not now anyway. I don't need to explain why. I introduce her to Levi outside the fish-and-chips joint and she understands immediately.

She looks him over, then says in this big, showy whisper, "Ooooh. Nice catch, darling!" It's classic Mimi.

I hug her goodbye. I don't know if it's easier this time

because she's in Mimi mode or because maybe, a little, we understand each other now—but it feels almost natural.

I wave as she pulls out onto the highway. It makes me nervous—she doesn't drive a lot. I'd feel way better if Tony were at the wheel but my guess is Ford Fiestas don't usually come with chauffeurs. I want her to be okay. She's my mother and I love her. (She's Mimi and I love her. She's Minerva and I love her.)

Levi puts his arm around my waist and says, "She's some character, eh? I feel like I've seen her somewhere before. What is it you said she does for a living again?"

I look at him and laugh. I've got an awful lot of explaining to do.

First, though, I'd like to see how jealous I can make Krystal.

Levi's okay with that.

54

The Making of Mimi (two-hour special presentation)

This Emmy Award–winning documentary manages to prove the impossible — that the truth about Mimi Schwartz is even more fantastic than anything the tabloids could have dreamed up. A must-see.

DISCUSSION QUESTIONS ON
NOT SUITABLE FOR FAMILY VIEWING

1. Over the course of the book, Robin has a number of her perceptions challenged. Name four things she believes at the beginning of the story that she realizes aren't true by the end. These can be facts, beliefs about herself or perceptions of the world around her.

2. Draw a picture (in words or images) of how Robin sees herself as the story opens and another picture showing what she actually looks like.

3. Robin is very, very rich. She can do whatever she wants with her life. Why do you think she chooses to spend it watching reruns of *You, You and Mimi*?

4. Why do you think the book is called *Not Suitable for Family Viewing*? Can the title mean more than one

thing? Does it have a different meaning to someone just starting the book than to someone who's finished it?

5. Do Robin and Levi have what it takes for a good relationship? What do you think attracts Robin to him? What does he like about her? What do they have in common? What are their differences?

6. Robin is horrified by the treatment the Bisters receive from the townspeople, but does she have the right to be so offended? Is she really innocent of prejudging others? Can you name several instances when Robin dismisses another person based on appearance or background?

7. A "red herring" is a deliberate attempt by an author to divert the reader's attention from something important in the book. Usually, this device is designed to keep people from guessing who the real guilty party is. Sometimes the red herring is a deceptive clue. Sometimes it's a false emphasis on something trivial. Sometimes it's more about the tone the author adopts. Can you think of five red herrings in *Not Suitable for Family Viewing*?

8. Red herrings are important, but real clues also need to

be planted throughout a book pointing to the actual bad guy. Looking back—make sure you finish the book first!—how many clues can you find that would lead you to the culprit? Are they well hidden? Too well hidden? Do you understand what led the perpetrator to commit the crime?

9. Write a commercial advertising the *You, You and Mimi* episode concerning the revelation about Mimi's background.

10. Mimi took great pains to hide her past life, but nevertheless held on to several small but meaningful keepsakes. If you were starting your life over, what would you hold on to and why?

Keep reading for an excerpt from Vicki Grant's upcoming novel, *Betsy Wickwire's Dirty Secret*!

PROLOGUE

Carly was leaning against the counter. Her hands were behind her back and her hair was swept over to one side. She was looking up at Nick. He was going to kiss her.

Betsy understood that immediately. It yanked her to a stop. She stood in the kitchen doorway like a cardboard cut-out of herself—flat, motionless, feeling absolutely nothing except the roots of her hair, which suddenly ached like thousands of tiny bruises.

She closed her eyes. No way. This couldn't be true. She was just thinking crazy things.

She opened her eyes and formed her mouth into a smile. Her teeth were so dry they caught on her lips.

"Oh, hi," she said, taking her Jitters apron off the hook by the door.

Carly's hand flew up to her mouth. Nick leapt back. Betsy dropped her apron and ran.

She ran with that painful fake smile still quivering on

her face. She ran out of the kitchen, through the coffee shop, onto the street. She didn't stop to get her purse or to pick up the tray of blueberry scones she'd sent flying or to tell the manager, who was just coming in himself, that she wouldn't be at work that morning after all. Betsy didn't think to do any of that. She couldn't think. All she could do was run.

Betsy played basketball and soccer. Normally, she was a pretty good runner, but now she was out of control. She looked like she'd caught her toe on something a few steps back and hadn't quite managed to get her balance again. She was pitched forward at the waist and doing that frantic outstretched-arm thing people do just before a face plant.

Any other time, had she seen a video of herself running like that, she would have laughed. She would have posted it on Facebook, sent it to all her friends, made jokes about it. That was one of the reasons Betsy was so popular. It wasn't just that she was pretty. She was a lot of fun too.

She wasn't laughing now. In fact, she wouldn't even have been aware of how ridiculous she looked if an older man walking his dog hadn't put out his arm and said, "Are you all right, dear?"

She stumbled to a stop. She stood there panting and confused, staring at him. Why was he looking at her like that? Who was he? Why was he even talking to her?

He put a hand on her shoulder and looked directly into her eyes. "Do you need help, honey?"

Betsy more or less understood the words but somehow the sentence didn't quite make sense. She realized this was weird. Still, her confusion seemed to bother the man more than it bothered her. Betsy could see from his forehead just how concerned he was.

"Can I call someone for you?"

He said it very slowly but he didn't have to. Call—that one word—was all it took. Everything became horribly clear.

Call someone?

Tell someone what happened?

Betsy pulled herself up straight, flicked the tears off her cheeks, and tried to sound reasonable. "No. No," she said. "Why? I'm—I'm just out for a jog."

The man looked at her face. He looked at her sandals. He rubbed the corner of his mouth with his thumb and said, "Well, okay. If you're sure."

She nodded until he took his dog and walked away.

Despite everything else going on in her head right then, Betsy couldn't help feeling sort of insulted. She wasn't the type of person who'd lie. Why did he assume she was lying? It was six-thirty in the morning. Lots of people were out jogging.

As if to prove her point, Betsy started jogging—rhythmically, not too fast, at what her old gym teacher used to call "a nice easy trot." She sensed that she looked fine or, if not fine, at least normal. No one was going to stop her again to see if she was all right.

That calmed her for a second. She realized that all she needed to do was blend in for a while until she could find someplace to . . .

To what?

She kept jogging but her heart burst into a sprint.

To hide?

To escape?

The truth erupted from her in a big honking sob.

To die.

It was the only thing that would work. She needed to die. She wanted to die.

She found herself running again. She couldn't see for the tears but everything else was in sharp focus. She knew she'd lost a sandal. She knew her mascara was all over her face. She was even aware enough at some level to realize that her howling sounded a lot like the animatronic dinosaur she'd seen on a junior high trip to the Museum of Natural History.

Betsy recognized she was making a scene. She just didn't care. Why should she? She had nothing left to care about.

She ran and ran until she was finally on her street, at her house, up the stairs, down the hall, in her bathroom. She slammed the lock into place, then threw herself face down on the cool, dewy floor.

In seconds, the whole family was up, scrambling for their glasses, their housecoats, calling to her, banging on the door, rattling the handle. *What? What's the matter? Is she crying or laughing? Bets! Open up! Did you hurt yourself? Is that blood on the stairs or dirt? Does anyone know what happened? Betsy, sweetheart, please! Talk to her, Mike. Tell her to come out. Betsy!*

Betsy closed her eyes, covered her ears and bit down on the bath mat to keep herself from sobbing.

The last thing she heard was her mother saying, "Someone call Nick. Call Carly. Find out what's going on!"

✳

Betsy Wickwire's life ended there.

It took her the whole summer to realize it was the best thing that had ever happened to her.

o o o